That One Night

CARRIE ELKS

THAT ONE NIGHT ALTERNATIVE PAPERBACK EDITION by Carrie Elks
Copyright © 2025 Carrie Elks
All rights reserved
110725
ISBN: 978-1-916516-35-9

Edited by Rose David

Proofread by Proofreading by Mich

Cover Designed by The Pretty Little Design Company https://www.theprettylittledesignco.co.uk/

This book is a work of fiction and any resemblance to persons, living or dead, or places, events or locales is purely coincidental. The characters are fictitious products of the author's imagination.

All rights reserved.

No part of this book may be reproduced in any form or by any electronic or mechanical means, including information storage and retrieval systems, without written permission from the author, except for the use of brief quotations in a book review.

CHAPTER One

EMERY REED PLACED the engagement ring in her fiancé's palm and stepped back, the weight of it still burning her skin.

"Seriously?" Trenton stared at her like she'd just slapped him. "You're really doing this?"

Her heart thudded painfully, but she forced herself to hold his gaze. "We agreed. If it didn't work out, we'd walk away without arguing."

"We?" He let out a humorless laugh. "*You* said that. I nodded. There's a difference." His voice was tight, jaw clenched. "You have no idea how bad this is going to look. You're walking away from ten years. Just like that?"

She didn't answer. What was the point? She'd spent three months trying to make it work. Again. Trying to ignore the app she found on his phone, the late-night messages, the excuses.

Now she was done. Even if it broke her heart.

"You don't have to worry about seeing me. Or things being awkward," she told him. "I'm heading home for the summer. To Hartson's Creek. My mom needs help getting the farm ready to sell."

It still felt strange saying that. *Getting the farm ready to sell.*

Her dad had only passed a few months ago. Everything was still raw. For her, for her mom. But the work had to be done, and Emery couldn't bear to let her mother do it alone.

"You're going to disappear back there and pretend none of this happened?" he asked.

She shook her head. "No. I'm going to try and start over."

To remember who she used to be, before she twisted herself into knots trying to be the perfect fiancée. The perfect daughter. The perfect everything.

Trenton stared at her, like he couldn't believe what she was saying. "Can we at least wait until the end of the summer until we tell people we've broken up and the engagement is over? Until my parents get back from their cruise. I don't have time to deal with this now. I have that project. It's important." He sounded almost dismissive. Like she was just another item on his to-do-list.

You never have time, she thought. *Not for me.*

He stepped forward, his voice softening, like he could sense a chink in her armor. "Come on. Let's keep it quiet until we've both processed it. Just for a few months. It'll be easier for both of us. You know that."

She knew it would be easier for him, that was for sure. And Trenton always put himself first. It just took her this long to realize it.

Sensing a chink in her armor, he went in for the kill. "Come on, Emery. You owe me this. After all these years."

She looked at the ring in his hand. The same one he'd given her after college, when the future had felt bright and uncomplicated. When she still believed in him. In them.

And just like always, guilt curled in her chest. Not because she was doing the wrong thing. She knew she wasn't. But because she was so damn tired of being the one who upset people. The one who caused ripples. And telling everyone now would feel like setting off a bomb.

Especially with her mom still grieving.

Especially in a town where everybody knew everybody.

And especially because *Trenton's family lived there too.*

Which meant she'd have to lie. Smile. Pretend, just for a little longer.

So she'd do what she always did.

She'd make it easier. For him, for her mom, for everyone but herself.

"Fine," she said quietly. "I won't say anything. Not yet."

"But it's over?"

She turned away before he could see the tears brimming in her eyes. "Yes," she told him, her voice low and ragged. "It's over."

ONE WEEK LATER

There was something bittersweet about standing in an empty classroom after the last bell of the year had rung. Emery gently pulled the final poster from the bulletin board, smoothing it out before placing it on her desk with the others she'd made months ago.

Everything was clean. Quiet. Done.

"Please tell me you're ready," Maisie called from the doorway, her tote bag slung over her shoulder, sunglasses pushed into her curls. "Because I'm one silent scream away from cocktails and freedom."

Emery glanced over with a tired smile. "I think I'm gonna skip it."

Maisie frowned. "You're going to miss the end-of-year celebration? The others are already at O'Hara's. They've got tequila and questionable karaoke. Come on, it's tradition."

"I'm not in the mood."

Maisie walked in and began gathering stacks of cardstock from Emery's desk, carrying them toward the supply closet. She didn't even have to ask where they went. After four years of teaching second grade together, and being best friends, Maisie knew Emery's system by heart.

"And you weren't in the mood last night either," she pointed out. "Or the night before that."

Emery followed her, locking up the cabinet after she'd stacked the last of her things. "Because I'm leaving tomorrow. I've got a long drive, and a lot of work waiting for me."

"You also just ended a ten-year relationship," Maisie pointed out, her tone gentler now. "You're allowed to wallow. Or rage. Or scream-sing breakup songs at an Irish bar."

Emery huffed out a laugh. "I'm too tired to scream-sing. And I don't feel like wallowing over Trenton."

Maisie paused, then gave her a look. "Good. Because I wasn't planning to let you for long. I'm still hoping you'll come with me to Europe, where you'll fall in love with a gorgeous Italian who doesn't own a single dating app."

"You know I can't." Emery's smile faded. "My mom needs me there to help her. The farm's too much for her on her own, and with Dad gone..."

Her voice caught. Just a little.

Maisie softened. "I know. I just hate seeing you tied in knots over this. Especially when you're still wearing that." She nodded at Emery's ring finger.

Emery looked down at the diamond that no longer meant anything. "It makes things easier. For now."

"Easier for who?" Maisie lifted a brow.

"My mom. She's still grieving. The last thing she needs is to worry about me too."

Maisie crossed her arms. "I still can't believe you agreed to this charade."

Emery couldn't quite believe it herself. But she'd given her word and she'd stick to it. Even if Trenton never stuck to his.

Muttering something under her breath that definitely wasn't school-appropriate, Maisie walked out of the closet.

Emery followed behind, trying not to smile at her friend's obvious annoyance. "It's not like I'll be seeing him," she pointed out. "He'll be in Charleston, I'll be in Hartson's Creek."

"But no guy is even going to look at you with a ring on that finger," Maisie said.

Rolling her eyes, Emery locked the closet behind her. And there it was, school was out for summer. "I have zero desire to start dating again."

"Not even a tiny desire?" Maisie asked, looking disappointed. "Surely there have to be some hot single guys in Hartson's Creek."

"Considering I've known 95% of the male population there since kindergarten, I think I'll pass."

Maisie narrowed her eyes. "So you're telling me you're going to spend your entire summer working on a farm, pretending you're still engaged, and not even making one bad decision?"

"I'm going to be too busy for bad decisions," Emery said firmly.

Maisie sighed dramatically. "That's what I was afraid of. Which is why…" She reached into her pocket and pulled out a crumpled piece of lined paper. "I made you this."

Emery took it, raising an eyebrow. "Is this a to-do list?"

"It's a fuck-you-Trenton list," Maisie said proudly. "Handcrafted. Emotionally charged. And guaranteed to jumpstart your post-breakup glow-up."

Emery glanced down at the blue-ink scrawl:

1. *Go skinny dipping*
2. *Get a tattoo*
3. *Get drunk at least once*

4. *Stay up talking all night*
5. *Dance on a bar*
6. *Ride on the back of a motorcycle*
7. *Have sex with a man who isn't your ex*

"Maisie!" Emery blinked. "I'm not doing these. Especially not number seven."

"Yes, you are." Maisie refused to take the list back. "You'll spend the whole summer meandering around the farm like a sad sack unless someone forces your hand. You need this. You need fun. Make some reckless decisions, you might even enjoy them."

"I'm not sleeping with a stranger," Emery said, though she couldn't quite stop the laugh from bubbling out.

Maisie rolled her eyes at her. "Okay. Because I'm such a generous friend," she said, pulling a pen from her bag, "we'll revise." She struck through number seven and wrote beneath it:

1. *Kiss a man who isn't your ex.*

The words made something flutter low in Emery's stomach. The kind of flutter that reminded her she hadn't kissed anyone but Trenton in nearly a decade. Hadn't even thought about it.

Until now.

"I'm serious, Em." Maisie's voice softened again. "You already did the hard part. You left. Now it's time to remember who you were before all of this. Before *him*."

Emery swallowed hard, her throat tight.

Maisie had been through her own heartbreak last year. When her boyfriend moved to Texas and left her behind, she'd cried for a week. Then she'd booked a solo backpacking trip through Europe. That's where she was headed tomorrow, until school restarted in the fall.

And Emery? She was heading back to a town she'd tried so hard to outgrow.

But apparently she was going with a list.

"Okay," she said, folding the paper in half and tucking it into her bag, because she was all out of fight right now. "I'll do it. I'll do your damn list."

Maisie beamed. "That's my girl." She pulled Emery into a fierce hug. "Now get out of here and go do something totally irresponsible. Preferably involving tequila."

Emery smiled against her friend's shoulder.

She had no idea what the summer would bring, but for the first time in a long while she wasn't just bracing herself for survival.

She was heading home to start again.

CHAPTER
Two

"HENDRIX HARTSON, why aren't you answering your phone?"

Hendrix looked up from the ground where he was repairing an irrigation line that had been leaking for a week, and tried to suppress a smile. His cousin Sabrina was pouting, her brows knitted the same way they used to when she didn't get her way as a kid.

At twenty-six, his junior by three years, she could just about get away with it.

"I'm busy," he pointed out, glancing at the water still trickling from the line. The sun was beating down, there was a farm full of animals that needed watering, and if he didn't fix this pipe soon, there'd be hell to pay.

And also, he didn't want to answer his calls.

Since he'd come home to Hartson's Creek a couple of months ago, his phone had become a millstone. Constantly buzzing with texts from his brothers, missed calls from his mom, and naturally, daily Snapchats from Sabrina. Because his cousin was way too cool for a regular message.

"I've sent you, like, a dozen Snaps this week," she said, rolling her eyes. "I even called you last night. And don't tell me you were busy then. There's nothing going on around here."

She huffed and looked around at the expanse of farmland, golden wheat swaying alongside rows of sunlit corn.

"It's so boring." She shook her head.

"I'll check my phone tonight," he said, even though they both knew he wouldn't.

"Liar." She sighed like the weight of the world had landed on her shoulders. "I remember when you used to be fun."

"When was that? Back in grade school?" he teased.

They'd always bonded over being the youngest in their loud, chaotic families. Her with three older brothers, him with two. At family parties they'd run wild, stuffing their faces with frosting, spiking lemonade with hot sauce. They once tied helium balloons to their Great Aunt Gina's dog to see if he'd float.

He didn't. And Aunt Gina had *not* been amused.

Finally stemming the leak, Hendrix stood, wiping his face with the hem of his dusty t-shirt and feeling the ache in his back.

"What are you doing out here anyway?" he asked.

Sabrina had never cared for farm life. Not like he had. From the moment he was old enough to help muck out stalls, he'd loved the rhythm of it. The animals, the sweat, the sun that soaked into your bones and made you feel like you belonged.

As a kid, it had been the one place he didn't feel like a screw-up.

And now that he was back, it was the only place people didn't expect him to be anything other than quiet and useful.

Well, except for Sabrina.

"I came to rescue you from your self-imposed exile," she said, flicking a glance at his dirt-streaked jeans. "There's a party Saturday night at Mariah's house. You remember parties, don't you? People. Music. Fun. Not smelling like you lost a wrestling match with a horse."

He smirked. "Didn't Mariah go to New York to be an actress?"

"That was Victoria. Keep up." She crossed her arms. "Are you coming or not?"

He opened his mouth, already searching for an excuse. The last thing he needed was to end up in a house full of twentysomethings drinking canned cocktails and live-streaming their bad decisions.

"It'll be fun," she coaxed. "Fireworks. Karaoke. Probably someone crying about their ex in the bathroom. It's basically a tradition." She grabbed his hand. "Come on."

"I can't." He shook his head, trying – and failing – to look remorseful. "I'll be working on my place."

The cottage his uncle had sold him needed everything repairing. Gutters, roofing, plumbing. Same with the neglected patch of farmland it sat on. Working his uncle's land was a paycheck. But building something of his own?

That was redemption. His future. And it was more important than parties.

"Mariah specifically asked me to invite you," Sabrina said, narrowing her eyes. "She's single. You're single. She makes a mean margarita. That's practically a Hallmark movie."

"Sabrina." His voice was a warning.

"What? I'm just saying, she'll be wearing a sundress and cowboy boots. Your kryptonite."

"Fixing irrigation lines and sleeping through the night are my kryptonite," he told her. "Have fun. Don't do anything I wouldn't do."

"Ugh." She rolled her eyes. "You're so boring now. What did they do to you in California?"

He paused, just for a beat, then shoved the wrench back into the toolbox.

"Nothing happened," he said gruffly. "Maybe I just grew up."

Sabrina snorted. "Wow. So this is what thirty looks like. Dad jokes and an early bedtime."

"I'm not thirty."

"Close enough." She smirked. "You've gone full Hartson. Might as well get cargo shorts and start grilling with unnecessary confidence."

A reluctant laugh rumbled in his throat.

"Enjoy your irrigation pipe, old man," she called as she turned to leave. "I'll go drink tequila and make terrible decisions for both of us."

He watched her boots kick up dust as she walked away, the swing of her hips saying annoyed, not angry. She'd cool off. She always did.

He'd message her later. Or maybe he'd finally open one of her Snaps.

Sabrina was his favorite cousin, after all. He loved her. But right now, he wasn't trying to be fun or social or the life of any party.

He was just trying to be good.

By the time the sun dipped low over the hills and the last of his tools were packed away, Hendrix's shirt clung to his back and his throat felt like sandpaper.

He took the long way home, cutting across the fields on his dirt bike. The scent of warm hay and earth clung to the air, carried by the breeze off the creek.

His Uncle Logan was out by the west fence, clipboard in one hand and wire cutters in the other.

Hendrix coasted to a stop and swung off the bike. "Leak's all fixed. Checked the whole line. There are no more holes."

His uncle nodded, satisfied. "That section's been bleeding for days."

"Not anymore. It's good to go."

Logan walked over, his strides easy, steady. He was tall like all the Hartson men, but carried a kind of calm Hendrix hadn't yet figured out how to fake.

"You heading home?" his uncle asked, looking up at the fading sun.

"Yeah. Might start on the gutters before it gets dark." Hendrix slung his gear bag over his shoulder. "Roof's next."

"You're putting in the hours."

"Trying to make it mine," Hendrix said simply.

"You already have." Logan clapped a hand on his shoulder. "And Court said to tell you dinner's on the stove if you want it. Meatloaf and cake."

"She doesn't quit." Courtney was his aunt. Like all his family, she loved to feed him up, despite the fact he was six-foot two and all muscle.

"She's a Hartson." His uncle shrugged. "It's how we love."

"I'll swing by and grab some cake tomorrow," Hendrix promised.

Logan nodded, then added, "Your mom cornered me at the store this morning. Wanted to know if I'd seen any unfamiliar vehicles at your place."

Hendrix groaned. "Please tell me you didn't answer her."

"I told her if you had a harem, you were doing a damn good job keeping it quiet."

"She's never gonna stop." Hendrix rubbed the back of his neck. "You'd think with Pres and Marley giving her grandkids left and right, she'd have her hands full."

"She's a mom," Logan said simply. "And moms worry."

"I know. But I'm doing okay." He paused. "Just… maybe not the way she wants me to be."

Logan nodded. "That's still okay. You don't have to be anything but who you are."

Hendrix started to reply, but Logan held up a hand.

"Oh, and Alice Reed called."

Hendrix winced. The farmer's widow living in the cottage opposite his seemed to enjoy making his life a misery.

"She says your 'infernal machine' is giving her hens palpitations." Logan smirked. "Apparently her daughter's coming home this week, and she doesn't want her disturbed."

That made Hendrix snort. "The woman times my coffee breaks like she's got a drone on me."

"She's got eyes everywhere and zero tolerance for nonsense. And she's your neighbor now," Logan pointed out.

"I'll drop off an apology card. Maybe some earplugs for her daughter."

Logan laughed. "Just don't rile her up. You've got enough going on."

With a nod, Hendrix kicked the bike to life. The engine roared as he took off through the pasture, the wind hitting his face and the last light chasing his shadow over the golden fields.

His muscles ached. His hands were raw. But for the first time in months, his head felt a little clearer.

He wasn't here to stir up trouble.

He just wanted a little peace.

And a chance to start over.

CHAPTER
Three

"ALL I'M SAYING IS that you look so pretty in a skirt," Emery's mom said, folding another dish towel and smoothing it out like it had personally offended her. "Cutoffs just look… messy."

Emery took a breath. She'd forgotten how traditional her mother could be. Apparently, cut-off denim shorts and a black tank top were a step too far for a proper young woman in Hartson's Creek.

"I mean, you used to love wearing dresses," her mom added, without looking up.

"I also used to think crimping my hair was a good idea." Emery kept her voice light, trying to remember that her mom was grieving. This wasn't really about shorts. Or even appearances. This was about control. Something her mother hadn't had for a while now.

The house still felt heavy without her dad. The chair he always sat in was empty. The space he used to fill so loudly and easily felt like a vacuum. Her mom had spent her whole life being a wife, a partner, a helpmate. And now she was a widow with a farm she didn't know how to run.

Thank god Jed Walker, her dad's longtime farm manager,

had stayed on past retirement to help keep things afloat until the property could be sold.

Emery's gaze flicked to the engagement ring still glittering on her finger like it had every right to be there.

God, what a mess her life was.

"It's ninety degrees outside," she told her mom. "It's too hot for anything but shorts."

Her mom sighed. "Maybe the air conditioning needs upgrading. It's been sluggish since April."

And there it was. The other elephant in the room.

There was no money for upgrades.

"You're selling the place," Emery reminded her gently. "There's no point getting a new system installed now."

"But it'll sell faster if everything's new," her mom said. "Maybe you could ask Trenton what he thinks?"

That name again. Her jaw tensed.

Of course her mom would bring him up. He was the golden boy. The wealthy one. The safe bet. And of course her mom would default to him when it came to anything practical.

"We've got it under control," Emery said, forcing a smile. "Let's just get everything organized so we can put it on the market."

She was sitting at the polished dining table, surrounded by stacks of paperwork her father had left behind. Or at least some of it. A lot was missing. And none of it was in order. But she had to make sense of it if she wanted the sale to go through without hiccups.

Her mom paused her endless glass-polishing, brow furrowing as she watched Emery.

"Is everything okay with you and Trenton?" she asked. "You haven't said much about him since you've been back."

Emery fought the instinct to flinch. She'd been home for less than twenty-four hours. But of course, in this house, silence meant something was wrong.

"Everything's fine," she lied smoothly. "Why wouldn't it be?"

"I just don't know if it's smart for you to be here without him. Don't you miss him? He can't be thrilled you're spending the whole summer away."

Emery stood and reached for her mother's hands, threading their fingers together. "He's okay with it," she said softly. "He's been swamped at work. You know how he is. And we both agreed me coming home was the right thing."

Her mom's face softened. "He's such a good man," she murmured. "Such a catch." Then her voice brightened. "Imagine. A Reed marrying a Montclair."

Emery looked down at the ring on her left hand again. It felt heavier by the second.

But she was doing this for her mom. Alice Reed had cried twice already since Emery arrived. Once when she found her dad's worn boots by the door, and again when she couldn't find the deed to the back fields.

Her mom needed stability. Hope. And not more heartbreak.

But still, she couldn't help the growing sense of tightness. As though the walls of this old farmhouse were slowly closing in. The air in here was too still. Too full of memories.

Unlike Emery, her mom had never left this town. She hadn't gone to college, hadn't lived anywhere but Hartson's Creek. She'd been raised on a farm and married a farmer. Her whole world was this land, this house, these routines.

Knowing about Emery's break up?

It could break her.

And Emery had already broken enough things lately.

"You know what?" she said, releasing her mom's hands and stepping back. "I'm going to take a walk. The realtor asked for some initial photos. I'll take a few while the light's still good."

"In this heat?" Her mom frowned. "You'll burn up."

Maybe she would. But right now, she needed to breathe.

"I'll be back in an hour," she promised, grabbing her phone and slipping in her earbuds before her mom could protest.

Outside, the sun hit her like a wall. She squinted toward the nearest field, where Jed was talking with a few of the farmhands. From the way they were herding cattle, it looked like they were rotating pastures.

Jed spotted her and tipped his cap, the sun glinting off his white hair. She smiled and waved back, grateful for his presence.

The Reed farm was just fifty acres now, much smaller than it used to be. Her father had sold off parcels of land over the years whenever money got tight. Most of it now belonged to the Hartsons next door.

But there was still enough land to get lost in.

She followed the dirt path that wound around the cornfield, the green stalks already waist high. In a few months, they'd be golden and ripe for harvest.

She veered toward the small copse of trees at the edge of the property that used to be her childhood escape. When she was little, she used to sneak back here whenever her parents were upset with her. Her mom never liked walking through the woods, and her dad was always too busy with the farm to track her down.

The moment she stepped beneath the canopy, the air turned cooler. Calmer. The sound of bugs and birds replaced the distant hum of farm life.

And there, just beyond the trees, was the pond.

Its surface glinted in the sun, water still and glassy. Fed by a tributary of the Hartson Creek, it had always been her favorite place on the property.

And today, it looked almost... magical.

A breath of wind stirred the surface. Somewhere, a dragonfly zipped across the edge.

And then, unbidden, Maisie's list floated into her head. That wrinkled piece of paper, still folded in the pocket of her overnight bag.

The first item.

1. Go skinny dipping.

She stared at the pond, heart thudding like it had something to prove.

She couldn't. Could she?

For a second she just stood there, thinking about how stupid that list was. Maisie had messaged her yesterday to say she'd arrived safely in London. She'd sent a photograph of herself, sitting in an English pub next to the sparkling River Thames.

I want you to tick one item off your list this week. Or there'll be trouble. ;)

Damn, she missed her, even if she could be a pain sometimes. It was only a matter of time before Maisie called her to see if she'd done as she asked.

She glanced around the woods. Jed and the farmhands were busy rotating cattle on the other side of the property. Nobody ever came back here. Not anymore.

She could do this. Just a quick dip. A rebel move. A silent "screw you" to the box she'd spent the last decade squeezing herself into.

Before she could think too hard, she tugged off her sneakers and socks, neatly tucking them aside. Her shorts and tank top followed. Then, standing in just her underwear, she hesitated.

Maybe this was enough. Technically, she could lie and say she did it—

No. If she was doing this, she was doing it right.

With a determined breath, she unhooked her bra, then shimmied out of her panties, folding them on top of the pile.

The water sparkled invitingly in the late afternoon sun. "Just do it," she whispered, more to herself than anyone else.

Because a good girl wouldn't.

And right now she was trying hard not to be one.

She walked forward, letting the cool water lap at her feet, then her calves and her thighs, until she pushed off and dove beneath the surface. A rush of silence enveloped her, the water soothing against her heated skin as she surfaced, blinking into the dappled light.

She floated for a moment, breath steadying. The ache in her chest loosened.

Was this what peace felt like?

For the first time in months, maybe years, she felt like herself.

At least until a loud bleat shattered the stillness.

"Maa."

She jerked upright, scanning the opposite bank.

Another bleat. Deeper this time.

And then she saw him. A goat, casually weaving his way through the edge of the woods.

"Oh no." she squinted. Definitely a billy. Probably feral. He had a smug look about him.

"Hey, cutie," she called softly, swimming closer to the edge.

The goat blinked at her, unimpressed. Then turned... and headed straight for her clothes.

"No," she groaned. "No, no, don't you dare!"

She swam hard toward shore, but it was too late. The goat was already rooting through the pile. With astonishing speed, he snagged her panties and tank top in his mouth – and to her horror, her bra too – and took off like a four-legged bandit.

"Get your mouth off my panties!" she shouted, scrambling out of the pond, slick water trailing down her bare skin.

He paused, looked at her as if considering her request... then bolted.

"Oh, you bad, bad goat!"

She lunged for him, grabbing at her bra, but he yanked it out of reach and darted past her, her clothing flapping like a banner of humiliation between his teeth.

Left with only her shorts, she yanked them on and took off in pursuit, one arm desperately covering her chest. Her bare feet slapped the earth as she chased him along the edge of the trees.

This was not how skinny-dipping was supposed to go.

And then, because things weren't already mortifying enough, she heard it.

The unmistakable roar of an engine.

She froze as a dirt bike came tearing down the trail beyond the trees, kicking up a cloud of dust. Her eyes widened in horror as the rider veered toward them, and the goat darted in the opposite direction, toward the road.

"Stop, damn you!" she shouted at the billy.

But of course he didn't. And she couldn't chase him that way. Not without being seen. And judging by the way the rider slowed, she had already been spotted.

The bike coasted to a stop, engine still idling, dust curling around the tires. And there she was, topless and soaked. Somewhere between dignity and disaster.

"Are you okay, ma'am?" the rider called with a low voice as he swung his leg off the bike.

"Don't come closer!" she yelled, gripping her chest like her life depended on it.

He didn't listen.

Of course he didn't.

The man walked toward her with easy confidence, his dark blond hair buzzed close to his scalp, his T-shirt clinging to muscles that didn't belong in a town like this. His eyes raked over her, amusement pulling at his lips.

She winced, feeling completely exposed. "You don't have to stare at me like that."

He didn't even blink. "It's kinda hard not to when a half-naked woman's running across my field."

Her stomach dropped. "Your field?" When did her dad sell that?

Before she could ask him, his eyes lit with recognition. "Wait... I know you. Emery Reed?"

She blinked, realizing exactly who this mountain of a man in front of her was. "Hendrix Hartson?"

Well. Her humiliation was now complete.

He'd been two grades above her in high school, all trouble and smirks and not enough time in class. A blur in her peripheral vision back then. The type she avoided. Too wild. Too everything.

And now he was standing in front of her, hotter than any memory, his lips twitching as he looked her over.

"Can you please stop staring at my chest?" she asked him.

He arched a brow. "To be fair, it's pretty hard not to right now."

His eyes caught hers, and for a moment she couldn't look away. His gaze was steady, appraising. Like he was trying to figure out what was happening here.

And before she could say another word, he grabbed the hem of his T-shirt and pulled it off.

Holy. Hell.

Tan skin. Sculpted abs. Shoulders that looked like they could carry half the farm.

Her mouth went dry.

He held the shirt out to her. "Take it. I won't look."

She grabbed it gratefully, the cotton warm from his skin, and turned away. Pulling it on, she couldn't help blushing at the way it brushed against her bare skin, or ignore the shiver that followed.

"I'll get this back to you," she mumbled, pointing toward

the old cottage across the lane. "I assume you own the cottage over there?" She could vaguely remember her mom telling her somebody had moved in.

He nodded. "I do."

She swallowed hard. "Thanks for not laughing at me. Too much."

He shrugged, his eyes dancing. "Give it time. I'm just working up to it."

They stared at each other for a beat too long. Something flickered between them, something hot and inconvenient. But before she could think on it anymore, he turned to mount his bike. "I should go. Frank has a taste for Victoria's Secret, apparently."

"Frank?" she repeated.

"The goat. I inherited him with the place. He's a jerk."

She laughed, despite herself. "You're telling me."

He kicked the bike into gear, the engine snarling beneath him. "See you around, Emery."

She watched him ride away, shirtless, dust trailing behind him like a damn movie scene.

Her pulse was still racing. Her body still buzzing.

And her stupid list was burning a hole in her mind.

Taking a deep breath, Emery tugged at the t-shirt he'd given her and turned to walk home.

That was definitely an interesting way to tick off number one.

CHAPTER
Four

WHAT THE HELL was wrong with him?

Hendrix dragged Frank back up the lane toward his cottage, closing the gate firmly behind him even though he knew his goat could bust out again in a minute if he wanted to.

The billy had been exactly where Hendrix knew he'd be. Leaning over the fence by Logan's field, posturing like a hormonal teenager trying to impress the nanny goats. Who, for the record, looked deeply *un*impressed.

Kind of like Emery Reed, when she'd caught him checking her out.

He hadn't seen her in years, not since she was that girl in high school who always had her nose in a book or was scribbling in a notepad for the school paper. She'd been a couple of years younger than him. One of the good girls, pretty and studious, and he'd never given her the time of day.

Now? She was all grown up. All curves and flushed skin and wide brown eyes that any man would have to drag his eyes away from.

Okay, not any man. Him. And he didn't drag his eyes. Not fast enough, anyway. He could still remember how soft and smooth her skin had looked, how her breasts swelled behind her arm as she tried to give herself some dignity.

How her stomach was taut, her hips flaring out as her body disappeared into her open cut offs.

She's engaged, asshole.

Yeah, he'd noticed that too. His eyes had gone straight to the ring, even while she was yelling at him to stop staring.

He vaguely remembered hearing something about her being with Trenton Montclair, one of the group of rich assholes he'd known in school. The kind of supercilious, smug piece of shit who treated everyone like they were beneath him.

Hendrix wrinkled his nose as he walked back to the cottage, Frank plodding behind him like he hadn't just wrecked the afternoon. Halfway up the road he'd discovered Emery's shredded black tank top and her lacy panties, the latter still mostly intact.

Of course Frank had saved the panties. Freaking pervert. His mouth dried as he looked at them.

They were little more than a scrap of lace, with a tiny bow at the front. He had to blink away the image of her wearing them.

And nothing else.

Christ. He tossed the ruined tank into the trash and took the panties into the laundry room, adding them to the overflowing basket. He'd wash them, fold them, and return them. Not because he wanted an excuse to see her again. He didn't. She was off-limits, for more reasons than he could count. But he didn't want her thinking someone else would find her panties lying in a field. Somewhere under the muscles and rough edges, he still had a sliver of decency.

Popping the top of a soda can, he drained half of it in one gulp. He'd take a shower, find a new t-shirt and get back to working on the cottage.

He'd had barely made it halfway to the living room when

he heard the front door creak open. No knock. No shout. Just the sound of an intruder with hooves.

"You have got to be kidding me," he muttered, heading back toward the hallway.

Frank. Of course.

The damn goat had wandered inside like he owned the place. His chin lifted, his beady eyes scanning the room like he was appraising the decor.

"You can go right back out the way you came in," Hendrix told him.

Frank let out a short bleat and took a few slow steps, ignoring him completely. Hendrix sighed. He'd agreed to take on Frank when he bought the place, figuring one goat couldn't be that much trouble. He hadn't realized the damn thing was Houdini in disguise with a lingerie habit.

Still, Frank made sense in a way most people didn't. He didn't talk back, didn't judge, and didn't care about Hendrix's past. And sometimes, Hendrix could relate to a creature who refused to be fenced in.

But stealing women's underwear? That wasn't the kind of rebellion Hendrix could get behind.

Not when it got *him* in trouble.

"Out. Now," he said, curling his fingers around Frank's collar and leading him to the door. Frank resisted for a moment, then let out a long sigh, like this was all beneath him, and allowed himself to be escorted out.

Hendrix walked him to the edge of the yard, giving him a gentle nudge back toward the pasture. Frank turned and pressed his cold nose against Hendrix's back.

"Don't give me the sad eyes," Hendrix said, rubbing his hand over Frank's fuzzy head. "You can't go around stealing underwear and expect to get away with it. Some women are off-limits."

Frank gave him a look that said he disagreed.

Hendrix let out a breath. "Yeah, I know. She was pretty.

But she's engaged. She's got her whole life planned out already. She's not for guys like us."

Frank flicked his tail, then trotted off without a backward glance, like he didn't believe a word his owner just told him.

"Oh my God, I wish I'd been there to see that," Maisie said, laughing down the phone line. Emery groaned, her cheeks still burning from the memory of standing almost naked in the middle of the field.

"Sooo... this Hendrix guy. Is he hot?"

"If you like that kind of thing," Emery muttered.

Maisie didn't miss a beat. "It doesn't matter what I like. I'm asking about you."

There was the sound of shuffling, like Maisie was getting herself comfortable. It was late at night in Europe, but jet lag had hit her hard. According to her rant when Emery answered her call, her body was still working on eastern US time.

She'd spent the last half hour gushing about how gorgeous English men were and how she'd already landed two tinder dates since arriving on European soil.

Emery felt a pang of envy, listening to her best friend's escapades. She missed her. She missed having somebody she could talk to and confide in.

Truth was, she'd only just got here and she was already feeling lonely. It was hard to feel that way when she was working. She loved being surrounded by her students. Her days were full of teaching and her nights full of grading and lesson planning during the school year.

But now, it was just her, the farm, and her mom. And all the stupid thoughts rushing through her head.

After putting Hendrix's t-shirt on, she'd managed to sneak back into the house without her mom noticing, thank god.

And she'd hidden his t-shirt under her pillow because she was pretty sure her mom would notice an item of man's clothing in the laundry.

Despite her embarrassment there'd been something else. A feeling harder to define. All she knew was that every time she thought about the way that man had looked at her, it made her body heat up.

When was the last time Trenton had seen her like that, unable to pull his eyes away? She could barely remember.

He certainly hadn't stared at her with dark eyes, looking like he wanted nothing more than to throw her over his shoulder and carry her to his bed.

"So what's next?" Maisie asked.

"I guess I avoid the guy next door for the rest of the summer."

Maisie laughed again. "I meant on the list."

"You know what's next. You wrote it." Emery pulled the list out of her pocket. After sneaking upstairs, she'd put a big tick next to *Go Skinny Dipping*. "Number two. Get a tattoo," she read out.

"You don't have to do them in order," Maisie said. "You're so regimented. The whole point of the list is to help you lighten up. You don't have to treat it like an assignment."

"Have you met me?" Emery asked her. "Of course I'm going to treat it like that."

"Yeah, you're right." Maisie sounded almost gleeful. "But maybe we should move them around. Put the tattoo later. I know you, you'll never do it."

"I don't actually want to do any of them," Emery told her. "Especially after what happened today."

"But isn't a tiny piece of you glad you did?" Maisie sounded almost sad. Like her plan wasn't working. "Isn't it nice to do something that you know your asshole ex would hate?"

Emery couldn't help but smile at her friend's vehemence. "Maybe…"

"Then try to do some more. For me. I hate being so far from you. I just want you to remember who you are. How much fun you can be when you don't have Trenton weighing you down."

"I'm trying," Emery told her. "I really am." She swallowed hard, because she knew Maisie was right. "I promise by the end of the summer I'll have them all done."

"Even number seven?" Maisie asked, sounding more than a little smug.

Kiss a man who isn't your ex.

Emery swallowed. "Even number seven."

The silence that followed wasn't empty. It was charged. Hopeful. And just a little terrifying.

CHAPTER
Five

HENDRIX HANDED each of his brothers a beer, then took a sip of his own. It was almost six, and he'd arrived back at his cottage to find them waiting for him, their cars parked in his driveway. Frank was nowhere to be seen, no doubt having found somewhere cool to sleep the afternoon away.

"To what do I owe the pleasure of this visit?" he asked Pres and Marley. They looked like they'd both come straight from work – Pres from the construction site, and Marley from the fire station where he was the chief.

And as much as he loved them both, he knew they wouldn't just casually drop in on their little brother for the fun of it.

"Mom asked us to check on you," Pres admitted sheepishly, taking a mouthful of beer. Pres and Marley were twins. Thirty-four, loud, loyal, and completely incapable of minding their own business. And like most twins, they came as a set. They were also both married with kids, much to their mom's delight.

He'd always been the wildcard, the one his mom lost sleep over. Even at twenty-nine, he was still the worry line on her forehead. All he knew was that she worried about him often. And he didn't like it. He just wanted to live a quiet life.

"Well you can report back that I'm fine," Hendrix told them.

"She's all worked up with this charity thing," Marley said, shrugging. She'd been working on creating a charity for the past two years, alongside their dad. From the start, as the three of them were growing up, their parents had made it clear they wanted their children to make their own way in life. That included them not inheriting their dad's money from his rock music career before he settled down in his hometown.

Hendrix was fine with that. He didn't want money he hadn't earned himself, and he knew his brothers didn't either. They both encouraged their mom to create the Hartson Foundation – her way of helping the homeless in West Virginia – by building shelters and apartments where those less fortunate could rebuild their lives.

"Mom hates you living out here all alone. She thinks you're lonely," Pres murmured, taking a seat on the swing that had been here when Hendrix moved in.

"She also thinks you're living in squalor," Marley added, his mouth curling at the thought.

"And she isn't wrong," Pres pointed out. "He *is* living in squalor. But he's not lonely. Didn't you see the pair of women's panties at the top of his laundry pile?"

"You're looking through my laundry?" Hendrix frowned. "You got some kind of dirty clothes fetish?"

Pres rolled his eyes. "I used your bathroom, remember? I had to pass your laundry room. So what is it? Are they yours?"

Marley chuckled.

"None of your business." Hendrix shook his head, glancing over at the Reed Farmhouse again. It had been a week since his encounter with Emery. He'd glimpsed her once or twice but nothing more.

Okay, there was more. But most of it was in his imagination. Maybe his mom was right, he was lonely.

But not for company. For feeling alive. For seeing a woman half naked in his field after losing her clothes to Frank.

For seeing *her*.

He blinked that thought away. He wasn't interested. No sir. And even if he was, she was taken.

By Trenton Montclair.

"So, whose are they?" Marley asked. He was the quieter of the twins. But apparently right now was when he chose to speak up.

"Nobody important." Maybe he should let them think he had company. They could report it back to Mom. She'd at least stop worrying for a while. But then... it felt wrong. Letting them think that those panties meant anything.

They belonged to Emery. And he was enough of a damn gentleman to not want anybody to think badly of her.

"Frank found them," he said. And he immediately regretted it.

"In your bedroom?" Marley asked.

"You having sex in front of goats now?" Pres added. The two of them started to laugh.

"He found them outside. Somewhere." For fuck's sake. Hendrix rubbed his eyes with the heels of his hands. He loved his brothers, he really did. But they were as nosy as shit.

He'd chosen to live out here because he wanted peace. But maybe peace didn't want him.

"Where did he find them then?" Pres asked, a grin on his face. "On your land?"

"I don't know. You know Frank. Wanders around."

"He's a ladies' man," Marley said.

"A ladies' goat," Pres pointed out.

"A nannies' goat, if you want to be specific," Hendrix said, feeling tired now.

"Yeah, well those panties didn't belong to a nanny goat. There are only two leg holes."

Marley frowned. "You think a goat's panties would have four leg holes? Wouldn't that be like a bodysuit?"

Pres blinked, like he was seriously thinking about it. "Hmm, that's a good question. All I know is that no goat was wearing those panties. They were delicate. Pretty."

"Will you stop talking about the damn panties?" Hendrix muttered. "They're not your concern."

Because seriously, they were making his head ache. And it was wrong. They were Emery's. Nobody should be looking at them. Especially not his asshole brothers. "And stop sneaking around, looking at my stuff."

"He's calling the panties his stuff," Pres said to Marley, completely unperturbed by Hendrix's outburst.

"I noticed." Marley nodded, looking almost serious. "He seems very attached to them."

"He probably takes them to bed at night," Pres agreed.

"Will you both fuck off?" Damn, he was tired. He loved his brothers, but right now he craved silence.

His brothers sniggered. "Just doing our brotherly duty." Pres cleared his throat. "You are being careful, right?"

"Jesus." Hendrix shook his head. "Now, was there anything else you wanted to talk about, or are you here just to sneak around the house?"

"Mom wants to know if you're ever going to come for lunch one Sunday. And Delilah keeps asking after you, too," Pres added. "She misses her Uncle Hendrix."

Hendrix winced at the mention of his eleven-year-old niece. He'd barely seen her since he came home to Hartson's Creek. "It's a busy time on the farm. And I work most Sundays."

"At least try some time. Mom cares about you, man. It hurts her when she only hears news about you from Uncle Logan."

Hendrix swallowed hard. "I'll try."

"Which means you won't," Pres said. "Come on. Just come for an hour. Or I'm gonna start spreading rumors about those panties."

Hendrix narrowed his eyes. "You wouldn't."

"No he wouldn't." Marley was always the peacemaker. "But please try to come. For Mom. We're meeting at their place after church."

Hendrix let out a breath. "Okay, I'll try." He meant it this time, and his brothers knew it. That's why they both took a mouthful of beer and nodded, not bothering to push the conversation anymore.

"Hey, who's that?" Pres asked. Hendrix followed his gaze over the road to the Reed farm, where Emery was standing on the porch, talking on her phone. She was wearing a pair of shorts and a tank again. No surprise with this heat. He noticed her legs had gotten more golden – she must have been working out on the farm.

He pulled his gaze away.

"Emery Reed," he murmured.

Pres' lips curled. "Don't let mom know a pretty woman's in the house next to yours."

"She'll be delighted to hear that pretty woman's engaged to Trenton Montclair," Hendrix pointed out. As much as for himself as for his brothers. Because there was something about Emery that pulled him in. Not just the fact he'd seen her half naked.

"Montclair," Marley murmured. "Isn't he the asshole that planted weed in your locker at school?"

Hendrix nodded. "The very same."

Because Montclair had been jealous that Hendrix was chosen for the varsity football team, and he hadn't.

The little shit had made it clear how pissed he was by getting Hendrix into so much trouble that his mom had been called in to see the Principal, causing her to miss their dad's induction into the Rock and Roll Hall of Fame.

It was years ago, but it still stung. The memory of his mom's disappointment still rankled. She'd been hurt by him and hated not being able to support his dad.

Marley wrinkled his nose. "What the hell does she see in a guy like that?"

"She probably likes the bad boys." Pres grinned.

"Shame though," Marley said. "She's pretty."

Yeah, she was. But she was also everything he'd sworn to avoid. Messy, complicated and tempting as hell.

But for once in his life, Hendrix was trying to be the kind of man his mom didn't have to worry about.

"Honey, is Trenton planning on coming to see you soon?" her mom asked, trying to keep her voice casual, even though Emery could tell there was something on her mind.

"I don't think so. He's having to work weekends to get everything done." It wasn't a complete lie. He was super busy at work – he always had been. But she hadn't spoken to him for the last week. For all she knew he was living his best life on the weekends.

The funny thing was, she didn't care.

"Actually," she said, because she wanted to shut this conversation down fast. "He said that he might have to fly west for a couple of months. There's a project in Arizona that needs his attention." She lifted a brow. "He's so sorry he can't be here."

"Oh." Her mom frowned. There was clearly something bothering her. Emery felt her jaw tighten. "It's just that people are asking questions."

"What kind of questions?" Emery asked. She'd been here for just over a week now, spending most of it collecting paperwork and trying to get as much detail about the farm as she could to answer all the realtor's requests.

"I saw Chrissie Fairfax at the dress shop," her mom murmured. "She was saying how strange it was that you were here and your fiancé wasn't. It's not like Charleston is a million miles away. He could at least come down on a Saturday afternoon to see you."

Emery's stomach tightened. For a minute she considered coming clean. But she couldn't stand the thought of the tears and the recriminations.

Through the window, she could see Jed gearing up to leave for the evening. It felt like the reprieve she was looking for. She jumped up from the table.

"I need to speak to Jed before he leaves," she told her mom. "I'll be back in a bit."

Her mom frowned. "Oh, of course."

Rushing out into the sultry early evening air, Emery found herself glancing at the farm cottage on the other side of the lane.

She hadn't seen their new neighbor since the day his goat had stolen her clothes. She hadn't laundered his t-shirt either. It was still under her pillow. Last night she'd pulled it out and smelled it like some kind of weirdo. The aroma of earth and cologne had taken her right back to the field. To the darkness in his eyes as he'd stared at her, standing half naked.

To the way she'd felt alive like she hadn't for a long, long time.

It was a good thing Trenton didn't know about *that*. He probably would have a hissy fit they would hear within a ten-mile radius.

"Hey!" she called out, spotting Jed standing over by the pasture, in a pair of jeans and an old t-shirt, the way most farmers dressed. He turned around, giving her a beaming smile.

"Hey, Emery girl. What's up?"

She forced a smile on her face, trying desperately to think of something to say.

Actually, I'm trying to escape from my mom and you're a convenient excuse.

Yeah, that wasn't going to work. "I was wondering how your family was doing," she said lamely.

He blinked, like he knew she was lying. "They're all good. We had another grandbaby. My youngest daughter's child."

"Congratulations," Emery said, genuinely pleased for him.

"Thank you." He beamed. "Want to see a picture?"

"Yes I do." She smiled while he pulled out his cell – an old battered iPhone that she would lay a bet once belonged to one of his six kids. His thick, calloused fingers took a while to find the photo, but when he did his smile widened even more as he held it out to her.

"They named him Samuel Jedidiah. After me." He looked proud as punch at that.

"He's a beauty."

"He really is." He cleared his throat. "And how are you doing with getting all that information you need?"

"I've found nearly all the paperwork. Dad's filing system left a lot to be desired."

"He was a doer, not a paper man," Jed told her.

"I don't suppose you know when he sold off the top field, do you? I need that information."

Jed rubbed his chin. "A couple of years back I think. Let me look through my own paperwork," he said. "Times have been hard. Costs keep going up and crop prices keep going down. Your dad made the decisions he needed to keep this place going." He looked at her, his expression soft. "Your mom, too. It's been hard on her, I guess. Trying to keep this place going when she has no idea where to start. It'll be good for her to move on."

"It will." She nodded. "Thank you for staying on and helping her. It means a lot."

"No problem, kid." He ruffled her hair and it sent a rush of warmth through her. "I'm glad you're back. You've made your mom happy, and I haven't seen her happy in a long while."

Her throat tightened. "Thank you."

"And she's so excited about your wedding. Maybe she'll get to show photos of her grandbabies around soon too, huh?"

There was that guilt again. Mixing with the feeling that she was letting everybody down. "Maybe," she lied.

He winked at her. "I'd better get home. You get this place on the market and get it sold before fall. That way your mom can start building her life before the year is over."

"That's the plan." If they could find somebody to buy it. "Have a good evening."

"You too, kid." He wandered over to his old, battered truck and climbed inside. She watched as he drove away. She was just about to walk back into the house when a loud bray came from the rocky lane, making her jump.

A goat – *the goat?* – was leaning his head over her mom's fence, his big bottom teeth on display as he called out to her. His eyes – yellow as the sun with a dark slash across the center – followed her as she walked over.

"Are you the panty-stealer?" she asked, keeping her distance because she didn't trust him not to steal the clothes off her body this time.

He let out a bray, then reared onto his hind legs like a horse, his hooves clattering against the weathered wooden slats of the fence. She was used to highly strung animals – what farm kid wasn't – but it still made her jump.

"Frank!"

Hendrix came storming out of the cottage and across the lane, a towel in his hand, his hair wet. He was wearing a pair of jeans and nothing else, his feet bare, just like his chest, which was covered in tiny droplets of water.

Everything inside of her clenched.

His eyes caught hers. And yeah, he caught her looking. At least she had the good grace to blush.

Not to be ignored, Frank started pounding his head against the fence.

"You're gonna have to stop flirting with my goat," Hendrix said, his voice thick. "He's getting unmanageable."

She laughed softly. "He's the same one then. Frank?"

"This is him. Yeah." He grabbed Frank by his collar. "I'm sorry if he disturbed you."

"He didn't steal my panties this time, so I'm gonna let him off."

"He ate half of one of my belts yesterday while I was working," Hendrix told her. "Just wandered into the house and had a feast."

"He gets into your house?" She frowned. Maybe she should make sure their front door was locked. She didn't put it past Frank not to sneak up on her mom.

Hendrix shrugged, looking amused. "Yep. I figure him having a nap on my sofa is probably better than flirting with the nanny goats. The last thing this world needs is a bunch of baby Franks."

It was stupid the way she blushed at the mention of something as natural as Frank mating. But maybe because she was thinking more about the owner than the goat.

He was stupidly masculine without a top on. His chest thick and muscled, his skin tan.

To distract herself, she walked forward and stroked Frank's face. He let out a low bray and pressed his muzzle against her chest.

"He's sweet when he's not stealing clothes," she murmured.

"He's sweet because he's got his face against your body."

Actually, it was against her breasts. Frank looked delighted at their softness. When she glanced up at him, Hendrix seemed pretty transfixed by them too.

What was it with men and boobs? She'd never understand it. But that didn't mean she didn't like the way he was staring at her.

"I should go back inside," she told him.

"Yeah." He nodded, his gaze still on her. "And I should probably go put on a shirt."

That made her smile. And then he smiled back at her and she felt a weird twist in her stomach. It went well with the shivers down her spine.

"I'll see you around, Emery," he murmured, pulling Frank away from her chest and walking him back to his own farm.

Her heart pounded as she watched him lead the goat into his yard, tickling him under his chin like he was fond of him.

And then she walked back into her own house.

CHAPTER *Six*

PULLING up outside his brother's house, Hendrix climbed out of his truck with a sack of rabbit bedding slung over his shoulder, a frantic request from his niece, Delilah, the second she found out he was at the farm supply store.

He could already hear chaos from inside.

One of his three-year-old twin nephews was crying. Or maybe screaming. Possibly both.

He knocked once, then let himself in, because that's how small towns – and his big family – rolled.

His sister-in-law, Cassie, was crouched in the hallway, wrangling a dripping-wet toddler who had only one sock and zero remorse.

"Oh hey," she said breathlessly, brushing a strand of hair off her forehead. She had the look of a woman on the edge. "We had a milk incident."

"I heard the banshee scream from the yard," Hendrix said, holding up the bag. "I got the message from Delilah. Figured her rabbit might want some bedding before she goes to sleep."

Cassie gave him a grateful smile and inclined her head at the stairs. "You're a lifesaver. She's in her room."

"Good luck with…" he gestured to the puddle forming beneath the toddler, "whatever this is."

Cassie sighed. "If you ever feel like becoming a live-in nanny, just say the word."

Hendrix laughed and headed upstairs. His eleven-year-old niece's door was half-open, soft light spilling into the hallway. He knocked gently before pushing it open.

The room smelled faintly of strawberries and sawdust. Posters of pop stars, planets, and one extremely dramatic horse covered the walls. In the corner, a fat white rabbit blinked at him from her hutch like she was the queen of it all.

Delilah was on the rug, painting her toenails a sparkly purple and wearing the look of someone with *Very Important Things* to do.

"Special delivery for Delilah Hartson," he announced, hoisting the bag like it was pirate treasure.

She lit up, jumping to her feet and throwing her arms around him before grabbing the sack. "Thanks, Uncle Hendrix. You saved my life. And Bun Bun's."

"I live to serve." He gave the rabbit a salute. "How's Her Majesty doing?"

"She kicked all her bedding out this afternoon. Mom said she has an attitude."

"She gets it from you," he teased.

Delilah stuck out her tongue. "That's rude. I'm a delight. You must be mixing me up with my brothers." Her face suddenly turned serious. "I miss Club Solo."

For a second, his mouth turned dry. *Club Solo* was the secret alliance they'd formed the week her twin brothers were born. Just the two of them against a world suddenly obsessed with multiples. He'd knelt beside her at the hospital, looked her in the eye, and told her he knew exactly what it felt like to be the odd one out, since he was the only brother of twins, too.

"I miss it too," he said softly. "I've been a crappy president."

She shrugged, looking delighted that he'd sworn in front of her. "You've been busy. Dad says you've been renovating your house."

He reached out and gently tugged the end of her ponytail. "Still. I owe you at least one emergency meeting. Maybe with cupcakes."

Her smile came slowly, but when it did, it lit up her whole face. "And a new secret handshake." She dropped her voice. "Twins are the worst."

"They are."

"Too loud. Too sticky. Too twinny."

"You said it, Vice President." He winked.

She giggled, then gave him a sly look. "So… I have some more news."

He sat on the edge of her bed. "I'm all ears."

Her voice dropped to a whisper. "I have a boyfriend."

Hendrix arched a brow. "Do you now?" Wow. She wasn't supposed to be growing up so fast. Pres was going to be so mad. He suppressed a smile at that thought.

"His name is Ben. He gave me half his cupcake at lunch," she said proudly, her cheeks pinking up.

"That's practically a proposal."

She grinned with delight. "He asked to walk me to library period. I said yes."

He sank onto the floor beside her. "Classic boyfriend move. Does your dad know?" God, he couldn't wait to see his brother's face.

"God, no. He'd just be embarrassing."

He tried not to laugh. "Okay. So what do you want from me? Uncle standard advice? Spy gear?"

She shrugged. "I just needed to tell somebody. And I knew you wouldn't freak out."

"I'm honored." He bumped her shoulder with his. "Want my two cents?"

Delilah nodded.

"If Ben's sweet, makes you laugh, and doesn't make you feel like you have to be anyone else... then he's a good one."

She nodded solemnly. "He said my sneakers are cool."

He gave her solemn nod. "Total keeper."

She smiled, then tilted her head. "How come you don't have a girlfriend?"

He lifted a brow. "Whoa there, kid. You're coming in hot with the personal questions."

"I'm just asking." Her gaze was steady. "You're funny, you smell good, and you're not ugly."

"Well, thanks," he said, laughing under his breath. "But I'm on a break from dating."

"Because of the California girl?"

He paused. Sharp kid. "Yeah. She wasn't who I thought she was."

"What happened?"

Hendrix paused. Yes, she was growing up, but there were some things above her grade level. Not that he wanted to talk about this anyway.

"Let's just say we didn't want the same things. I figured it out late, but better than never."

Delilah nodded, like she understood more than she should. "Mom says the best relationships are built on friendship."

"Your mom's smart."

Delilah gave him a long look. "So maybe you just need a new friend."

He didn't reply right away. Instead, he reached out and tucked a lock of hair behind her ear. "Maybe I do."

She leaned into him, resting her head on his arm. "You're gonna be okay, Uncle Hendrix."

"Yeah," he said quietly. "Thanks kiddo. I'm trying to be." And that was all he could hope for right now.

―――

Emery stared at her phone, her brows pinching. This morning she'd sent over the last of the paperwork she'd managed to find to the realtor.

Jed had helped a lot. He'd talked her through the crop schedules and helped her find the employment contracts for the farm staff, and she'd finally laid her hands on the updated title deeds and farm plans that had been drawn up after her dad had sold off the pond and the surrounding land.

She re-read the email the realtor had sent back to her, her throat tight.

Emery,

Many thanks for sending these through. I noticed there's an agricultural lien on the livestock. Can you send the details through as no sale can proceed until this is settled?

Kind regards,

Richard Houseman
 WV Country Realty

She had no idea about this lien, but it obviously wasn't good news. Turning in her chair, she called out to her mom, who was making iced tea in the kitchen.

"Do you know anything about a lien on the livestock?"

"What dear?" Her mom didn't turn around.

"A lien. A loan. Do you know who dad took it out with?" And more importantly, how much he took out. Why did this have to be so difficult?

"I've no idea, honey. Your father was in charge of the finances." She carried over a glass of sweet tea and put it in front of Emery. But there was a strange look on her face.

"Do you know where I might find out? There's nothing about it in the farm's bank statement."

Her mom let out a sigh. "Do you really need it?" she asked. "Can't we sell the farm and sort it out later?"

"That's not how it works, Mom. The realtor needs everything." Emery pressed her lips together. "Would Jed know about it?"

"No. We promised we wouldn't tell…" Her mom trailed off, realizing she'd given too much away.

"What's going on?" A shiver snaked down Emery's spine. "What kind of lien is it?"

Her mom stood stock straight, like she was trying to hold herself together. "Maybe you should talk to Trenton," she finally said, like it pained her to say the words.

"What would he know about it?" Emery asked, confused. "Is he involved in the loan?"

"He asked us not to tell you. Daddy promised him. We didn't want you to worry about the farm when you were so busy," her mom murmured.

Emery felt her whole body tense up. "Did Trenton loan you the money?" she asked.

Her mom sighed. "Yes, I think so."

For god's sake. Emery winced. "How much?"

"Daddy needed to buy some new livestock," her mom told her. "We had a bad year. Or a bad few years." She shifted her feet. It was so obvious she was embarrassed. But why the hell did Trenton get involved?

Yes, he had money. She knew that. But it felt like control, not money.

"How much did he loan Dad?" Emery tried to keep her voice soft.

"I don't know." Her mom really looked like she was about to start sobbing.

"A hundred dollars? A thousand? *More*?" She knew it was more. Farm equipment and livestock didn't come cheap.

"I really have no idea." Her mom started to cry. "And does it matter? He's going to be your husband. He wanted to help. Family helps family. He just didn't want to worry you. Asked us not to say a thing."

Of course he didn't want her to know. This was all a power play to him. Another way to show her how much control he had. "Mom, I need to find it all. The paperwork, the amounts."

"But why?" Her mom didn't seem to get it.

"Because we have to declare and resolve any debts on the farm before we put it on the market."

"Trenton never told us that."

Emery swallowed hard. "No, he probably didn't. But you can't sell the house without resolving this."

"Maybe you could speak to him," her mom said, twisting her bracelet around her wrist. "Ask him if he could sign away the debts early."

Emery winced. Her head was starting to hurt. "I don't think I can do that."

"Why not?"

She had no answer to that. At least not one that wouldn't cause more problems than it would solve. "I'll speak to him," Emery agreed, because right now there was no other way. "Just find me that loan agreement. Please."

"Okay." Her mom nodded. "I'll look this afternoon."

"Thank you."

"Why did you loan my parents money without telling me?" Emery asked Trenton later that afternoon when she'd finally brought herself to call him.

Her mom had found the paperwork in an envelope in her dad's dresser. She'd handed it to Emery, her eyes full of embarrassment. And for the last hour she'd seethed every time she looked at it.

"Hello to you too. How are you?" His voice was smooth.

"The loan?" she asked again. "Why did you give them so much money without telling me?"

Because now she knew how much it was in total. Just shy of eighty thousand dollars.

"Your parents asked me not to," Trenton replied, echoing her mom's words of earlier. "It was all going to be written off once we were married. And once I took control of my trust fund," Trenton continued. "Now that's changed, of course."

"I'm going to need you to sign the lien away," she told him. "We need it closed before I can put the farm on the market."

"You want me to sign it away before it's repaid?" he asked. There was a frown in his tone.

"Yes. We'll pay the money back once the farm is sold."

"But how do I know you'll do that?" he asked her.

Annoyance rushed through her. "Because I'm giving you my word."

"You also gave your word that you'd marry me," he pointed out. "And look what happened there."

"And you agreed to be faithful," she retorted. It was one thing agreeing to do this stupid charade just to keep their parents happy. Another to know he held something over her mom. "Please don't be difficult," she said softly. "I just need this thing to be resolved."

"I'm not being difficult. I'm a businessman. Speaking of which, I'm late for a meeting."

"Trenton…" she started to argue back, but he'd already hung up. All that was left was a buzzing on the line and the fury rushing through her body.

Letting out a sharp cry, she threw her phone onto the floor, the crack of plastic against hardwood echoing through the quiet room.

Her chest heaved as she paced across the kitchen, fists clenched at her sides. Every part of her was shaking with anger and frustration.

She'd bent over backward not to cause waves. Stayed quiet to protect her mom. Agreed to a lie that made her sick.

And Trenton was still holding all the power.

"I should have gone to Europe," she muttered, hating this tangled web of lies that she was caught up in.

Because right now, she had no idea how to get out of this mess.

As she picked up her phone she saw the stupid list stuffed into the back of it between her phone and the case. She'd been looking at it earlier, mostly because Maisie had messaged her from Edinburgh, telling her that she'd decided to stay and marry a Scotsman.

She was joking, or at least Emery thought she was, but it still made her feel wistful. Like the world was going on without her. And here she was, stuck in a mess that felt impossible to get out of.

That's when she saw it. The most easily attainable thing on her friend's list. And the one that she needed to do right now.

3. Get drunk at least once.

Hendrix peeled off his sweat-soaked shirt and slung it over his shoulder as he climbed down from the roof, muscles burning, chest slick and golden in the dying sunlight. Another repair done. A hundred more to go.

The land still needed prepping. Trenches needed to be dug, soil was waiting to be balanced, and he had a list of crops he planned to buy for fall. But tonight his body had hit its limit. Dust clung to his skin, his jeans were stuck to his thighs, and the only thing he wanted more than a shower was a cold beer on the porch.

A goat's bleat sounded in the distance.

"Don't start, Frank," he muttered. "You're not the one hammering nails in ninety-degree heat."

He stepped onto the porch, cracked open the screen door, and grabbed a beer from the fridge. Popping the cap, he wandered back underneath the wooden overhang, tipping his head back to take a long, satisfying mouthful of beer, the ice cold liquid soothing his overheated body.

The kind of peace you only got in a small town wrapped around him like dusk.

Frank gave a little bray.

"What's up, bud?" Hendrix asked. But then he saw what the goat was looking at.

A very determined Emery Reed was walking across the lane that separated her farm from his. She was wearing a pair of shorts that exposed her smooth, tan legs, and a t-shirt she'd tied up at the waist to expose a thin sliver of her taut stomach.

"Be good," Hendrix murmured to Frank. "We don't want to make the pretty lady mad tonight."

Truth was, as she got closer, he could see there was already a frown on her face. What had he done this time? He'd barely seen her all week.

"If you're coming to talk about Frank, whatever he's done isn't my fault," he told her as she reached the bottom of the stairs. Frank, deciding to be a gentleman for once, stepped aside so she could walk up them.

She tipped her head to the side. "I didn't come about the goat." She let out a sigh. "I just wondered if you had a beer you could spare. My mom keeps a sober household."

He blinked, because he hadn't expected that. "Yeah, I've got a beer you can have." He walked inside and grabbed another bottle from the refrigerator. When he came out, she was sitting in one of the chairs on his porch, tickling Frank beneath the chin.

"There you go." He passed the open bottle to her.

"Thank you," she muttered, then took a long swig from the rim. By the time she stopped swallowing, almost half the bottle was gone.

"Bad day?" he asked her.

"Something like that."

He took one of the other chairs, letting his long legs stretch out in front of him. "Want to talk about it?"

She shook her head. "Not really." She sighed, like she had the weight of the world on her shoulders. Then she looked at him, their eyes catching. "Do you ever wish you could go back in time and make different decisions?"

The corner of his lip quirked. "I don't think that deeply." It was a lie, but the last thing he wanted to talk about were all his bad choices. Especially with her, the woman who seemed to have it all together.

She looked around at the fields stretching into the distance. The light was waning, the sun an orange ball skimming the edge of the horizon. "Don't you ever get lonely out here?" she asked him.

He shrugged. "I don't have time to think about being lonely."

"But this is what you want? Your own farm?"

"Yeah." He nodded. "I like working outside. Being in charge of my own time." He took another mouthful of beer, noticing she'd almost finished hers. "Anyway, it's hard to get lonely when you're related to half the town."

She nodded, frowning like she was taking his words in. "Is it nice having a big family?"

"Sometimes." He smiled softly. "It was fun growing up, being surrounded by my brothers and cousins."

"And now?"

"It's good, as long as they're not poking their noses where they aren't wanted." He loved them all fiercely. But yeah, they could be nosey assholes when they wanted to be. "Are you lonely?" he asked her, more because he didn't want to talk about himself than actually being interested in her answer.

She ran the tip of her tongue over her bottom lip. It was fuller than her top lip. Shaped like a perfect bow. "I'm an only child. Nearly everybody I went to school with has moved away. It's strange," she told him. "My mom has more friends here than I do."

"What about your fiancé? Won't he be coming to visit?" His jaw tightened at the thought of that ass. "Or are you going back home soon?"

"I'm staying for the summer," she told him. "Getting the farm ready to sell. And no, Trenton won't be coming here. He's busy." Weird how she didn't seem to sound like she cared a whole lot about that.

And what guy was too busy to spend time with the woman he was marrying? That was messed up. But it also wasn't his business. If Montclair wanted to neglect his fiancée, that was *his* problem.

"How about you?" she asked him. "Do you have a girl-friend?" Her words were a little slower. Like the beer was having more of an effect on her than it should.

"Nope." His reply came out in a long two syllables.

Their gazes locked and it sent a jolt through him. He could see the interest in her eyes. The same kind of curiosity he saw in his cousins and brothers every time they wanted to know every damn detail of his life.

Hendrix Hartson. Family fuck up. Always entertaining.

"Can I have another beer?" she asked him. "Actually, do you have anything stronger? Maybe whiskey?"

He wanted to laugh. "No, I don't have whiskey." And if he did, he wouldn't give it to her. She was so obviously a lightweight. "One more beer. That's it. Then I'm cutting you off."

It took him a minute to grab two more bottles, getting rid of the old ones in the recycling bin. This time when he came back out, she was on her phone, tapping on the screen as Frank lay at her feet.

"Everything okay?" he asked, handing her the bottle.

"Everything's good." She took a sip, a smaller one this time. "Have you ever stayed up all night talking to somebody?"

He started to laugh. "Where did that come from? And no, I've never stayed up all night talking. I like my sleep too much. And I can't be exhausted and work with farm equipment."

She nodded. "Yeah, that's what I thought." She took another mouthful, then let out a sigh. "Damn stupid list."

"What was that?"

"Nothing." She smiled a little hazily at him. And for the first time he noticed she wasn't wearing her engagement ring. Her eyes caught his, and he pulled his gaze away quickly.

But not before something passed between them.

Something that felt suspiciously like trouble.

―――

Woo hoo at getting another item ticked off. So did you ask him about staying up talking all night? – Maisie

. . .

I tried. But he made it obvious it was a no go. I'm not sure why I'm doing this stupid list, anyway. – Emery

Because you know it's good for you. And you love me. And I need entertainment when I'm on the sleeper train to Vienna and the people in the next bunk are singing football songs. Maybe you should try number seven with him. – Maisie.

Shut up. And go to sleep. I've already ticked two off the list. That's one a week on average. I'm killing this thing. – Emery

I knew you would. I should have kept number seven as it was. – Maisie

I'm glad you didn't. You know I don't like to fail. – Emery

Exactly. – Maisie

CHAPTER
Seven

"HEY MOM, did you hear that Hendrix has a pretty new neighbor?" Pres asked, sending a sly look at Hendrix, who was minding his own damn business, eating the barbecue their dad had cooked.

"Emery Reed?" their mom replied, not missing a beat. "Yes, I heard." She pressed her lips together. "And I also heard she's engaged to Trenton Montclair, so that's a no-go."

She sounded almost sad about that, like setting him up with her would have been a good idea otherwise. Hendrix sent his brother a dirty look. Sometimes it felt like the three of them had never grown up.

"Don't make me regret coming over here," Hendrix warned him. Pres shot him a dirty grin. Most of the family was here, despite the clouds starting to form a grey canopy over the blue sky. There was a storm warning for later. He'd head home after this and make sure everything in the farm was secure.

"Trenton Montclair," their dad said, deep in thought. "Wasn't he the one who…"

"Yes, he was." Their mom's voice was low. "And the less said about that the better. Who wants cake?"

"I haven't finished my burger yet," Marley pointed out. Nor had anybody else for that matter. There were about twenty members of his family there, sitting around tables in his parents' backyard. Marley and Presley and their families, along with their cousins Michael and Grace were here, as well as Sabrina, who was entertaining them all with stories of her recent dates.

"He doesn't need somebody who's engaged. I already told him I could set him up with my friends," Sabrina said, biting off a mouthful of burger. She had a glint in her eye that Hendrix knew meant trouble. But then trouble and Sabrina went together like a gin and tonic.

"I'm fine, thanks," Hendrix told her.

"Mariah is sweet," Sabrina said. "She still asks after you even though you're a bore."

"Which one is Mariah?" his mom asked his cousin. Hendrix internally groaned. He wasn't interested in any of Sabrina's friends. They were too young. And even if they weren't, the thought of dating anybody his cousin confided in was way too horrific.

"She's the one who trashed her dad's car driving home from a bar," Michael said, winking at his sister.

"Eek." Their mom wrinkled her nose. "Maybe not then."

"There's also Lila," Sabrina mused. "She's been single for a while."

Hendrix's eyes met Marley's. For once his brother looked sympathetic. He'd been through this himself before he'd settled down with Kate and her kids.

"Didn't Lila get caught setting fires last year?" Grace asked.

"Well, yeah, but she had a legitimate reason," Sabrina answered, shaking her blonde hair. "She'd found her ex in bed with another woman. She took a pile of his things and set them on fire."

Jesus Christ. "You know what?" Hendrix said. "I'll find my own girlfriend, thank you."

Delilah patted his hand, in an 'I've got this' kind of way. "Why are you all trying to set him up anyway?" she asked her aunts. "You keep telling me not to bother with boys. To be a strong independent woman." She folded her arms across her chest, looking older than her years. "So why can't Hendrix be a strong independent man?"

Pres lifted a brow.

"She's gonna be trouble," Marley said to him.

"Already is." Pres looked resigned.

"If you're really not interested in Mariah, maybe you should try online dating," Sabrina told Hendrix, ignoring her niece and cousins. "I've met so many guys on there."

"What guys?" Michael asked. "Who are they? Do Mom and your dad know?"

Sabrina rolled her eyes. "Of course not. I'm not an idiot." She looked at Hendrix. "I'll come over next week. Make you a profile."

"Over my dead body," he replied. "Thank you, but no thank you." Even if he wanted to online date – which he didn't – there was no way he was putting his love life in Sabrina's hands. He loved his cousin fiercely, and he'd fight to the death for her.

But he trusted her about as far as he could throw her.

"Shame about Emery Reed," Pres murmured. "She looks exactly like Hendrix's type."

His mom's gaze landed on Hendrix.

"Oh honey, she's engaged. You don't want to be getting the reputation of being a home wrecker," his mom said.

"I'm not a home wrecker." He frowned at being accused of something he hadn't done. "I barely even know the woman." And he definitely wouldn't be admitting that she got drunk on his porch with him the other night. He glanced over at his brother, shooting him a dirty look because Pres knew exactly what he was doing. Shit stirring, mostly.

"Guys don't get called home wreckers," Grace said, thankfully pulling the attention away from Hendrix. "The double standards are so annoying when it comes to cheating. They get called studs."

"True story," Sabrina said, poking her tongue out at Hendrix. "I hate that so much."

"Me too," Kate, Hendrix's sister-in-law agreed. "And don't get me started on the way dads get called great when they do the bare minimum of taking care of their own kids."

Marley choked on his burger bun. Pres hit his back, and a lump of bread flew out of his mouth.

"I hear ya," Cassie agreed. "Double standards all round."

Christ, Hendrix was getting a headache. "There you go," he told his mom. "There's nothing to worry about. Now, can I enjoy my food in peace?"

"I just want you to be happy," his mom said, looking hurt. "After everything…"

"I know," he said quickly. "And thank you. I am happy." He shot a look at Pres. "And as for you…"

"What?" Pres asked, looking innocent.

"It wasn't that long ago you were in my position. Or you," he said to Marley.

"And you gave as good as you got whenever Mom tried to set us up," Marley pointed out. "I remember you teasing me about Kate."

"You two fought about it, as I recall," Pres said, grinning.

"You fought over me?" Kate asked, looking confused.

"He gave me a nuggie trying to get me to admit I was attracted to you." Marley laughed, and Kate reached out to squeeze his hand.

"I hate the way you boys fight," their mom said, shaking her head.

"Boys will be boys," their dad murmured. He was the one who taught them how to fight, after all.

"It's all a load of macho bullshit if you ask me," Sabrina said. Grace and the other women nodded. "If you just talked things out you wouldn't get into so many problems."

"But where would the fun be in that?" Pres asked.

"Talking of macho bullshit, anybody want a beer?" their dad said, standing up. "Women included, of course."

———

The sky was streaked with layers of pink and red with smudges of dark gray that only seemed to be getting worse as the sun slowly slid toward the horizon. Hendrix had spent the last hour moving his uncle's cattle safely to the barn, and now he was home, checking that his own place was ready for the summer storm the forecasters had promised was coming.

From the corner of his eye, he could see Emery crossing the lane and walking his way. He immediately bristled. He was still salty after Pres teased him at their mom's place and the accusations of being a home wrecker.

As he'd been leaving his mom had asked him if he was okay, and if he knew dating a taken woman was wrong.

Of course it was wrong. And he wasn't dating her, anyway. They were barely friends. But the memory of his mom's worried face still played in his mind.

After the mess last year, and all the mistakes he'd made over the years before, the last thing he wanted was to cause her more pain.

So yeah, he was avoiding Emery Reed. And for good reason. He closed up the shed where he'd put Frank, because as much as the goat was a pain in the ass, he didn't want him getting caught in the storm.

"Hey," Emery called out. She was smiling, and it hit him in the gut. Her gaze dropped to his arms, taking in the rolled up denim shirt he was wearing, as his tan, hair flecked arms locked up the shed.

"You ready for the storm?" she asked him once she was standing a couple of feet away.

"Just put Frank away." He kept his voice low. Trying to let her know he wasn't interested in conversation.

"You think it'll be bad?" She frowned like she noticed the way he wasn't being friendly. It made him feel like an ass.

"Probably not. Just the usual storm." He caught her eye. "Is your generator ready in case you need it?"

"Jed checked it this morning. It's good to go." She looked over her shoulder at the shed where the generator was housed. "Though hopefully we won't need it."

"Always good to be ready. Good luck tonight." He turned away, ready to walk back into his house.

Emery cleared her throat. "Is something wrong?" she asked before he made it to the front steps.

"What?" He turned to look at her.

Her pretty brow furrowed. "You seem distracted. Is everything okay?"

He sighed. Why were women so damn perceptive? "Everything's fine, Emery," he told her. "Why wouldn't it be?"

"I don't know." She shifted her feet. "I guess you look angry. Did I do something wrong?"

Ah fuck it. He was going to have to say something. And he hated that.

"You're an engaged woman," he finally managed. "You probably shouldn't be talking to me."

She recoiled, like he'd slapped her in the face. "What?"

"Would your fiancé like you talking to me?" he asked her.

For a second she said nothing. He could see the hurt in her eyes, though. And it made him feel like an asshole of the highest order.

And when she did speak, he felt even worse. "So I'm not

allowed to talk to members of the opposite sex anymore?" she asked him. "What kind of sexist bullcrap is that? And anyway, why would I care?"

He blinked at her words. They sounded way too much like his cousins and sister-in-laws. "People talk. You have a reputation to uphold. I'm just thinking of you."

"Sounds like you're more worried about your own reputation," she shot back.

"I don't have one, Emery." And wasn't that the damn truth?

She twisted her hands together. "You make it sound like I'm doing something wrong. Talking to you." She jutted her chin out, clearly hurt. "And not once have I done anything wrong."

He sighed. She was right, she hadn't. It was him. All of this. He'd never been good with words. Never known what to say. He was a man of action, not pretty sentences.

And yeah, she'd done nothing wrong. But maybe *he* had. Maybe he'd thought about her in a way a man shouldn't think about a taken woman.

"I don't know what to say. I just think it would be better..." He trailed off, running his hands through his hair. "If we didn't talk."

A gust of wind lifted *her* hair, and his eyes fell on the exposed curve of her neck. This time she didn't meet his gaze. Instead, she gave a curt nod.

"Okay then," she said, her voice low. "I guess I'll see you around." She turned, her shoulders held high as she walked across the lane back to her mother's farm. He watched her leave, hyper aware of every movement she made. The way her sneakers kicked up the dust on the road, the way her hips swayed.

He could feel the wind whipping up the further she got from him.

"Emery," he shouted. The loud call of his voice made her stop, but not turn to look back.

"Make sure you close everything up," he shouted. "The storm will be here soon."

But she just walked back into her house.

CHAPTER
Eight

"FRANK!"

Emery sat bolt upright in bed. She'd been sleeping fitfully since about nine o'clock, thanks to the sounds of the storm lashing against the house. They matched the dark thoughts in her head.

She'd spent most of the night alternating between hurt and anger. How dare he accuse her of improper behavior? His twisted double standards were such bullshit. And yet they'd hit something deep inside of her, something that made her feel like she deserved them.

She'd fallen asleep fuming. But now she felt disoriented, hearing the rain still hammering against the window. And something else. Something that she couldn't quite catch.

"Frank! Where the hell are you?"

She could barely hear the words over the sound of the storm. Frowning, she sat up and put her feet on the wooden floor then padded over to the window, yanking open her curtains.

Rain was blasting against the glass, and she had to lean forward until her brow touched the cool glass to see through the torrent. Her breath fogged the surface as she frowned, her eyes focusing on Hendrix's house. The door was open and the light glowing through revealed the silhouette of a man standing at the top of the steps.

Emery pulled her window open and rain immediately covered her face. "What's going on?" she yelled, but the wind swallowed her words. *Was Frank missing?* That goat was a pain in the ass, but like Hendrix she had an affinity for animals.

Every farmer knew that your livestock worked hard for you and in return you protected them.

"Dammit." She slid her feet into her sneakers at the foot of the bed and ran down the stairs, being careful to keep her movement light, because the last thing she needed was to wake up her mom.

When she opened the front door Hendrix wasn't at the bottom of his steps anymore. His front door was closed, too. For a second she hoped that Frank had come to him, but then his door opened again and Hendrix ran out. The light was bright enough for her to see that he was wearing a pair of shorts and sneakers. No shirt, though he was pulling a raincoat around his shoulders.

"Has Frank taken off?" Emery yelled from her own doorstep. Hendrix frowned at the sound of somebody else outside. Then his gaze fell on her, taking her in.

She was wearing way less than him. Tiny shorts, a camisole, sneakers, and nothing else. At least she had a top on this time.

"Go back inside," he yelled back.

But of course, she didn't. She and Frank, they had an understanding. And on the farm, neighbors helped neighbors, no matter if they were asses who had demanded you don't talk to them.

She grabbed an old raincoat of her dad's from the hook in the hallway and ran out of the house, pulling the door closed behind her. Her shoes squelched against the path as she went to join Hendrix in the road. A river of rainwater was running down the middle.

"Dammit, I told you to get back inside," he shouted when she was close. "Just turn around."

Ignoring him, she pulled her hood over her head. "Where do you think he went?" she yelled. Rain was plastering her face, her hair.

"I've no idea. He must have gotten spooked. I got woken up by a loud bang, and when I looked out, the door to the barn was open."

A spooked animal was the worst kind. "Then I guess we should start looking." She slid her hand inside the raincoat. "You got a flashlight?" she asked, fiddling with her phone to illuminate the area in front of her.

"Yeah." He had a bigger one. One of those heavy metal flashlights that you could probably kill somebody with if you needed a blunt instrument.

"We should split up," she suggested. "I can head toward the pond and you can look on the road."

"We're not splitting up. You're going inside."

Shaking her head, she started jogging down the road, her feet splashing in the puddles, her skin shivering at the coolness of the water as it clung to her legs. Yes, it was a summer storm, but a few minutes ago she'd been snug as a bug in her bed, not soaked to the bone.

"For fuck's sake," Hendrix said behind her. She could hear the thud of his feet catching up with her.

"I'm serious," she told him. "You need to go the other way. We'll find him in half the time."

"And what about you?" he asked. "What if you end up slipping on your ass and getting hurt?"

She rolled her eyes. "Let me worry about me. Where would you go if you were a goat scared for your life?"

He blinked like she'd just asked him the hardest math equation he'd ever heard. "I don't…"

"Where's his happy place?"

"In my house." He lifted a brow.

"Other than that?" Her lips were wet from the rain. Her whole body was. It was pouring down so thick and fast.

"My uncle's farm. With the other goats."

"Then go there. I'll head to the pond because we know he likes it there." She glanced at her phone. "I'll meet you back here in twenty minutes."

"I don't like this."

"Nobody said you had to. Now go." She gestured at him like she'd gesture at Frank. "Seriously, get out of here."

God, he was as stubborn as she was. But thankfully, after a few seconds of staring at her, he did exactly as she asked, turning on his heel and running down the lane, heading for the main road that led to his uncle's farm.

As for Emery, she headed back toward the copse of trees. "Frank, you'd better be nice to me after this," she muttered. But she had a feeling that he'd be exactly the same.

"What's going on?" his uncle shouted from the doorstep of his own farmhouse. He'd been out checking on the animals when Hendrix jogged up the road toward the paddock where the goats hung out when the weather was nice. Tonight, like Frank should have been, they were locked up in their shed. A glance over at it, through the rain, told him that Frank wasn't there.

Not unless he'd learned how to pick a lock.

"Frank's missing," Hendrix told him. "Have you seen him?"

"No. You sure he came this way?" Uncle Logan asked, frowning.

"No idea," Hendrix admitted, wiping the rain from his

face. "You know what he's like. It's like looking for a needle in a haystack."

"Did you have him secured?"

"He was in the shed. Burst out, I'm guessing the thunder spooked him."

"Ah hell. And there's no sign of him at your place?"

Hendrix shook his head. "Not around the house. Emery Reed's looking for him near the pond."

"Alice's girl?"

"That's her. She heard me shouting. I must have woken her up. She came out to help."

Logan nodded but said nothing. Like he could hear Hendrix's unease at leaving her alone.

And yeah, he did feel uneasy. Yes, she'd grown up on a farm – unlike him – and she'd made it clear she could hold her own. He believed her, too, but it still felt wrong. Especially after the way he'd spoken to her earlier.

I just think it would be better if we didn't talk.

Despite the rain lashing down his mouth felt dry at the memory of her expression when he'd said it. Sure, she'd tried to hide her reaction, but the hurt still molded her features.

Christ, he felt like an ass. Especially since she'd come out in the storm to help him find his goat, even if she had every reason not to.

"I'll take a look around here," Logan told him. "You head back to your place. Knowing Frank, he's probably gotten into your house and started a fire in the fireplace."

His lips twitched, mostly because he could picture that scene. "Thank you," he told his uncle. "I appreciate it."

"It's what we do here." His uncle lay his hand on Hendrix's arm. "We take care of each other."

Yeah, he was starting to understand that. And maybe it wasn't so bad after all. Right now, it felt more like a gift than anything else.

Leaving his uncle, he ran back to the road. Mud splashed

his legs, rain soaked his clothes. But he didn't stop until he got to the lane.

And that's when he saw Emery. Leading Frank back through the last of the trees toward the pasture.

His muscles loosened with relief.

She was almost exactly at the place where he'd first seen her. Half naked, her arm partially covering the curve of her breasts. Then, he'd thought it was funny. And yeah, he'd lusted after her. What full-blooded man wouldn't? The woman was gorgeous.

But now he felt something different. Something deep in his belly. And he ran as fast as he could toward her, his heart slamming against his chest.

"You found him!" he shouted when he reached her. She was clinging onto Frank's neck. The goat gave the softest of brays before his knees folded and he collapsed onto the ground.

It felt like Hendrix's heart fell with him.

"He was in the water," Emery told him. "He was so scared he was shaking."

He was *still* shaking. Hendrix dropped to his knees, stroking Frank's nose. "It's okay, buddy. Just a storm." He looked up at Emery. "You're shaking too."

"I had to wade into the pond."

He winced. "Go home, take a shower. Get yourself warm." His voice softened. "And thank you. Thank you for finding him."

"You're going to need help getting him back to the house," she said, her voice making it clear she wasn't going to argue with him.

She looked stubborn and wet and glorious. He felt desire pulse through him.

"I'll manage." He squatted down, patting Frank's nose again. "Hey buddy, we need to get you home," he murmured, sliding his hands down Frank's body, one hand curling around his front legs, the other around his back.

Frank was a medium-sized goat. Not huge, but not a baby either. He had heft, and it took Hendrix's whole strength to lift him. Frank started to protest, and he heard Emery murmur to him, her hand stroking his face as Hendrix came to a stand.

It took all of his concentration to carry Frank across the muddy field, Emery still calming Frank down as they slowly made their way back to the house.

"Nearly there," she told him. "Where are you going to take him?"

"Into the house."

"Of course." She ran ahead of him, opening the door. "Where are your towels?" she shouted.

It was weird how welcome her question was. Like she was telling him he wasn't in this alone.

When was the last time he hadn't felt like it was him against the world?

"In the laundry room. Down the hallway on the left."

She ran in, and he gently laid Frank on the ground. The goat looked up at him, his golden eyes hazy as he tried to work out where he was. There was no fire in the grate – not even logs waiting to be lit. The West Virginian heat required air conditioning in the summer, not burning wood.

"I got these," Emery said, carrying a pile of old towels into the living room and dropping to her knees next to him. Between them they got Frank dry, then wrapped him up.

"Do we need to call the vet?" she asked him when Frank laid his head down on the now-wet rug and closed his eyes.

Hendrix shook his head. "I'll watch him tonight and reassess in the morning." He looked at her, taking in the way her soaking hair clung to her cheeks. Her skin was pink from warming up, but her pajamas were wet and muddy. She looked like she'd been rolling around on the ground.

He assumed he did, too.

"You should go home," he said again, his gaze lingering on her face. Mostly because he didn't trust himself to look below her neck. Despite the mud and rain, she looked stupidly enticing.

And she'd saved his goat. Wasn't that the thing? He'd tried to push her away but now he wanted her even more.

She's engaged, dumbass.

He tried to seize on those words, keep them in his head.

"I can stay here, with you and Frank." Her voice was soft.

He shook his head quickly. He didn't trust himself. That was the truth. He was already a hair's breadth away from touching her. He wanted to pull those wet clothes off of her. He wanted to pull her into the steaming shower with him.

He wanted to slide inside of her until they were both breathless and aching.

As a kid, he'd never wanted what the other children had. He'd never felt jealous of a new toy or a pair of sneakers.

But right now all he could think about was how much he desired her. He wanted this woman who was taken.

And that, he knew, was the reason he'd tried to push her away. Not for her reputation. But because he wanted her and he couldn't have her.

And now she needed to go home. *Now*. Before he did something he might regret.

"You're wet and muddy. Go get cleaned up, get some sleep. I'll let you know how Frank is in the morning," he promised. It was a miracle that he kept his voice even.

"You're wet and muddy too," she pointed out. She had that stubborn sound to her voice again. But instead of infuriating him, it enticed him.

"I'll take a shower in the morning."

"No you won't. You'll take one now while I stay with Frank, then I'll go home. Not before." She folded her arms across her chest. Despite himself, his gaze dipped.

"You're not going to let this go, are you?" he murmured.

"Nope."

His lips twitched. He'd been brought up around enough strong women to appreciate them. And to know when he was beat. "I'll be five minutes."

"Take your time." A smile pulled at her pretty mouth. "Frank and I have some chatting to do."

Shaking his head, he stood, walking barefoot over to the laundry room to grab a fresh towel to dry himself with. He slid his dirty, goat hair-covered hands under the faucet to clean them before taking a black towel from the pile on the shelf.

And that's when he saw them. Her panties. How the hell had he forgotten about them? He gave an internal groan, because not only were they in full view of anybody who walked into the laundry room, *but she'd just been in here to grab some towels.*

Christ, he hoped she hadn't seen them.

———

Emery stroked Frank's hair as he exhaled softly, his eyes closed, his body laid out on the dry towels. In the distance she heard the rush of water coming from Hendrix's bathroom.

She'd never been inside this cottage before. Back when she was growing up it had belonged to an old farmhand of the Hartson's – a loner who kept to himself. Her dad used to nod to him, but he'd refused all offers of dinner or trips out to the town, much to her mom's disgust.

The cottage was much smaller than the farmhouse she'd grown up in. And all on one floor. There was the living room, where she and Frank were, with whitewashed walls and a big brick fireplace. The rug was Persian, a red and gold pattern, and the sofas looked lived in but comfortable, with tan leather casings.

Behind the larger sofa was the kitchen. Again, it was nothing fancy, but looked like it functioned well. A huge fridge-freezer, a range, and plenty of workspace if you needed it.

To the right was the door to the laundry room. Hendrix must be using the bathroom next to the laundry, because he hadn't emerged from the hall.

Her cheeks pinked up. She'd seen the pair of panties in his laundry pile, and at first she'd felt a tiny bit jealous, assuming they belonged to another woman.

But then she'd realized they were hers. She wasn't sure what to think about that.

The door to the bathroom opened and Hendrix walked back out in a pair of sweatpants and nothing else.

"I'm clean and dry."

"I can see that." She pulled her lip between her teeth. His eyes met hers, and she could see amusement in them. "Frank is still asleep," she told him.

"Which is what we both should be doing. The rain has eased off a little. I'll grab us a couple of dry raincoats and make sure you get home safely."

"I can make my own way home," she told him. "You stay here with Frank."

"Are you always this aggravating?" he asked.

"You'd have to ask my friends about that." She rolled her eyes at him, but there was still a smile on her lips.

"And your fiancé."

Wasn't that just a bucket of cold water dumped over her? "I guess."

"You guess?" He frowned. "Surely the man you're going to marry knows you better than anybody else."

She shifted her legs. "Of course he does. I just…" She shook her head. "It doesn't matter."

He walked over to where she was with Frank, his body

looking huge as he loomed over them. She could see the little droplets of water clinging to his skin.

"Why does it feel like you always walk around half naked?" she asked him, changing the subject because she didn't want to talk about her engagement – or lack of it – right now.

"You're one to talk."

She bit down a smile. "That was a dare," she said.

Hendrix blinked. In the half light his eyes looked almost black. "You were the only one there. Who dared you to go skinny dipping? Frank?"

The goat gave a little snore. God, she loved that sound.

"It was on a list," she admitted. "My friend gave it to me before I came home. She dared me to complete them all."

His brows lifted. "What kind of list?"

"A…" Okay, she couldn't tell him it was a fuck-Trenton list. "She thinks I should go a little wild. Before…"

"You get married."

"Something like that." It wasn't quite a lie. It wasn't the truth either. And that sat way too heavy on her.

Hendrix hunkered down on the other side of Frank from where Emery was sitting. He patted the goat's neck. "He feels warmer." His gaze flickered to hers. "So your friend…"

"Maisie."

"What did she put on this list?" he asked.

"Well, go skinny dipping, obviously. And get drunk." She pulled her lip between her teeth, remembering the night she drank with him. "Those are the only two I've done."

"Two beers doesn't exactly constitute you being drunk," he pointed out.

"Stop raining on my parade." She pouted at him. "And I'm not a big drinker."

He shook his head. "What else is on there?" he asked her.

"Get a tattoo."

"Of what?" Hendrix looked genuinely interested. And yeah, there was still the unspoken panty situation between them, but she liked how easy this felt. Two friends, chatting. Not the guy who told her to stay away, or a guy that her ex hated.

Just two people and a goat in a living room. Your everyday kind of situation.

Emery shrugged. "She didn't specify. But I'm thinking a firefly."

"Why a firefly?" He tipped his head to the side. Up this close she could see the dark shadows of his beard growth on his jaw.

"My dad used to call me that when I was a kid."

He nodded. "What else is on the list?"

"Ride on the back of a motorcycle."

His mouth twitched. "You've never done that?"

"My dad hated them. Trenton too."

"Then you definitely need to do that."

She almost laughed. Damn, it felt good to be laughing. When was the last time life felt this easy?

"And dance on a bar," Emery said.

"So skinny dip, get drunk, get a tattoo, ride on a motorcycle, and dance on a bar," Hendrix murmured. "Not exactly pushing the boat out too far."

"Oh, I forgot. Also to stay up talking all night. And maybe it is for me." Her gaze held his and he lifted a brow.

"Is that it?" he asked.

She let out a soft breath, remembering Maisie's list. Of course there was something else. But she couldn't tell him that one. Not just because she'd have some explaining to do about why an engaged woman would kiss somebody else.

But because right now, with him half clothed and her own clothes sticking to her body like a second skin, it felt too intimate.

"That's it," she breathed.

"Seriously? Nothing more… dangerous?"

"Getting a tattoo is pretty dangerous." She folded her arms over her chest and he grinned. "I could get all sorts of infections," she said, her voice serious.

"You're such a good girl," he murmured. The way he said it sent a tingle down her spine. And between her legs, if she was being honest.

"What does that make you?"

"What do you want it to make me?" he asked. There was no way he couldn't feel this. The throb of attraction that made her skin feel too tight and too hot. His eyes were trained on her lips as she exhaled again.

Like he was trying to learn every curve and dip of them. Or maybe he was just trying not to look at her skimpy clothes.

"I think you like to be bad," she murmured. "And you do it well. But underneath all that hard assedness, there's a good man."

He shook his head. "Your opinion of me is way too high." It came out raspy.

"A bad guy doesn't go out in the middle of a storm to save his goat," she said, watching as he patted Frank's fur.

This time when he looked at her she could see the heat in his eyes. Could feel it, too, deep inside of her. Neither of them looked away. She knew she couldn't if she tried. And she didn't want to try.

Her heart slammed against her chest.

"Emery…" His voice was as soft as silk. The kind of voice that made her want everything she couldn't have. That made her want to hear his murmurs, close against her ear, as he moved inside of her. "I'm sorry about earlier. I was a dick. I didn't mean it." He shook his head, looking like he was trying to think through his words. "What I said…"

"It's forgotten," she told him. "It's okay."

"No it isn't. But I'll make it up to you," he told her.

"How?"

"I don't know. I'll think of something." He took a deep breath. "But in the meantime, you need to go home."

CHAPTER
Nine

I'LL SIGN AWAY *the lien at the end of the summer. Once you've followed through on our agreement. Please send a 'Y' to confirm you understand. – Trenton.*

Emery stared down at her phone, fuming. She'd been trying to call Trenton for days, to discuss the stupid lien and work out how they could resolve it.

And of course he'd been ignoring her calls. He must have eventually gotten annoyed at her, deigning to send her a text message. One that looked like something you'd get from a doctor's office, not from the man she used to love.

Reply 'Y' to agree? He could go take a running jump into a river.

God, she wanted to kill him.

Since the night of the storm she'd spent most of her time making phone calls, trying to work out a way she could put the farm on the market with the loan attached to it.

The short answer was, she couldn't. She'd even looked into getting a loan of her own, but she couldn't get that much money unsecured. Whatever route they took, it was going to delay the sale considerably.

There was no way she could get everything done before the summer was over and she had to go back to work. It had already taken her almost a month to get all the documents she needed. Time ran slower in West Virginia, especially when it was this hot. Nobody was in a hurry to get things done.

Gritting her teeth, she deleted the message. She wasn't going to let him get to her. Not when he seemed to want to control everything else. And then she shoved the phone in her pocket and wandered down to the yard to check on the chickens, smiling when she saw Hendrix outside his cottage.

Since the storm, she'd only seen him a couple of times. She'd gone to his house the next morning to check on Frank. The vet had just left and given Frank the all clear – with the suggestion of putting a bigger lock on the shed. Her eyes had met Hendrix's when he recounted that particular conversation and they'd both laughed.

She had a feeling that nothing would keep Frank from getting out of that shed if he desired to escape. He could probably learn to pick the lock if he wanted to.

The only other time she'd seen Hendrix was when he'd called her over and given her a gift to say thank you for her help in finding Frank. It had made her smile that he'd given her a bottle of whiskey.

"You can hide it underneath your bed," he'd told her. "In case you ever need to get drunk again."

But apart from that, he'd barely been home. Too busy working on his uncle's farm, she assumed. You didn't get through a storm like the one they had without needing to make some repairs.

Hendrix noticed her outside the chicken coop and walked across the lane, leaning on her fence as he smiled at her. He had a blue cap on his head to block out the beating sun.

And yeah, her heart did a little pitter patter at the way he was grinning. Like he didn't have a care in the world.

"How's Frank?" she asked him.

"Still an asshole."

Her mouth twitched. "Glad to hear he's back to normal." She tipped her head to the side, shading her eyes with her hand. Because the sun was really hot today.

"What are you up to this morning?" Hendrix asked her.

"Avoiding working." It was stifling inside and her mom was throwing a fit about the chickens refusing to lay eggs, so sitting on the porch had been her only option. She was almost to the end of the farm finances. But now that she knew where the black hole in them came from she had less enthusiasm for them.

Still, they needed to be done. Loan from Trenton Montclair or no loan from Trenton Montclair, this farm still needed to be sold.

"Sounds like a good way to spend the day." He had this little smile that made her pulse heat up. "Want to do some avoiding working with me? I'm heading into Ashford Gap. Gotta pick up some supplies."

"I thought we weren't supposed to be spending time with each other." She smiled to let him know she was teasing. Because they were over that.

He ran the pad of his thumb over his jaw. "I have an ulterior motive. I said I'd make it up to you, remember?" He lifted a brow. "My friend Jack runs a tattoo shop in the Gap. He's usually booked out for months but I called and he said he could fit you in. I figured you might want to tick off another item from your bucket list."

She blinked. Yes, he'd said he'd make it up to her, but she hadn't expected this. Or the way he looked at her with such stupidly boyish enthusiasm.

"Today?" she asked. It was sweet, but she'd assumed

she'd have time to prepare herself for something as big as a tattoo.

"Yep," he said. "Are you feeling brave enough?"

"Will we go on your bike?"

He shook his head. "No. You're not completing two items in one day. Plus, I need the truck to bring my supplies home."

"You have rules about *my* list?" she asked him, trying not to smile.

"If I'm helping you complete it, then yeah."

"Is that what you're doing?"

He lifted a brow. "Didn't I just say that?"

She took a deep breath. "I'm not sure I'm ready to get a tattoo."

"That's fair." He nodded. "But come with me anyway. I'll introduce you to Jack. You can talk it through and decide what you want."

Damn, he was being so reasonable. And the truth was, she *wanted* to go with him. "Give me a second," she told him. "I should tell my mom I'm leaving."

"You gonna tell her where you're going?"

Emery laughed. "Nope."

Luckily, her mom was still in a funk when she ran inside, trying to cool herself with a hand held fan. "Mom, I'm heading out to meet a friend," she told her. "I'm catching a ride with one of the hands."

Not a lie, not the truth. The story of her life.

"Okay." Her mom nodded, frowning at something on the television. "See you later."

Well, that was nice and easy. A surge of optimism rushed through her as she quickly checked herself in the mirror, smoothing out the frizz around her brow with her hands, and quickly sliding a slick of lipstick on.

Not for him, she told herself, but for her. It was the first time since she'd arrived that she was actually going out of town. Why hadn't she done this before?

When she ran back outside, Hendrix was waiting in his truck. The windows rolled down, rock music pumping through the air from his stereo. He had aviator sunglasses on, his cap turned backward so he could see a little better.

"Ready?" he asked as she climbed into the passenger side of the cab.

"Yep."

"Then let's go."

He waited for her to fasten her seatbelt before he revved up the engine, steering the large truck down the road while rock music pumped out of his stereo. From the corner of her eye she could see him mouthing along to the music.

She could smell the scent of whatever body wash he'd used before he'd picked her up, too. Low notes of musk that made her body tighten.

"I haven't been to the supply store for years," she said as he pulled onto the main road. It was funny, but even the way he drove was laid back. Like it was as easy as breathing.

"It hasn't changed," he told her.

She used to love visiting the store with her dad. The owner would always give her a popsicle in the summer and a chocolate bar in the winter, while he'd take her dad on a tour of their newest stock. The two adults would discuss the latest seeds or newest vehicles, while she wandered around the clothing, or hung near the pet supplies, hoping against hope her dad would get the hint and buy her a hamster or gerbil.

Of course he never did. Told her he had enough animals to worry about, then he'd ruffle her hair. *"But you're my favorite animal of all, kid."*

It looked different than she remembered when they pulled up outside. The shop must have been rebuilt in the past few years. It was a bigger, red-painted warehouse with a white roof and porch along the front, built to look like a huge barn, complete with a half-size windmill to the side of it.

Hendrix cut off the engine and jumped out of the car,

walking around to her side before she had time to pull at the handle. He offered her a hand to climb down, and the heat of his palm against hers made her feel sweaty.

Okay, the heat made her feel sweaty. But he definitely wasn't helping.

"We'll only be five minutes," he told her. "I just need to pick up a new pump and a couple of troughs. Then we can head over to Jack's."

She swallowed hard. "About that…"

"You chickening out?"

"No. I'm still thinking about it."

He gave her a half smile. "Well, you can think a little more while we shop."

He'd reached the glass doors to the tattoo parlor before she caught up to him.

"Remind me how you know Jack again?" she asked, sounding breathless from running to keep up with him. "Because you don't have any tattoos."

"How do you know I don't have any tattoos?"

She rolled her eyes, the ghost of a smile on her lips. Damn, she was pretty when she smiled.

She was also pretty when she didn't smile. And wasn't that a pain?

"Because you seem to enjoy parading around the farm half naked. I'm thinking of setting up a website, calling it *Only Farms*."

He coughed out a laugh. "Imagine my uncle on that."

"He's a good-looking man. There's an audience for a silver fox." Her smile widened. "But you still haven't answered my question."

"I have a tattoo," he told her, deadpan.

She blinked, like she was blindsided. "Where?"

"Never gonna tell you. If the sun doesn't see it, nor will you."

He liked the way her mouth dropped open. "Is it on your ass?"

"Nope."

"Your upper leg?"

"Nahah." He shook his head, enjoying this way too much. Her cheeks were already flushed as she looked down at the button on his jeans.

"No. Not there," she muttered.

"Was I supposed to hear that?"

"Is it there?"

"Where?" For some reason he wanted to hear her say it. A dirty word. She was so damn straight and proper. He wondered what it would be like to see her lose it and go wild.

You'll never know, asshole. She's not yours.

"You know where."

"Say it and I'll answer your question." They were full-on facing each other now. She drew closer.

"You're such an idiot."

"Say it, Emery."

She took a deep breath, shaking her head like she couldn't believe she was doing this. Especially in public. "Seriously," she muttered. "Do you have a tattoo on your cock, Hendrix Hartson?"

The way she said it made him full-on laugh. The kind of belly laugh that hadn't forced its way out of his mouth in a long, long time. She looked appalled and intrigued all at the same time.

"Yeah," he gave her a huge grin. "Of a whale. Life size."

"Shut up!" She batted his arm with her hand. He grabbed her wrist to stop her from doing it again, his fingers curling around her soft skin.

Her breath stuttered and damn, he couldn't stop looking

at her. It was some kind of exquisite torture, being this close to her, knowing he couldn't have her.

Her raspberry pink lips parted, her gaze locked with his. And for a minute he swore his heart stopped.

"We should go in," he said, his voice thick.

"We should. We don't want to miss our appointment with Jack." She nodded, not moving her arm from his grasp. He looked at the way his fingers made a bracelet around her wrist. She was so pale and so perfectly delicate. He wanted to break her and then put her back together.

He swallowed hard. "You ready for it? To go talk to Jack?"

"Yeah. And I've decided I'm doing it. I'm getting a tattoo today."

It was his turn to look surprised. "Seriously? What happened to 'I'm not sure I'm ready to get a tattoo.'?"

"I figure life is too short to start over thinking things."

Funny, because he'd only just started overthinking them.

"If I want a tattoo, I'm gonna get one," she told him, sounding resolute. "I don't give a damn what anybody thinks."

A smile pulled at his lips as he gently released her wrist. His fingers flexed, like they were already missing the touch of her. "You still planning on getting a firefly?" he asked her.

He was glad this was working out. After the whole debacle of telling her they shouldn't talk, followed by her heroism at saving Frank, helping her with this list was the least he could do.

It might even be fun.

"Yeah, I think I will. It's small so it won't hurt, right?"

"Right," he agreed, lying through his teeth. "You'll be fine."

CHAPTER
Ten

"OH MY GOD, oh my God, oh my God." She could barely breathe as the high-pitched wail escaped her lips. "Ow ow ow." It felt like the needle was hitting bare bone. Or a nerve.

She wasn't sure who looked more amused at her screaming – Hendrix or Jack. All she knew was that she was never doing this again. That needle hurt worse than breaking her wrist when she was eight.

"Want me to stop?" Jack asked her.

"No," she said through gritted teeth. "Keep going." Then she glared at Hendrix who was trying not to smile. "And you can shut up. This is all your fault."

That just made him smile even more.

It took almost an hour for Jack to finish coloring in the tiny firefly they'd agreed on. And yes, he'd warned her that it would be painful, because the skin on her ankle was thin and close to the bone. But she'd managed to keep the screams to whimpers, and she'd grabbed hold of Hendrix's hand tight, squeezing it hard enough for him to lift a brow.

She wasn't sure which of them was the most relieved once Jack had finished adding the ointment to her skin and covered up the tattoo, giving her a leaflet about caring for the freshly inked skin.

"By the way, I was wondering, does Hendrix have a tattoo?" she asked Jack as she slid the care instructions into her purse.

From the corner of her eye she saw Hendrix smile at her question. Because no, she didn't believe he had a whale on his dick. But she also wanted to know if he did have one somewhere.

"Don't tell her," Hendrix said.

"I'm afraid I have to keep strict customer confidentiality," Jack said, looking from her to Hendrix, an amused tone to his voice. "I could tell you but then I'd have to kill you."

"I'm gonna find out," she warned Hendrix.

He lifted a brow, not looking afraid at all. "I have no doubt of that."

Traffic was busier on their way back to the farm, mostly because it was almost rush hour. Hendrix played rock music again, that cap back on his head, and she felt that familiar flush on her body as she looked at him while he concentrated on the road.

"You want me to drop you off outside your house?" he asked her.

"No, it's fine. I'll walk home from yours. It's not exactly far."

"I can drop you off at the end of the lane if you want," he told her. "If you'd rather your mom didn't see you walking home from my house."

She opened her mouth to say maybe that was a good idea, but then closed her lips. Why the hell should she be embarrassed if her mom saw her walking back from his place? They were friends. There was nothing wrong with that. She was allowed to talk to people, dammit.

"Nah, it's all good. Once she sees the tattoo she'll forget all about that, anyway."

"You're not going to keep it covered up when it's healed?"

"Nope." She shrugged. "It's pretty. And I went through a lot of pain for this. There's no point in going through all that if you're going to hide it."

"It *is* pretty," he murmured.

Her skin tingled at the way he said it. She wondered what it would be like if he told her *she* was pretty?

Truth was, she'd probably melt. "Thank you," she murmured as the truck rumbled over the muddy tracks to his farm. The earth had dried hard, and the movement made her bounce up and down.

His gaze dropped to her chest, to the way her breasts moved with her body, then quickly moved it back to her face.

A loud bray from Frank greeted them when Hendrix opened her door and helped her climb down from the truck. She walked over to the goat, stroking his jaw.

"Is it of a goat?" she shouted to Hendrix.

"What?"

"Your tattoo?" she said. "Is it a goat?"

"You're not gonna let this go, are you?"

"Hendrix, you just watched me scream like a baby for an hour. The least you can do is let me see your tattoo."

"You want to see it?" he stepped closer, and her hand stilled on Frank's face. The goat looked peeved at her attention being interrupted.

"I didn't say that."

"Yes, you did. You said exactly that." His eyes were dark as his hands curled around his belt buckle, slowly undoing it.

"Hendrix!"

He started to laugh. "Damn, you're easy to scare. No, you're not seeing it. A man likes to have a hint of mystery. And anyway, I'm saving it for *Only Farms*, remember?"

"You're an ass. And you don't have a tattoo."

"If that's what you want to believe, go with it." He

reached down to tuck a curl of her hair behind her ear. His fingers felt hot against her neck, sending a shot of pleasure through her body.

"I hate you." Her breath caught in her throat.

"Good." He smirked. "You're gonna hate me even more when that tattoo hurts like hell in the middle of the night."

She looked down at the tattoo, all wrapped up to keep it clean. "If it hurts, I'm coming over here and banging your door down."

He opened his mouth to reply, but then he looked over her shoulder. "Your mom's watching." He took a step back, like he knew it looked bad for them being this close.

Emery looked over her shoulder. Sure enough, her mom was on the porch, pretending to plump the cushions on the swing.

"I should go," she said reluctantly.

"Yeah." He nodded. "Thanks for keeping me company this afternoon."

"Thanks for listening to me scream."

The way his eyes narrowed made her realize exactly how bad that sounded.

But then he winked and gave her a grin. "Go home, firefly."

"I'm leaving." She smiled back at him, because he could have made it so much more embarrassing. And just as she turned on her heel she muttered, "Goat dick."

"I'm not gonna lie," Maisie said, a grin all over her face as she talked to Emery on a video call. "This guy sounds like perfect number seven material. Either the original or amended version." She wrinkled her nose. "Though I like the original the best."

"He thinks I'm engaged," Emery pointed out. "So that's not gonna happen."

It had been a week since their trip to the tattoo parlor. Apart from a couple of meetings in the lane – where Hendrix had asked her about her tattoo and whether it was healing – she'd barely seen him. And yeah, she'd thought about going over and drinking all the beer in his fridge again, but her mom had been a lot more present the last few days. She'd notice if Emery went over there and she wasn't ready for that drama with her mom.

Instead, she'd settled for swigging at the whiskey bottle under her bed and thinking about how he made her breathless. There was something about the way he looked at her that made everything in her body tighten up, including her ribcage, making it difficult to inhale.

"So tell him," Maisie said. "It's not like you owe your asshole ex anything. Call the agreement off. You're a free woman. That gorgeous hunk of a cowboy is a free man."

"He's not a cowboy, he's a farmer," Emery told her.

"Ah, same thing." Maisie wrinkled her nose. She was sitting in her Airbnb in Barcelona. She'd found the perfect rental, including a great Wi-Fi connection that meant she could video call instead of just audio. She'd already given Emery the tour, and it looked beautiful. The apartment was built in the last century but had been updated, so along with the tall ceilings, floor-length windows, and beautiful parquet flooring, it had a modern kitchen, great internet connection, and air conditioning – which Maisie had raved about.

It had been a last-minute cancellation, which meant her friend had picked it up for a steal. And she was so clearly loving every minute.

"It doesn't matter whether he's a cowboy or a farmer, it still can't happen."

"You need to stop thinking about everybody else and

think about yourself. Just go for it. What's stopping you? You haven't heard from Trenton, have you?"

"No. He's too busy working on that real estate project in Charleston." Thank god that above all things Trenton was a workaholic. The thought of that lien on the farm was still making her feel nauseous, though. She hadn't told Maisie about it. Mostly because she knew her friend would be outraged. And she couldn't cope with that.

Maisie didn't know Trenton like Emery did. He'd make her mom's life a living hell if she didn't keep this going until the end of the summer. After that, well, then she'd be free.

It wasn't too long away. And she'd always been a patient woman. Once she'd gotten her mom moved into a new place, then she could concentrate on her own life.

"At least tell me you've ticked another item off the list," Maisie said, scooping a forkful of salad into her mouth. It was almost two o'clock in Spain, seven in Hartson's Creek. Emery's mom was watching a rerun of *Law and Order: SVU*, and Emery had closed up the chicken coop for the evening and was sitting in her bedroom, cross-legged on her childhood bed.

"It's only been a week since I ticked off the last one," Emery pointed out. "The tattoo has hardly stopped itching. I don't think I'm ready for more pain."

"It's been a month since you got home. You're not even fifty percent of the way there," Maisie pointed out. "I knew we should have agreed to a penalty if you didn't do them all."

"The list is the penalty," Emery pointed out. "I don't think you could give me anything worse if you tried."

Maisie grinned. "I bet I could. I tell you what, if you don't do another one this week, I'm changing number seven back to the original."

"That's not fair." Emery's chest tightened. "I'm doing my best."

"I know. But this is for your own good. So that's it. Either tick another one off the list before I call you next, or seven is back to doing the dirty with a guy."

"I'm really good at avoiding calls," Emery pointed out. Her friend knew her way too well. She'd done the easy things. Heck, even the tattoo seemed easy compared to the other items. She didn't want to ride on the back of a motorcycle, dance on a bar, or find somebody to stay up talking to.

And she definitely didn't want to kiss a random man.

Okay, she did. But she couldn't. And she was almost certain he wouldn't want to kiss her back.

"I'll track you down one way or another," Maisie promised. And Emery knew it was true.

"Okay," she sighed. "I'll try. But you're not changing number seven back."

"How's the tattoo?" Hendrix called out to her from the middle of the dirt road a couple of days later. It was early evening. Her mom had gone into town to meet up with a friend for dinner, and Jed and the farmhands had gone home, leaving her blissfully alone for the first time in days.

She'd checked on the chickens and poured herself a glass of iced tea, and was sitting on the deck while she went through her emails. There was one from the realtor, suggesting he come over next week to value the farm, pending putting it on sale when the lien was released.

Though she hadn't given him the details, she'd hinted that it should all be sorted within a month. That is if Trenton held up to his side of the deal.

Hendrix was sitting on his motorcycle, having just ridden back from his day job at his uncle's farm. His jeans and t-shirt were covered in a coating of dry earth.

"It's still a bit itchy," she shouted, lifting her leg to show him her fresh tattoo. He kicked the stand on his bike and walked over to the fence that separated her mom's farm from the road, leaning on it.

"Let me look at it."

She felt that familiar pull, the one she was trying really hard to pretend didn't exist. But she stood up anyway, walking to where he was standing. "You can come in," she told him. "My mom isn't here."

"Didn't she teach you not to invite strangers in?" he asked her, grinning. But he still walked over to the gate and unlatched it, striding to where she was standing.

"Hard day?" she asked.

"Had a couple of sheep escape. Spent most of it riding around the farm looking for them."

"Has Frank been talking to them?" She grinned.

"I wouldn't put it past him." He tipped his head to the side, his gaze sliding down to her ankle, where the firefly was etched into her skin. "You been putting the ointment on it?"

"Yes, Dad."

He laughed softly. "Let me look at it," he murmured, as he dropped to his haunches. She looked down at the top of his head, curling her hands because she had this desire to drag her fingers against his scalp.

"Can I touch it?" he asked her, looking up through eyelashes so thick any woman would kill to have them.

"Sure." She nodded, trying to keep her voice even.

But then his rough finger pads grazed her skin, and dammit, she started to wobble.

"Steady," he said softly, like she was an animal reacting to his touch. He slid his hands down her calves, reaching her ankle, tipping his head to the side like he was assessing every inch of her.

Thank God she'd shaved her legs this morning.

"The redness has gone." His voice was still gentle. She liked it way too much. "There's some flaking. The scab is peeling off. That's what's making it itchy." He looked up at her again. "Have you been scratching it?"

"Been trying not to."

"Good girl."

She hated the way she reacted to that. Her body felt heavy and light at the same time.

He slid his hands back up her legs, his lips parted. His fingers lingered on her calves, and for a second there was complete silence.

"Can I ride your motorcycle?" she blurted out.

He blinked. "What?"

"The list. My friend's list. I need to tick another one off." *Before she changes number seven and I'm hitting on you like a cat in heat.* "I need to ride on the back of a bike."

"The back?" he frowned. "Why not the front? Isn't the list meant to be about empowerment?"

She hadn't told him that. And yet he'd realized it. The thought made feel dizzy.

"It is," she told him, aware that he was still touching her legs. "But I can't operate a motorcycle, so I guess this is second best."

"I'll teach you."

"Huh?" She was way too distracted by the way he brushed his fingers further up her legs. It wasn't obvious that he realized he was caressing her. But every cell in her body was aware.

"I'll teach you how to ride."

"Now?"

He shrugged. "Now's as good a time as any." He glanced over at the swing where she'd been sitting. "Unless you have better things to do."

"No." She said it so quickly it made him smile.

"Good." He inclined his head at his cottage. "I'm gonna head in for a shower. Meet me at my place in ten."

Her throat felt dry as he stood and started walking away.

"And Emery?"

"Yes?"

"Put some pants on. And a sweater with sleeves."

"For protection?" she asked.

He smirked. "Exactly. We wouldn't want your pretty body getting scratched."

CHAPTER
Eleven

STEPPING under the steaming hot spray, Hendrix closed his eyes and took in a long breath. What was he thinking, offering to teach her to ride? It had been bad enough touching her. The softness of her skin had made his dick harder than an iron bar. And the way she'd looked down at him, her lips parted like she wanted to say something, but didn't know how, made him want to stand up and kiss her until they were both breathless.

She's taken, asshole.

Yeah, he knew. This whole thing was a bad idea. But then he'd always been the king of those.

It was just his way of making things up to her, that was all. There was no way he was changing his mind and watching her happy expression melt off her face again. They were friends. He was doing what friends did.

It would be fine.

By the time he walked outside, in a fresh pair of jeans and an old band t-shirt, she was waiting for him in his yard, her arms around Frank's neck, the goat nuzzling against her soft chest.

He never thought he'd be jealous of a damn goat.

"Does this work?" she asked him, turning to look at him. Like he'd told her to, she'd changed into a pair of jeans and a black long sleeve sweater.

He wasn't sure what he liked more. The fact she'd done as he'd asked her, or the fact that she was still looking at him like the sun shone from his ass.

What else would she do if he asked her? He pushed that thought down.

"Yep." He held out the helmet he'd grabbed from his room. "Put this on."

"*You* don't wear one," she said, looking at the black shiny covering.

"That's because I'm an idiot. And you have more brains than me. Put it on."

Of course she did it. He tried to ignore the desire pulsing between his legs. He took her hand, leading her to the bike he'd left in front of the porch stairs. He wheeled it into the lane, turning it so that it was facing away from the main road. They had at least a hundred yards of straight road ahead of them, more than enough for her to learn to ride.

He turned to look at her, gesturing at the bike.

"Sit on it."

She reached for the handlebars, her fists delicate as they curled around the metal, then hitched her leg up and over the seat, settling onto the leather. His jaw tightened. God, she looked perfect on his bike.

He should have jacked off when he was in the shower. Because right now all he could think of was dragging her toward him and kissing her.

Ignoring the pulse between his thighs, he walked up behind her, so close he could smell the sweet floral notes of her shampoo from the strands of hair below the helmet. His chest pressed against her back as he reached around her, circling her with his arms so he could hold on to her hands that were gripping the bars.

"You need to have a bend in your arms," he told her, moving them until he could see the ninety-degree angle she needed for control.

"Okay," she breathed, moving with him.

"This is the throttle," he murmured in her ear, twisting the right handle bar. "It makes the bike go faster." He moved her fingers down. "The front brake," he told her, squeezing her hands to show her how to hold it. "You use this to slow the bike down."

"To slow it down," she muttered. "Got it."

"The clutch," he said, moving her left hand. "You use this to disengage the engine. That way you can shift gears with your left foot." He slid his hands down her denim clad leg, showing her how to move it. Then he did the same to her right leg. "This one is the brake."

"I'm never going to remember any of this."

He laughed softly. "You're smarter than me. You'll be fine."

She turned to look at him, a strange expression on her face. "I'm not smarter than you."

"I think we both know you are. You went to college. Got a degree. I'm pretty sure you can ride a motorcycle." He stood and took her right hand, pressing her thumb against the red plastic button jutting out of the handle. "Kill switch. It stops the engine. Use it if you need to."

"What if I crash?" she asked him.

"You're not gonna crash. You're careful. You'll go slow."

She swallowed hard, like she was taking his words in. "Maybe this is a bad idea."

"What are you afraid of?" he asked her, his voice thick.

"Dying mostly."

"I'm not gonna let you die, Emery. I'm just teaching you how to ride a bike." He rocked the handlebars, showing how easily it moved. "This movement means it's in neutral. A good time to start it up." He flicked on the kill switch. "Remember where the clutch is?"

"Left hand."

"You're a fast learner." Of course she was. "Now turn it, and I'll kick on the engine."

"You won't let me get hurt, will you?"

"I got you." He watched as she twisted her hand, and he kicked the engine on, smiling as she jumped at the way it roared to life. His bike wasn't gentle, it wasn't smooth. It was an angry beast.

"Okay?" he asked her.

"No."

Dammit, he could see that from the way her body was trembling. "Listen, I'm gonna climb on the back," he told her. "I'll be right behind you. You've got this."

He feel her body relax as he climbed on to ride pillion behind her. He had to get close, his chest pressed tight against her back, so he could cover her hands with his.

"I'm gonna kick the stand away. Then we're gonna turn the clutch and you'll press your left foot on the pedal to go into first gear. Once we've done that, you'll hear the engine change and we're gonna turn the throttle. Okay?"

She nodded and he kicked the stand, keeping them steady with his feet on the ground. He softly covered her clutch hand with his, turning it as she pressed her left foot down.

The engine immediately engaged. "Turn the throttle softly," he told her. "Once the bike moves, you put your feet on the rests." He covered her right hand with his, slowly twisting it. Her back was stiff against him, her knuckles bleached white from holding the throttle so tight. The bike jolted forward, and she let out a soft yelp. He kept his hand steady on hers as it jumped forward again, slowly turning it more, until the bike was moving smoothly, his body caging hers as they went.

"Hendrix Hartson, don't you let go," she screamed at him. He could hear the fear in her voice.

It made him want to hold her tighter.

"I'm here, sweetheart. I'm not letting go." He squeezed her hands. "But we're gonna need to brake. You ready for it?"

"No!"

He started to laugh again. Damn, he liked this woman way too much. "Squeeze the brake," he told her. "Softly."

"I hate this," she cried out, but she still did as she was told. A little too hard, actually. She started to yell as they lost speed too quickly, making them skid. He took control of the handlebars, riding into it, feeling the bike turn as their speed dissipated, her body cradled by his as the wheels kicked up dirt.

And when they finally came to a stop, he could hear the way her breath was rapid and out of control.

He kicked the stand down, Emery caged between his arms. He was still holding her hands as her body slumped back against his.

"I hate motorcycles," she muttered, her helmet hard against his chest.

"That's a shame, because we need to turn around and ride back now."

"I'm not riding anywhere. I'll walk."

He threaded his fingers into hers, squeezing them. "You've got this," he told her. "It'll be easier this time. And then you can mark another thing off your list."

"I hate you."

"No you don't." He was still grinning. "Now, I'm going to turn us around, then we'll try again."

———

It was almost midnight and she couldn't sleep. Adrenaline was still coursing through her, despite it being hours since her bike lesson. Her mom was home now. Emery could hear the soft hum of the television coming from her bedroom. Another thing they shared – an inability to sleep.

Not that she cared right now. She was too busy feeling like she could conquer the world, thanks to Hendrix. He'd spent almost an hour with her, teaching her to ride, before she'd heard the rumbling in his stomach and realized he hadn't eaten dinner yet. So he'd gone back to his house and she'd strode happily back to her place, feeling like a new Emery. A badass motorcycle-riding first grade teacher with a tattoo on her ankle.

She couldn't wait to tell Maisie that she'd ticked another item off the list. But she'd do that tomorrow. Her mom's bedroom was too close for her to get away with that discussion right now.

Rolling onto her side, she pulled out the white t-shirt that was still under her pillow. There was no excuse for it to still be there. She'd changed the bedding more than once since the skinny dipping incident. Yet each time, she'd tucked it back where it had come from because she didn't have the energy to wash it and give it back to him.

Or that's what she told herself.

It was warm from where she'd been lying on it. And it still smelled of him. If she closed her eyes she could picture herself sitting in his car, the two of them listening to loud rock music as he drove her to the supply store.

Almost like she'd conjured it up just by thinking about it, the rumble of a car engine outside cut through the silence of her bedroom. It was getting closer, enough for her to hear the thrum of music coming out of the vehicle's open windows. She rolled over and got to her feet, padding across the floor and pulling the corner of her curtain open.

Because, no, apparently she wasn't above spying on her super hot neighbor.

But instead of seeing Hendrix's car pulling into his earthy driveway, she could see a small convertible. Red.

With a woman driving it.

A glance at her watch told her it was right before midnight. Her mouth felt dry as the woman – a blonde wearing a tiny, strapless black dress and high heels – walked up the path to the farm cottage. She looked young, though it was hard to see from here.

It gave her the smallest sense of satisfaction to see those ridiculously high heels get caught in a dried up divot of mud, making the blonde stumble.

But before she could even relish in it, the door to Hendrix's cottage opened and the man himself was standing in the frame, the glow of his living room light behind him. There was a smile pulling at his lips as he said something to the blonde who giggled.

And then threw herself into his arms.

Emery's stomach twisted. And she knew she didn't have any reason to feel jealous. If he wanted to entertain young, blonde women in the middle of the night, he had every right to. Just because he was helping her with her list, it didn't mean he owed her any kind of loyalty.

He also had every right to expect she wouldn't be spying on him, yet she couldn't look away.

The blonde pulled back from him, saying something that made him laugh. Then he grabbed her hand and pulled her inside, closing the door so that Emery couldn't see what they were doing anymore.

Which was a good thing. A really good thing. She shouldn't care. He was single, unattached. He didn't owe her any explanations, and he absolutely didn't owe her any loyalty.

But it still felt like a knife in the gut as she let the corner of the curtain drop, and walked back to bed, her heart feeling heavy.

Pulling the covers back over her, she stared up at the ceiling, at the cracks in the white paint, her eyes wide open. If she thought about it hard enough, maybe this would be a good thing.

It was obvious she had a crush on the man. One she shouldn't have, not just because everybody thought she was engaged, but because her life was a mess. She had no relationship, no home, and until she managed to figure out how to clear her mom's debts, she had no way of untangling herself from the man she hated.

Hendrix was with somebody. Whether it was casual or serious, it didn't matter.

He was just trying to be her friend. It wasn't his fault that she'd read more into it.

It was fine. Tomorrow was another day. The sun would rise, the world would wake up.

And somehow, she'd find a way to stop having feelings for Hendrix Hartson.

CHAPTER
Twelve

THE RED CAR was still in his driveway the next morning.

Not that Emery was looking. Okay, she totally was. She'd lain awake half the night listening for the rumble of the engine as it left, but there had only been silence.

Whoever it was, he clearly wanted them to stay the night. Which meant it wasn't just a booty call.

"Stop it," she muttered to herself, as she pulled on a pair of cutoffs and a t-shirt, because the sun was already beating in through the crack in her curtains. It was obviously going to be another hot one.

"Honey, can you fetch the eggs?" her mom asked as she walked down the stairs. "I need to make some cakes for tonight."

"What's happening tonight?" Emery asked her.

"Chairs," her mom reminded her.

"Chairs still happens?" Emery's eyes widened. She'd forgotten all about the spring and summer ritual the townsfolk of Hartson's Creek had. They'd meet in grassy field by the creek in the center of town every Friday evening, for gossip and cake. Everybody brought their own lawn chairs – hence the name – and whether you were a man, a woman, or a child, you'd meet friends there to talk or play with.

"Of course it does. I just haven't been feeling up to it for a while." Her eyes met Emery's and she knew her mom was talking about her losing her dad. "But a few of the women from the stitching club are going. Asked me if I'd join them."

"That's nice." It really was. As much as her mom drove her wild, it was good to see her getting out again. Maybe coming home had been a good idea, after all.

"You could come, too, if you'd like." Her mom suggested. "I'm sure they wouldn't mind."

"Oh, no. You go spend some time with your friends. You'll be able to enjoy yourself a lot more without me there." Before her mom could try to persuade her, Emery grabbed her shoes. "I'll go get those eggs now."

Just as she expected, it was already hot outside. The kind of blue-skied day that made you forget that storms existed. She felt the heat of the morning sun on her face as she walked down the porch steps to make a left to head to the chicken coop where hopefully there were enough eggs to keep her mom distracted for a while.

"You recovered from last night?"

She looked across the lane to see Hendrix standing by his bike. She wasn't sure if he was leaving to head to work, or if he had just come back.

The red convertible was still there, though. She quickly pulled her eyes away, not waiting him to notice.

"Just about." She forced a smile onto her lips. "I gotta go get some eggs." *And not talk to you. Because you had a woman in your bed and it's killing me.*

He frowned, like he knew she was trying to blow him off. But really, this felt excruciating. Not just because she'd embarrassed herself by lusting after him when he was taken.

But because the woman he was taken by was in the house right now.

"You sure you're okay?" he asked.

"I'm fine." It came out terser than she'd planned. Enough to make him wince. "I'm sorry, I'm just so busy. I really have to go."

He looked her over for a moment. Like he was trying to figure out what the hell was wrong with her. But then the door to his cottage opened and *she* walked out.

The beautiful blonde was still wearing the black dress she'd had on when she arrived last night, but over the top she had a huge denim jacket on that looked like it belonged to Hendrix. It was way too big for her tiny frame.

Emery watched, her mouth dry, as the blonde walked over to Hendrix and gave him a huge kiss on the cheek. "Thanks for last night," she said, her voice sultry. "I owe you."

Slowly, she turned her head, her brows lifting when she saw Emery standing there less than thirty yards away. Her mouth formed a little 'o'. "Who's this?" she asked Hendrix.

He let out a long breath, like he really didn't want this to be happening.

Ditto, babe. Emery wasn't exactly enjoying this either.

"Sabrina, this is Emery, the neighbor I was telling you about. Emery, this is Sabrina."

"You're the one who got a tattoo?" Sabrina asked.

And somehow it felt worse that he'd told her about that. Like he was betraying her, even though he wasn't.

"Yeah." Emery nodded. And to her surprise the blonde's mouth lifted into a full-on grin.

"I've heard so much about you. Well, as much as this ass is willing to tell." She full-on slapped Hendrix in the stomach, making Emery's eyes widen. "Which isn't much, because like his brothers, he's a complete loudmouth until you ask him a personal question."

"I don't answer because you talk too damn much," Hendrix grunted. "And what's with the criticism after I just did you a favor?"

Sabrina rolled her eyes. "I would have done it for you." She looked over at Emery. "I was on a date last night. And I didn't want to go home, so Hendrix let me stay the night."

"You were on a date?" Emery asked, the lift in her voice betraying her surprise.

"Yeah." She let out a sigh. "But then it all went a bit wrong. He got called into work on an emergency. But I'd already told my parents I wasn't coming home, so I opted to hide out here."

"Yeah, well, the next time you want to lie to Uncle Cam and Aunt Mia, don't involve me," Hendrix muttered.

"You have to help me." She pouted at him. "We're family."

"So are Marley and Pres. Go bother them."

"Wait, you're family?" Emery asked, trying to place the blonde. She knew most of the Hartsons, she'd grown up with them.

"Oh Lord, you don't remember me." Sabrina started to laugh. "I was a couple of grades below you in school. Wait…" She looked at Hendrix. "Did you think I stayed with him and… eww. He's my cousin."

"I didn't think…" Oh, what an idiot she was. She vaguely remembered there were some female cousins in the Hartson family, but she hadn't remembered Sabrina specifically. It had been a long time since she'd been in school.

And Sabrina was now a bombshell.

"Hendrix told me he'd taken you to get a tattoo," Sabrina continued, ignoring her cousin as she walked closer to the road. "Can I see?"

Trying to ignore the relief rushing through her, Emery lifted her ankle and Sabrina leaned closer, letting out an 'ooh.'

"Did it hurt?" she asked Emery.

"Like hell."

Sabrina laughed. "I thought it might. This is why I can never get a tattoo. I don't like pain."

"I'm not the biggest fan either," Emery told her. She could feel the warmth of Hendrix's gaze as he watched them talking.

"It's pretty though," Sabrina said, standing up and stretching her arms. "Well, it's lovely to meet you," she told Emery.

"Right back at you." It was strange how happy she felt now that she knew Sabrina was another Hartson. But she didn't want to think about that too deeply right now. She was too tired after her fitful night of sleep for that. She nodded at Hendrix, who was looking at her with a strange expression. "I'll see you around."

"Yeah, you will." His gaze didn't falter.

Her heart did, though. It did a little leap as she turned around and walked to the chicken coop, still feeling the heat of his stare on her back.

"Wow, she's sweet," Sabrina said to him, as he walked her back to his car. "And cute. You didn't tell me that."

"I didn't tell you anything about her," he pointed out. Because the last person he'd choose to confide in would be his cousin. He loved her, but she had a loose tongue. Sabrina and secrets didn't go together.

"You told me she was lonely," Sabrina pointed out. Because yeah, he might have asked his cousin to find a way to be friends with Emery. He still remembered that night on the porch when she'd admitted to having no friends here.

"I did. Thank you for being nice to her." He opened her car door for her, but Sabrina didn't climb in. Instead, she gave him an interested look.

"She has the hots for you," she told him.

"Shut the hell up."

"She does," Sabrina insisted. "Did you see how weird she

was until I told her we're cousins? She was jealous. And then suddenly she was all sweetness and light." Sabrina grinned. "Oh, I love a good neighbor love story."

"Can you keep it down?" Hendrix said, frustrated. Sabrina always talked too loud. And too damn much. "She's taken, remember?"

Because he did. Even if he wished she wasn't.

"When has that ever stopped you before?" his cousin teased.

But he didn't smile. It wasn't funny, not really. "I'm reformed," he said, keeping his voice even. "Now go home. Before your parents send out a search party."

"You were more fun when you were trouble," Sabrina told him.

"You could try being good, too."

She started to laugh. "Don't be silly. There's no fun in that." She rolled onto her tiptoes and kissed his cheek. "Thanks for letting me stay."

"Try not to do it again."

"You know I will." She winked at him. "Laters, taters."

She climbed into her car and he closed the door, waiting patiently until she started the engine and drove away. When he looked over at Emery's house, there was no sign of her.

Good. That was good. After last night's lesson, the last thing he needed was to spend more time with her.

Even if she was all he could think about right now.

———

"So all we need is for the lien to be removed then we can go full steam ahead," the realtor told Emery, as she walked him back to his car. It was Monday afternoon and he'd spent most of the day with them, measuring the rooms in the house, taking photographs, then doing the same with the farm as Jed took him around.

He'd stopped for lunch – her mom made a quiche and a potato salad that had made his eyes bulge, and then during the afternoon he'd gone through all the paperwork with them, and given his valuation. It was less than she'd hoped for, but more than enough for her mom to buy a little house in town and get settled.

And then Emery could start concentrating on her own life. Even if the thought of that right now made her stomach twist.

"I should have the lien resolved before the end of the summer," she told him. After all, Trenton's parents were due back from their luxury cruise in August. And as soon as they were home, he'd tell them about their relationship ending, then remove the lien with an agreement that his loan would be repaid after the sale.

Or at least that's what she hoped. And what she'd emailed him, suggesting that they do it all at the same time. But he hadn't answered her. She wasn't sure if he was salty at her lack of a 'Y' in response to his message the other day, or if he was genuinely busy.

She tried to push it to the back of her mind. If she started chasing him too hard, that would make things worse.

"Excellent," the realtor said, clicking the button on his key to unlock the car. "I'll have the listing ready to go. Just call me as soon as it's done."

"I will." Emery nodded as he nodded his head to her then closed his driver's door.

When she walked back into the house, her mom was in the kitchen, her back to Emery. It took her a moment to realize her mom's shoulders were shaking.

"Mom?" she said, walking toward her. That's when she heard her sob.

"I'm sorry. Ignore me. I'm just…" Her mom gulped in a breath. "It's a lot to get used to, knowing somebody else will own this place."

Emery took her into her arms and held her tight. "Of course it is."

"I've lived her for so long. I don't like imagining what it'll be like to be somewhere else." Her mom's voice was muffled as she cried into Emery's shoulder. "Your dad brought me home here the day that we married. And this is where I had you." She looked up, her eyes red-rimmed. "I'm so sorry that you're having to do so much to help me."

"It's okay." Emery's voice was low. "You're my mom. Of course I'll help you."

"I just feel so useless. He was asking all those questions and I didn't know what to say. Your father always dealt with everything."

"I know." Emery touched her mom's cheek. "But it's all going to be okay. You'll move into your new place, make new friends. Start living again. It'll be different, but you'll be fine."

"I'm so happy you have Trenton," her mom said. "So you don't have to feel like this. All alone. Nobody should feel this way."

Emery's stomach contracted. "You don't have to worry about me. I'm fine."

"How was he when he called last night?" her mom asked. Because Emery had taken to pretending to talk to him a few nights a week to keep her mom's worries at ease. She was actually turning into a good liar. Which wasn't necessarily what she'd wanted from life.

"He's fine. Just very busy."

"The sooner we put this place up for sale and you can go home the better," her mom said.

Emery hated lying to her. But it wouldn't be for much longer. Once the lien was gone, everything would be okay. Her mom could move on, and so could Emery. Whatever moving on looked like.

All she knew was that she wouldn't rely on a man the way

her mom had relied on her dad. The fall was just way too hard.

CHAPTER
Thirteen

"EMERY!" The high-pitched voice made her jump. She'd been talking to Jed about a tractor that needed repair – more expenses that the farm didn't need right now. He gave her a nod and started walking toward the field where the farmhands were waiting for him, and she turned around to see the owner of the voice standing next to a red convertible.

Sabrina Hartson was waving at her, a huge smile on her face. Emery couldn't help but smile back. The woman's natural positivity was infectious.

"Hi." Emery walked over to where Sabrina was standing. "How are you?" she asked her, genuinely happy to see her.

"I'm good. But I'll be better if you agree to come out with me on Friday night." Sabrina wiggled her brows.

"What's happening on Friday night?" Emery asked her, still smiling. Because the thought of going out with people her own age felt invigorating. Yes, she got to chat with Maisie, but the oceans between them made Emery miss her friend desperately.

Sabrina clapped her hands together. "It's karaoke night at the Moonlight Bar in town. A few of my friends are going. I want you to come too. They're all excited to meet you."

Weird how warm that made her feel inside. It felt good to be bonding with this woman. Like it was the dawn of a new day.

"I can't sing," Emery admitted. "Will that be a problem?"

"Don't worry, most of my friends can't either," Sabrina told her, shrugging. "Anyway, you don't have to sing. We're just going to drink cocktails and check out the hot men. So are you in or what? It's going to be fun."

From the corner of her eye she could see Hendrix's dirt bike heading down the farm road toward them. She hadn't seen him for the past few days. It had felt like he was avoiding her, truth be told, but maybe she was being too sensitive.

He didn't owe her anything. If anything, it was the other way around. He'd helped her finish another item on her list after all.

"What's going on?" he asked as he came to a stop beside Sabrina's car.

"I'm just asking Emery if she'd like to come out with me and the girls on Friday." Sabrina shrugged.

Hendrix looked from his cousin to Emery, like he wasn't surprised. "Where?"

"To the Moonlight bar." Sabrina lifted a brow at him. "Karaoke night."

Hendrix looked at his cousin a moment too long. Like he was trying to work out her intentions. "I can drive you," he told Emery. "If you'd like."

"You're coming to karaoke too?" Sabrina asked, looking appalled at the thought of it. Emery bit down a smile.

"Pres and Marley keep hassling me to play pool. Seems as good a day as any to head into town and make them happy."

Sabrina rolled her eyes at him. "Shut up. You just want to make sure we behave." Sabrina looked over at Emery. "He's such a killjoy."

She didn't look like she cared, though. Emery got the impression that nothing bothered Sabrina.

Maybe she should try being a little more like that.

"Yeah, well we'll meet you there." He looked over at Emery. "Won't we?"

"We will." She nodded, grinning. Her day was already looking up.

"Whatever." Sabrina shook her hair out. "Your moods are so swingy they belong on a kid's playground." She poked his chest with her finger. "Just make sure you get her there on time."

Hendrix's eyes met Emery's. "I will," he murmured. And it made her heart gallop.

Because yes, he was just driving her to the bar to meet up with his cousin. It wasn't a date or anything. But he wasn't avoiding her, either. Whatever it was that was happening between them, she liked it. Way too much.

Hendrix was running late, dammit. A baler had jammed, and he'd spent the last hour fixing it, sweat soaking his skin. And by the time he'd gotten home he was covered in sticky dirt and bits of hay, and needed a long, hot shower.

Being late was the last thing he needed, because he didn't want to give his cousin another excuse to be annoyed at him. She'd already called and given him hell for offering to drive Emery.

"I thought you wanted me to be her friend," Sabrina had complained.

"I do. I also want to make sure she gets home okay."

"You're so aggravating," she told him.

"Right back at you. I'll see you Friday at seven."

Truth was, he didn't want Emery walking into the bar

alone. He didn't want other guys looking at her and thinking she was fair game.

She *was* engaged, he reminded himself. That's why he was feeling protective of her. Not because he wanted her.

Squeezing that thought out of his mind, he pulled his dark t-shirt over his head and made a vain attempt to get his damp hair under control. His muscles ached. Before the baler broke he'd spent most of the day wrangling his uncle's cattle, moving them to a shadier spot. A few of them hadn't wanted to comply so he'd spent too much time coaxing them, then dragging them. And then he'd cleaned out the cattle sheds, then forking hay from the delivery van into the barn.

He rolled his head from side to side to loosen the muscles in his shoulders. A year or two ago he would have planned to drink his way through the pain, but the fact was he had to be up early in the morning to do this shit all over again.

Truth be told, he loved it.

Grabbing his keys, he strode out of his little farmhouse, automatically looking to his left to make sure Frank's shed was closed tight. That had been another chore – repairing the door, installing a new lock, and making sure that Frank was comfortable in there.

When he got to his gate he stopped, unsure whether he should go over and knock on her door. Emery hadn't told him not to, but he knew her mom was high strung. He didn't want to cause any more problems than she already had with that relationship.

Before he could make a decision the door opened and she walked out.

And his heart damn near missed a beat.

She was wearing a red silk dress, the bodice cut in a crossover that skimmed her chest, giving him a delicious hint of the curves hidden beneath it. The skirt was short and tight, with a slit on her thigh.

Her eyes met his and he could barely breathe. Her hair

was glossy in the warm evening light, her dark waves tumbling over her shoulders. She curled her fingers around her black purse and walked down the steps. And he grinned, because even though she was dressed up to the damn nines, the woman was still wearing sneakers.

His eyes darkened as he strode across the road to open the gate for her. The smell of her perfume filled his senses. Floral but delicate. It made him want to ride a steed and win her hand.

"You're gonna create mayhem in the Moonlight Bar looking like that," he said, his voice thick.

A half-smile pulled at her lips. "Should I take that as a compliment?" she asked. She genuinely looked unsure.

Did she really not know how beautiful she was?

"Yes, you should. You look…" he let out a breath, shaking his head. Fuck, he couldn't find the right words. He never could. He was a do-er, not a talker. "So damn good."

Yeah, that wasn't right. But her smile still widened, like she knew his words had a different meaning.

"You don't look so bad yourself," she replied softly.

Hendrix looked down at the dark jeans and black t-shirt he was wearing. The shirt was cotton, light, because it was still so damn hot outside.

But the truth was, he'd wanted to wear something she'd like. Wanted her to enjoy looking at him. He wasn't a vain man, but he knew that heads usually turned when he walked into the bar.

He also knew that when they walked inside tonight, the heads wouldn't be turning to look at him. And he was more than okay with that.

"We should go," he murmured. "Before Sabrina sends out a search party." He put his hand on the curve of her back, feeling the warmth of her through the silk. This close, it was impossible not to think of kissing her.

She's marrying another guy.

Taking another breath, he steered her toward the passenger side of his truck, helping her into the cab. Her legs looked so damn enticing as she crossed them once she was situated. Supple, warm. With the lightest of tans.

Closing the door, he took his time walking around to the driver's side, needing it to center himself. Emery in cut-offs and a tank was one thing. Hell, her wearing barely nothing after skinny dipping was pretty good.

But seeing her like this? Dressed up so damn classy that he knew she was out of his league? That was something else all together.

He started the engine as soon as he climbed in, determined to make the drive as fast as he could. It felt dangerous to be alone with her like this. Dangerous to his self control and dangerous to her engagement.

He wasn't stupid, even if he'd tried to make his cousin think he was oblivious. He knew when a woman was interested in him. Even if she shouldn't be interested.

Especially then.

"Can I choose the music?" Emery asked as he pulled onto the farm lane.

"Go for it."

She leaned in, the short sleeve of her dress riding up to reveal her toned arms. Her biceps brushed his as she pressed the button to search for another station, and it made his jaw tighten.

"Sorry," she said, giving him a genuine smile. Like she thought she'd done something wrong.

"Not a problem."

She chose a 70s soft rock station. Boston was playing. "More than a Feeling" blasted out of his stereo.

"Do you mind if I open the window?" she asked.

"Works for me," he told her. "Nature's air conditioning beats man's."

So she did. And the image of her sitting in his truck, her

hair lifting in the breeze, her lips singing along, seared itself into his vision.

And into his brain. Permanently.

As a kid he'd been a punk. The kind of annoying little shit that made his brother's lives hell. And then, as a teenager, those hormones had surged like a damn tsunami. He'd discovered his looks, that girls liked his swagger, his self assurance.

But most especially they liked his driver's licence and his ability to borrow his older brothers' trucks.

Friday nights were date nights. And he dated his way through town. Until that day when everything changed, and he became a social pariah. No self respecting parent would let their daughter go out with him after that.

He was known as the wild one. The dangerous one. The one good girls avoided.

And Emery was a good girl. He had no doubt about that. She'd worked hard during school, dated one guy, got her college degree, and gotten engaged.

Their roads couldn't be anymore different.

"How's the tattoo?" he asked her, trying to break the silence. And ignore the weird sensation in his chest that happened every time he looked at her.

She looked down at her ankle. "It's so pretty. It makes me smile every time I look at it."

He swallowed, because *her* smile made *him* smile. And wasn't that all kinds of messed up?

"They say it's addictive. You gonna get another one?"

She laughed lightly. "That kind of pain is definitely not addictive. I'm all about the pleasure."

Her cheeks pinked up, the way they always did when she said something she kind of regretted. He was getting to know her. Starting to learn her tells, the way a poker player could watch your face and figure out what kind of hand you had.

"Me too," he murmured, pulling into the town square. "And here we are. Welcome to the pleasure dome."

There was a parking space right to the left of the bar, and he pulled in, cutting off the engine. The place was already busy. It always was on a Friday night. Full of workers spending their paychecks and wanting to relax after a hard week.

Full of guys wanting to find a woman without having to swipe on a damn phone app.

The low hum of music escaped through the door as they walked toward it. And yeah, his hand was soft on her back again, because the urge to protect her was strong.

"I'm gonna be in the pool room," he told her. "If anybody gives you any trouble, come get me."

There was a smile playing at her lips. "The only trouble I'll get in is if I try to sing. Rotten vegetables will be thrown at me."

He shook his head. "You have no idea how good you look, do you?"

Her lips parted as she stared at him. "Maybe you should tell me."

He wanted her. Wanted to drag her home and keep her there. Like some kind of caveman staking his claim.

"I don't have the words."

"How do you usually tell a woman she looks pretty?" she asked him, her voice breathy. She tipped her head to the side, her lashes fluttering as she waited for his answer.

He lifted a brow. "I'm more about showing than telling."

Oh, that made her blush. And he liked that way too much.

"Now go have a good time. But not too good a time." He opened the door for her. "If Sabrina starts acting a fool, let me know."

"She's a wild one, isn't she?"

"She has the Hartson blood in her."

"Hey!" a voice shouted from the corner. His cousin was

waving at them. Okay, she was waving at Emery. "We're over here. We have drinks." Sabrina pointed at the glasses stacked up on the table.

Oh boy. This wasn't going to end well.

"Stop looking so worried," Emery told him. "I'm a big girl. I can handle your cousin."

"Just don't let her lead you astray."

Emery wrinkled her nose, her eyes shining as they locked with his. "Now you're making it sound fun. Go." She pushed his arm, a laugh rumbling from her throat. "Chill out. And have a good time, too. You deserve it."

Before he could say anything else, she rolled onto her tiptoes and pressed her soft lips against his cheek, her breasts grazing his arm. His body froze for a moment. Then he reached down to steady her, his hands curling around her hips.

And then she was gone, walking over to Sabrina's table, as his cousin stood and threw her arms around Emery, introducing her to her friends.

He was glad his cousin was taking Emery under her wing. The woman deserved to have a good time.

Just not too good.

CHAPTER
Fourteen

THE MUSIC STOPPED and everybody cheered. Emery couldn't help but grin as Sabrina flounced back from the podium where she'd just belted out a karaoke version of 'I Need a Hero', her voice as thick and sultry as Bonnie Tyler's.

And from the way she was stopped several times by guys as she headed back to their table, it was clear a lot of them were trying to volunteer to be her partner for the night.

"How was I?" Sabrina asked as she took the seat next to Emery.

"You were fabulous." Emery grinned at her. "And that's not me just trying to inflate your ego."

"That's good," Mariah, one of Sabrina's friends commented. "Her ego is big enough as it is."

"For that, you have to buy me another cocktail," Sabrina told her, grinning because she knew it was true. "And I can't help it. It's the Hartson side of me. I swear the big dick energy my cousins have has turned into big…"

"Pussy energy," Mariah said, smugly.

"BPE. Whatever." Sabrina shrugged. "And you still owe me that cocktail."

"I just ordered a round," Emery told her. "It was my turn."

They were on their fourth. Maybe fifth. And definitely the last for Emery. Her head was starting to feel fuzzy. She liked the buzz, though. The way she couldn't stop smiling.

The way she felt freer than she had in a long time.

Truth was, she kind of wished she had Sabrina's confidence. Maybe she was right. You were either born with it, or you weren't.

Or maybe it had been squeezed out of her by a million different compromises. Making herself fit the mold of being the best daughter to her mom. The best fiancé to Trenton. But it didn't matter, because now she was getting it back.

"Are your cousins going to sing tonight?" Lila, a blonde who worked at the local diner, asked Sabrina.

"No, thank God. They'd embarrass the rest of us." Hendrix's older brothers, Presley and Marley – along with Pres' wife, Cassie – sang professionally in a band.

"How about Hendrix? Maybe we should get him up on the stage?" Mariah asked.

"You're only saying that because you have a crush on him," Lila replied, elbowing Mariah in the side.

"Shut up." Mariah shook her head. "You know that was when I was younger. I'm over him."

"Did you hear he took Emery to get a tattoo?" Sabrina asked, a sly smile pulling at her lips.

All eyes fell on her. Mariah frowned momentarily, replacing it with a smile like she was trying to show she didn't care.

Emery felt bad. "It's not like that," she told her. "He knew it was on a list my friend gave me. So he introduced me to his friend who's a tattoo artist."

"What list?" Sabrina asked her.

"It's a long story." Emery was having to speak loudly to be heard. "But my friend from work knew I was coming home this summer and wanted me to get out of my comfort zone. So she made me a kind of to-do list."

"What else is on it?"

Oh no, what was she getting herself into? Those cocktails had a lot to answer for. "Skinny dipping. Which I already did." And no, she wasn't going to tell them about her meeting Hendrix almost naked. "And the tattoo, of course. Get drunk." She looked at the cocktails. "Which really doesn't seem to be a problem."

"What else?" Sabrina asked.

She wrinkled her nose, trying to remember one that wouldn't cause problems. Like admitting she enjoyed riding on a motorcycle with Hendrix way too much. "Dance on a bar counter."

As soon as she said it, regret washed over her. Because of course Sabrina's eyes lit up like Christmas had come early.

"Oh my God," Sabrina said. "That's amazing. We can do that tonight!"

"Seriously, it's meant to be," Mariah added.

Emery looked at the bar. It was covered with drinks. People were leaning on it. "I don't think she meant somewhere like this."

"Then where?" Mariah asked, because there was no other bar in Hartson's Creek.

"Coyote Ugly," Sabrina said, and they laughed. But she was clearly thinking things over, because her eyes were narrow.

"It's fine. I'll do it another time." Or not do it at all. Because the idea of dancing on a bar, being watched by everybody, made her want to break out in hives. It was one thing to go skinny dipping with nobody watching. Or getting a tattoo from a guy who did it day in and day out.

But to be the center of attention here? Dear god, no thank you.

"I'm gonna ask Ryan," Sabrina said, standing.

"No." Emery shook her head quickly. "Don't do that."

"If you don't do it here, where are you going to do it? Come on, I'll do it with you. So will the others."

Mariah shrugged. Lilah grinned.

And Emery thought she might be sick any minute now.

"Third time champion." Marley grinned, holding his pool cue aloft like he was celebrating a major win. "You guys might as well go home. I'm on a streak tonight."

"Don't confuse luck with skill," Pres retorted, shaking his head, because this game had come down to the last ball. Which was more than could be said for when Hendrix played Marley in the last round. He'd barely potted a thing. Been too busy thinking about what was going on in the main bar.

Too busy popping his head around the door to check that *she* was okay.

And she was. She hadn't seen him checking on her, but Emery looked like she was enjoying herself. She was laughing with his cousin, talking to Sabrina's friends. And thankfully, all the women at the table were making it clear to any assholes who approached them that tonight was strictly a ladies' night. No ardent suitors invited.

"Sure, let's call it luck," Marley said, the smile still pulling at his lips. "The more I play, the luckier I get."

"Maybe if you'd been lifting roof tiles for eight hours today you'd be singing another tune." Pres rolled his shoulders, groaning. He worked as a contractor. Owned his own business. Mostly he coordinated the work, but if a tradesman didn't show up or got sick, he was the first to take over.

"Sure, old man, blame your muscles if that makes you feel better."

"I'm only older than you by five minutes." Pres narrowed his eyes.

Marley shrugged. "Sometimes that's all it takes."

Hendrix shook his head at his brothers. They had their own bond. It was impossible for them not to. And yeah, sometimes he felt a little excluded, despite their attempts to make him feel a part of it. It wasn't something they did on purpose, he knew that.

But he couldn't exchange a glance with Pres and know exactly how he felt like Marley could. Or wince in real pain when his twin was in an accident the way Marley had that time Pres had fallen from a roof.

Maybe that's why he felt so lost for so long. Looking for something that he could never have. When your only frame of reference growing up was that your brothers had the kind of bond that could never be broken, you either sought out the kind of intimacy that could give you that or you avoided it.

And Hendrix had avoided it like a professional. Causing his mom even more heartache.

"So what's your excuse?" Marley asked, looking at Hendrix. "You're not even putting up a fight today."

"He's too busy thinking about a woman," Pres murmured.

Hendrix rolled his eyes. They hadn't stopped joshing him about driving Emery to meet up with Sabrina and her friends since he'd walked through the door to the pool room. Even though it would have been super weird for them to be traveling from their houses opposite each other to *exactly the same place* and home again without sharing a ride.

"Get out of here." He shook his head, mostly at his lame riposte.

"Whatever happened to there being nothing between you two?" Pres asked. "First you're taking her to Jack's place, then you're driving her here."

"We're friends." And that was it. Because there was nothing going on between them. Not even if every damn day his heart beat faster whenever he saw her from across the road.

"And she's engaged," Marley pointed out. And for some reason that made Hendrix's jaw tighten.

"So where's her fiancé?" Pres asked. "How the hell is he letting her out of his sight for this long if everything between them is a-fucking-okay?"

That thought had occurred to Hendrix before. And then he'd pushed it away like it was poison.

"Doesn't he live and work in Charleston?" Marley murmured.

"It's not that far away. Would you leave Kate for that long?" Pres asked his brother. "Because if Cass was living and working somewhere and I was somewhere else you can be damn sure I'd be driving to see her every weekend, no matter how far away she was."

"You drove to New York after all," Marley murmured. Hendrix grinned, because he remembered that particular episode. It was in the early days of Pres and Cassie's relationship. His brother had this guilt about it, because his first wife – and the mother of his daughter – had died three years earlier, and Cassie was his kid's dance teacher.

He'd tried so hard not to fall for her, but the chemistry between them was instant. It still hadn't stopped Pres from behaving like an idiot, though, and insisting Cass take an opportunity in New York when she was offered it.

And then he'd realized what a fool he was to let her go, so he'd bundled his daughter, Delilah, in his car and driven the hundreds of miles to Manhattan so he could declare his love for Cassie.

Hendrix let out a long breath. In so many ways it had been easier for his brother. Yes, he had to overcome his own demons, but they were both single. They were so obviously in love with each other.

Whereas Emery Reed was engaged – and presumably in love with – another man. This infatuation, if that's what you wanted to call it, with her was all on his side.

Even if sometimes it felt like it wasn't.

And wasn't that the most dangerous thought?

"There's definitely something weird between them," Pres agreed.

"Can we get on with playing a game, please?" Hendrix replied, shaking his head. "If I wanted an in-depth discussion on my love life, I'd have gone to see Mom."

Pres had the good grace to snicker.

"Have you talked to her?" Marley asked Hendrix.

"Mom? No."

"I mean Emery. Have you asked her why that asshole hasn't visited her since she's been back in town?"

Hendrix frowned. "No, why would I?"

"Because the way I see it, there's one of two reasons for his absence." Marley grabbed the rack, lining the plastic triangle up in the center of the blue baize. "Either he doesn't want to see her, which means their relationship is in trouble. Or…" He hunkered down to pull the ball release, the sound of them rolling to the front of the table echoing through the room.

"Or?" Hendrix prompted. Not because he was interested, or at least that's what he was telling himself. But because he wanted this conversation to be over.

"Or she doesn't want him to come see her. Which also means their relationship is in trouble." Marley filled the triangle with the balls. "Now who's up next?"

"You go again," Hendrix told Pres.

"You sure?"

"He just wants to see you pout when you lose again," Marley teased.

Sure, that was the reason. Not because Hendrix wanted to think about what Marley had just said. Marley was the quieter of the twins, but not because he didn't have things to communicate. But because he thought a lot. Pres, on the other hand, tended to blurt things out before they even reached his brain.

"Either way, she's still engaged," Pres pointed out.

"Can we shut up about it now?" Hendrix asked them. "If somebody overhears they'll think you're being serious. And I don't want rumors flying around about things that aren't true. She deserves better than that."

Pres and Marley exchanged one of those stupidly annoying glances he could remember from growing up with them.

"What?" Hendrix asked, shaking his head.

"You're fucked, man," Marley murmured.

"Absolutely and completely," Pres agreed, grinning.

"What the hell is that supposed to mean?" A frown pulled at Hendrix's brow. He should have stayed home. Hell, he would have, if she wasn't here.

And no, he wasn't her keeper. He just cared, that was all.

As a damn friend, in case you were wondering.

"It means you're not worried about us spreading gossip because it might harm you. Or stop you from getting some female action," Marley said, still unable to hide his enjoyment. "But because you're *worried about her reputation*."

"Shut the hell up and play the game," Hendrix muttered.

"Completely fucking besotted," Marley agreed.

Before Hendrix could tell them they were delusional, the door to the pool room opened, and a young guy ran in.

"There's some girls going full on stripper in there," he shouted to his friends playing at another pool table. "They're dancing on the bar. You gotta come see."

Marley froze. His eyes met Pres' again. At exactly the same time they both said, "Sabrina."

And then all three of them rushed to the bar area like the whole place was going up in fire.

CHAPTER
Fifteen

MAYBE MAKING a fool out of yourself in front of a full bar of revelers wasn't everybody's idea of fun, but Emery actually found herself smiling and enjoying this.

And she got to mark another item off her list. There was no way Maisie would believe she'd actually gone through with number five on the fuck-Trenton list, but dammit she had.

The loud throb of music had her hips swinging to the rhythm. Next to her Sabrina was dancing like she was made for it, getting down low, lifting up again, causing the guys to whoop and reach out for her every time she leaned over to blow them a kiss.

Emery, on the other hand, was happy to dance with her hands raised up, her dress swishing around her thighs as some talented guy with the mic sang out the chorus to Bon Jovi's "Livin' On a Prayer".

"Come on," Sabrina shouted in her ear. "We need to get dirtier." She grabbed Emery's hands, facing her as she swung her hips low, encouraging Emery to do the same.

"Let me take you home tonight," one of the men standing at the bar shouted up to Emery. She rolled her eyes at Sabrina.

"Sorry, gentlemen," Sabrina called back to him. "Tonight is ladies' night." She leaned into whisper to Emery, "You look so beautiful. Look at them all watching you."

And they were. A whole cluster of men were cheering them on. But this wasn't about them, it was about her. About feeling free to do all the stupid stuff she should have done when she was younger.

She'd been so busy trying to be somebody that she wasn't, that she forgot about finding out who she was.

Not that she would ever be the kind of person who willingly jumped on a bar to dance. But how would she have known that unless she tried? And until the end of the song, she would try.

She'd let the music fill her up as adrenaline flowed through her veins. She'd let her body move the way it wanted to, not because she wanted male attention, but because it felt good.

"Uh-oh," Sabrina called out. "They look mad." She didn't sound worried at all as her cousins approached them. Pres and Marley had their eyes narrowed, staring at their younger girl cousin.

Hendrix, however, was looking straight at Emery.

And she liked the way he looked at her. Like there was nobody else in the room except the two of them. She locked her gaze with his, her breath escaping through her lips as she kept dancing.

For him. Only for him.

That's how it felt.

He kept walking forward, people parting like waves in front of him as though they knew he'd barge through if they didn't. And not once did his eyes waver from her. His jaw was tight, his body tall, his shoulders held so damn proud it made her body ache.

And once he was at the front of the crowd, standing only inches away from her, she felt like she was on fire.

Sabrina opened her mouth – presumably to remind him it was ladies' night – but when she looked at the expression on his face she closed it again. Her eyes moved to Emery's face, like she was trying to work out what was going on.

Good luck with that. Emery had no idea herself.

All she knew was that every time this man was close she felt like she was somewhere between flying and falling. Maybe it was the adrenaline, or the sudden effect all of those cocktails had on her thought process, but whatever it was, she was certain how she felt about him.

She wanted him. She wanted him to want her. To touch her. To kiss her until neither of them could breathe.

She was the teenager she'd never been. Hormones surging through her like they were an alien force.

And all through this revelation, he didn't move a damn inch. Didn't try to stop her, didn't try to encourage her down.

Just stood guard in front of her. His eyes never wavering. Completely locked on her face the way her gaze was set on his. It felt like everybody else in the room had faded away, that the spotlight was just on the two of them.

She swayed her hips and his mouth parted, letting out the softest of breaths, like he couldn't keep it in.

She couldn't remember the last time she felt this in control. Like she was taking her life into her hands at last. There was nowhere else she'd rather be right now than here, dancing, looking at him.

Wishing for everything she couldn't have.

The song came to an end and everybody cheered. Sabrina lapped it up, her hands waving in the air. "Who's gonna catch me?" she shouted, launching herself into the air like a rock singer. A dozen guys ran forward like bridesmaids trying to catch the bouquet, jostling each other to be the one to have her in their arms.

With the attention firmly on Sabrina, Hendrix stepped forward and held his hands out to Emery. She let him reach for her, his palms warm and strong as he lifted her down from the bar. And when her feet touched the ground, he didn't let go.

"Another one from your list," he murmured. And it made her heart heat up. He remembered. Not only did he remember, he actually looked pleased she'd achieved it.

"Yeah," she said, grinning at him, feeling a little dizzy and breathless. "How did I do?"

Sure, she was fishing for compliments. Blame the alcohol.

"You looked like an angel. A dirty angel."

She laughed.

Another singer had taken the mic. A familiar country song replaced Bon Jovi and couples started to fill the dance floor. From the corner of her eye, she could see Sabrina arguing furiously with Pres and Marley.

"Dance with me," she whispered to Hendrix.

He shook his head. "I can't."

The way he said it, like she'd asked him to go on a killing spree with her, felt like a bucket of ice water being thrown over her body. It actually made her shiver, and not in a good way.

Oh, she'd forgotten about the sting of rejection. In all the glory of taking control she'd forgotten about the way this back and forth could hurt.

Like a knife stabbing her heart.

"You're engaged," he muttered. "It would be wrong."

Trying to find a hint of dignity, she lifted her head up to look him in the eye. "If you're so worried about me being engaged, why did you keep my panties?"

Okay, those cocktails were working. Why did she bring that up now?

Hendrix's jaw twitched. She'd pissed him off. She could tell that from the way his eyes narrowed and his lips pressed together in a thin line.

"You know what? It doesn't matter. I want to go home,

anyway." And she did. She wanted to curl up in her bed and smell his damn t-shirt and forget about the mess her life was.

This was the problem with alcohol. Or maybe it was just the problem with her. She messed everything up.

Right now, she felt like she was in a labyrinth of her own making. Every time she tried to find the exit, she ended up deeper into the maze.

No matter what she did, she couldn't get out of it.

"I'll just say goodbye to my brothers." Hendrix nodded.

Oh, he thought she wanted him to take her home? Oh, hell no.

"It's fine. I'll find my own way back. I'll get a cab."

"In this town?" He lifted a brow. "You'll never get one. Don't be silly, I'll drive you."

Sometimes, all you had left was pride. "I'd hate for you to have to drive home an engaged woman," she told him, unable to keep the annoyance out of her voice. "People will talk."

He blinked at the way she threw his words back at him. "That's not what I meant. You're being unreasonable."

Yeah, she was. But she'd spent a lifetime being reasonable. Doing the right thing, being the good girl. And look where that had gotten her?

He reached for her arm, his fingers curling around the top of her bicep. His palm was warm. Strong. She hated that she loved it. "Stay here," he told her. "I'll be right back and I'll drive you home."

She didn't nod. She didn't say okay. But like everybody else in her life, this man expected her to obey him. And why wouldn't he? She always did what she was told.

Watching him walk back to the pool room, where no doubt his brothers had disappeared to, she let out a low breath.

What an idiot she was. Thinking he felt the same way she

did. Why would he? He thought she was engaged to a man he disliked intensely. A taken woman.

The thought of sitting next to him in his truck for the drive home made her stomach tighten. She couldn't do it. Couldn't let him drive her because he was being nice. Couldn't watch the way the tendons on his forearms twisted as he turned the wheel. Couldn't look at his profile as he drove, admiring the razor-sharpness of his jaw and the way his nose was so damn straight.

She walked over to the table where some of Sabrina's friends were standing and giggling, and grabbed her purse.

"Can you tell Sabrina I had to go?" she asked them over the noise of the Karaoke.

"Sure." Mariah was too busy laughing at something one of her friends was saying to pay much attention. And that was a good thing. Emery didn't want to explain. She didn't want to do anything.

She just wanted to go home.

The door to the pool room was still shut. *Good.* That gave her enough time to make an exit without him noticing.

She'd walk to the curb. And if there were no taxis there, she'd walk home. At least she'd have her dignity.

And with that thought she headed straight for the door leading to the outside, feeling the warm night air wrap around her as she stepped onto the sidewalk.

Emery wasn't where he'd left her only a couple of minutes ago. Of course she wasn't. Hendrix let out a low curse, already annoyed because his brothers had decided to tease him when he told them he was leaving.

He was trying to do the right thing here. Why was everybody making it so damn difficult?

Yes, he found her attractive. Okay, he thought about her

every damn night. Imagined the way her lips tasted. Imagined the way *she* tasted.

And the panties. Shit, she knew about them. He felt like shit, keeping them when he knew she was taken.

But he also had enough common sense to know it could only ever be a thought. There was no graceful way out of this situation that didn't end up with somebody getting hurt.

He should have stayed away from her. He knew that. He'd always known that. God knew, he'd tried.

And then he'd wavered. Well, this time it would be different. He'd drive her home and that would be it. They both knew this thing between them was a ticking time bomb. Even the thought of her sitting next to him in the cab of his truck – those lithe, tanned legs stretching out, that red dress making the most of every curve she had – was making his neck feel hot.

Sighing, he walked over to the table where she'd spent the evening. Sabrina was talking to her friend, the two of them giggling.

"I thought you'd left," his cousin said to him as he leaned in to ask her where Emery was. Because she certainly wasn't at the table.

"Just about to. Where's Emery?"

Sabrina blinked. "No idea."

"She said she was leaving, too," Mariah told Sabrina. "I was supposed to tell you that."

"So where is she?" Hendrix frowned, looking around the packed bar. Another Karaoke song had started up, and the singer was murdering the ABBA song. Christ, he was getting a headache.

"I don't know," Sabrina replied. "Maybe she got lucky with another guy."

"She's engaged," he reminded her.

Sabrina gave him a slow grin. "She sure wasn't acting like it when she was staring at you."

His jaw tightened. And yeah, he wanted to defend her, even if there was a kernel of truth in his cousin's words. Emery wasn't acting like she was engaged. Or maybe that was just wishful thinking.

"Maybe she went to the bathroom," Mariah suggested.

"Can one of you go look?" His voice was tight.

"Why are you so annoyed?" Sabrina asked him. "A girl is allowed to spend some time getting ready, you know?"

He took a deep breath. He was on his last string of patience here. "I'm not annoyed. She just said she wanted to go home and now she's not here."

"Men." Mariah rolled her eyes at him. "Always expecting women to be at your beck and call."

"You know what?" he said. "I'll go check for myself."

He turned and strode away, hearing his cousin and her friends laugh softly at him. And yeah, maybe they were right. He wasn't even sure why he was so pissed. He just was.

He'd been feeling that way a lot recently. Ever since a certain somebody moved into the house opposite his.

It took a hot minute to get to the bathrooms. The door to the ladies' room was open. A line formed through the doorway and out into the bar.

"Listen," he said to the woman at the end. "I'm trying to find my friend. Do you know if she's in there? Emery Reed?"

"I've no idea." She shrugged.

Damn it. "Emery?" he called out, his voice loud enough to carry into the bathroom. "You in there?"

"Whoa," another women in the line said. "He's angry."

"But hot," her friend replied. "I'll be Emery," she said to him. "You can call me anything as long as you call me."

For God's sake.

"There's no Emery in here," a voice called out from in the bathroom.

The Moonlight Bar was full, but it was also compact. If she

wasn't in the bathroom, then she wasn't here at all. She must have left the way she'd threatened to.

Annoyance rushed through him as he strode across the room to the front door, pushing it open. Taking a deep breath of fresh air, he looked around. And that's when he saw her in the distance, walking away from him.

"Emery?" he called out.

She didn't even flinch. Just kept on walking.

"Wait the hell up."

Still nothing. He ground his teeth together, unlocking his truck and sliding quickly into the driver's seat. Sure, he could run after her, but then they'd be arguing in the street.

Instead, he started up the engine, reversing out of his parking space, and gunning the engine to catch up with the small, female form disappearing into the distance.

It didn't take long. Even in those tennis shoes she was walking at a steady, almost slow pace. His breath caught as he looked at the expression on her face. She looked so damn sad it was killing him.

He hit the window button and called out to her.

"Get in the truck, Emery."

And damn if she didn't just jut her chin out, the way Frank did when he was pissed. "I told you, I can walk myself home."

CHAPTER
Sixteen

HENDRIX TOOK A DEEP BREATH, but it did nothing to clear the annoyance rushing through him.

"Please get in the damn truck before I drag you in."

Her mouth dropped open. Good. At least she was aware of his intentions.

"What are you, a caveman now?"

"I'm a man who worries about your safety and wants to make sure you get home without getting hurt. Somebody needs to. Because your fiancé so clearly isn't."

She laughed, though there was no amusement to it. "We live in the asscrack of nowhere, Hendrix. What do you think's going to happen to me? Will I get abducted by a horny goat?"

His mouth twitched. "I told you I'd drive you and get you home. And I'm going to do it."

She hadn't stopped walking. The truck was barely moving, only going four miles an hour at best, as he kept at her pace.

"What are you planning to do?" she asked him. "Drive at that pace for an hour? It'll make you crazy."

Yeah, it would. He liked speed, not crawling. "If I have to."

"You don't have to." She finally stopped and he hit the brakes as she turned to look at him through the open passenger window. "You don't have to do anything. I'm nothing to you, remember? You couldn't even bring yourself to dance with me."

"You're behaving like a brat," he told her.

She sighed. "I know. And I hate it."

His mouth twitched again. "Then stop it."

"I can't."

What kind of reply was that? "Why not?"

"Because if I stop, I'll start overthinking. So if it's all the same with you, I'll be a brat and make you hate me and then maybe my life won't be such a damn mess." Her voice broke at the end of her words.

And he broke a little too.

Just as he opened his mouth to form a reply – *any reply* – that would make her stop looking like she was about to cry, she took an about turn and ran through a gap in the hedge along the road, into a field.

Damn, she was going to take a shortcut. The kind of shortcut his truck couldn't follow her in. Yes, she was heading in the right direction for home, but she'd have to run through fields and jump a river to get there.

He was going to kill her. But first he was going to catch her. "For Christ's sake," he muttered, cutting the engine and wrenching the car door open, slamming it behind him as he ran toward the gap.

He could see her, ten yards ahead. Damn, that woman could run. But he could run faster. He knew it and she knew it.

"Emery, if you don't stop running I'm gonna make you regret it," he called out, thundering after her.

She didn't stop, though. Didn't even look back. Just kept running.

Adrenaline rushed through his body. The kind of adrenaline he knew he shouldn't like. But it forced his muscles tighter, made his gait wider, made him faster than she could ever hope to run.

"Is this about the panties?" he yelled. "Frank's the one who stole them. I just didn't know what to do with them when I found them." Okay, it was a half-truth. But she needed to stop storming away from him.

It took him less than thirty seconds to catch up with her. And no, he didn't throw her over his shoulders, because yes, his body was full of testosterone right now, but his momma also brought him up to have some manners.

Instead, he ran in front of her, making her curse as he turned and reached for her arms.

"Let me go," she told him breathlessly. Her chest was rising and falling like she wasn't used to using this much energy all at once.

"I will if you stop running," he told her. He was a little breathless, too, but it made his voice low and thick. Her eyelashes fluttered at the way he sounded.

"And if I don't?" she murmured. He noticed she hadn't pulled away from him. Not yet, anyway.

"Then I guess I'm running with you. All the way home."

She blinked, like she wasn't expecting that. Maybe she'd expected him to be a caveman, too.

Yeah, well he wasn't the cliché she thought he was.

"Your truck is on the side of the road," she pointed out.

"I'll have to come back to get that afterward," he told her. "And then I'll be doubly pissed."

Her jaw trembled, like she was trying not to laugh. "Or you could just let me go home alone. That could work."

"Nope. It's the truck or the marathon. Your choice."

"Four miles isn't exactly a marathon."

"When was the last time you ran four miles, Emery?" he asked her.

Her brows dipped, like she was actually trying to remember. "I did the couch to five K thing a few years ago. Well, I started it. And then I decided I liked the couch part better."

He couldn't help it. He grinned. And she rolled her eyes at him.

"But I can certainly walk it," she told him. "*Alone.*"

And then, before he could answer her, she put her hands on his chest and pushed him. Like she thought that would give her the edge to start running without him. Normally, that kind of push wouldn't make him move an inch. He was strong, he was balanced, and as annoying as she was, she was far less powerful.

Physically, at least.

But she took him by surprise. Enough for him to step back, his heel clipping whatever rock had seen fit to nestle into the ground behind him. Maybe it was the way the adrenaline was still rushing through him, or maybe it was the way her hands felt so soft on his chest.

Whatever it was, he lost his balance spectacularly. He stumbled back, his arms shooting out in a vain attempt to regain his equilibrium, before he fell back into the grass, his body hitting the ground with a thud.

From this position, the sky was an almost perfect blue-black, yellow stars twinkling like pinpricks in the velvety heavens.

"Oh my God!" Emery muttered. "Oh crap, I didn't mean to."

She dropped to her knees next to him. "Hendrix, I'm sorry. I didn't mean to push you. Are you okay?"

He frowned. "Where am I?"

"Oh no." Her breath was coming rapidly now.

"Who are you?" he asked her.

"I'm Emery. I live across the street from you." She reached out to touch his head. "Does it hurt? Do you have a concussion?" She was leaning over him, her face close to his. He could feel her breath on his skin. "Stay here. I'll call somebody. An ambulance." She stroked his hair softly, and it felt good.

"Or you could get in my truck and let me drive you home," he growled, capturing her wrist in his, pulling her even closer toward him.

"You asshole! I thought you were hurt." She frowned at him, and he couldn't help but start to laugh.

Christ, she was so pretty. And so close. He could feel her thighs against his as she leaned over him. Her mouth parted as she glared at him.

He wanted to pull her closer. Wanted her body on top of his. Wanted his mouth on hers.

Instantly, he was hard.

Releasing his hold on her wrist, he took a deep breath. "You need to move," he told her gruffly.

"Why?" he could feel her breath on his face as she spoke. "Are you sure you're okay?"

He shook his head slowly. No he wasn't. He was so far from okay it wasn't funny. "If you don't move, I'm going to kiss you."

"Oh."

"So please move," he muttered. "Before I lose my goddamned mind."

She was still staring at him. Her legs were still touching his in the most maddeningly delightful way. And he was aching for her.

"What if I don't want to move?" she asked him.

Yeah, he was definitely losing his mind.

"Then I'll move you." It wasn't a threat. His tone was more playful than that. Like it already knew what his heart was feeling. What his whole body was feeling. A flicker of interest washed over her face as she pulled her plump bottom lip between her teeth.

Did she know how beautiful she was? He didn't think so.

He got the impression that life had beaten that out of her, one painful experience at a time.

"Try it," she whispered, her chest lifting as she inhaled sharply. Like she'd forgotten to breathe until her lungs began to protest.

Yeah, well he knew that feeling. It was all over him. It made him forget who he was, who she was.

It was like his mind was a desert except for this feeling that washed through him. This need. This ache.

To kiss her.

"You want me to move you?" He had to ask one more time. He wanted her permission. Needed it.

"I want you to try."

A slow grin pulled at his lips as he looked at this vision of complete loveliness hovering over him. He could feel the tips of her hair tickling the skin of his jaw. Could smell the sweet notes of her perfume.

But most of all he could feel her excitement. She looked like nobody had flirted with her like this in a long, long time. He pushed that thought to the back of his mind because that road led to too many difficult discussions.

"Hold on," he murmured. "Because if I try, I always succeed."

He reached for her delicate wrists, closing his hands around them like they were bracelets, pulling her body against his, because if he was doing this, he was doing it so she didn't get hurt.

She didn't fight him, didn't protest. Her face was blushing, her breath coming faster.

She liked this as much as he did.

"Do you have any idea how aggravating you are?" he asked her, lifting one of her arms to press his warm lips against the inside of her wrist. The skin was so thin he could see the blue of her veins beneath it.

"I can be more aggravating," she said, and it sounded like a promise.

"I've no doubt of that." His grin widened as he slid his hand down her back, then twisted their bodies like he was a wrestler pulling her underneath him, his hands sliding between her body and the earthy ground, to make sure the impact didn't hurt her.

And suddenly she was the one looking up at him, her eyes wide like he'd actually taken her by surprise.

It was only when he felt her body rock against his that he realized she was clinging to him. Her arms were around his neck, her legs were wrapped around his hips. Her dress was pulled up so high he could see the edge of her panties.

"What are you going to do to me now?" she whispered.

"What do you think?" His voice was a rasp.

He lifted his head, looking straight into her eyes. His mouth was a breath away from hers. Her legs weren't clinging to him anymore, but they were on either side of his, her thighs pressed against his hips.

When his mouth claimed hers, it was like every firework in the world was exploding around them. He started the kiss softly, like he was exploring, his hand cupping her face, his mouth moving against hers until they were both breathless. But then she kissed him back, her fingers scraping his back, her tongue sliding against his, her body rocking, like it had a need that had to be sated.

He scraped his teeth against her lip, pulling it, sucking it, his hand sliding down her neck, down her side, cupping her soft breast. Her nipple was hard, and he teased it with the pad of his thumb, until she let out a soft groan that was warm against his mouth. It made him want more.

Made him want everything.

Running his hands along her hips, he feathered his fingers down to her thighs, finding the spot just below her panties.

The damn end zone. The goal. Her skin was warm, soft.

He could imagine it against his face as he took her to oblivion. Scratching her with his beard, teasing her with his tongue.

Her fingers slid through his hair, scraping his scalp as he kissed her again. Then he trailed his mouth along her jaw, down her throat, and she let out a mew like a trapped kitten.

He kissed the dip where her throat met her chest.

"You're so damn perfect," he told her. And they weren't just words, they were real ones. How had he kept himself from touching her for this long? He had no idea, but somebody should give him a damn medal for restraint.

"Hey! Everything okay there?" a voice called out from the distance.

He lifted his head up. "Shit," he muttered. Then he pulled her dress down to cover what he could of her.

CHAPTER
Seventeen

"THAT'S IT?" Maisie asked, sounding almost disappointed. "He just drove you home? Nothing else?"

Emery frowned. "I thought you'd be pleased. I crossed off two items. I achieved number seven. Isn't that the pinnacle?"

"It would be if you didn't seem so down about it."

Yeah, well she couldn't help it. Going from the high of feeling Hendrix Hartson's lips on hers, his hands caressing her body, to the sound of a stranger calling out had been pretty much like falling down to earth from a great, great height.

The man had seen Hendrix's truck abandoned on the side of the road and thought there was a problem.

And there was. A big problem. She couldn't stop thinking about the way his mouth moved desperately against hers.

He'd driven her home silently, after explaining to the good Samaritan that they'd heard a hurt animal. All lies, but the stranger had just shot them a knowing look and left.

Hendrix clearly didn't want to talk about what had happened. He'd put the music on high and pressed his foot down on the gas, his jaw tight as they drove home. And he'd dropped her off in the road right outside her mom's house, waiting until she'd made it inside before he drove to his own farm.

She hated the way he wouldn't meet her gaze. She couldn't read him at all. It was like he'd closed down and she couldn't pry her way inside the steel box encasing his thoughts.

"I think I might've messed things up," she confessed. "He'd made it clear he didn't want to touch me at the bar. And then I behaved like an idiot and practically forced him to chase me."

"You didn't force him to do anything. He's a grown man," Maisie pointed out. They were on the phone this time, instead of chatting by video call. Maisie was at the beach with some friends she'd made traveling. When they were both silent, Emery could hear the murmur of the other sun-worshippers and the occasional crash of the water hitting the shore.

It was almost four o'clock in the afternoon and she hadn't seen Hendrix all day. He must have left before she'd got up, because there was no sign of his bike outside when she'd looked out of the window. If he'd been in the yard, if he'd even been home, she would've tried to talk to him.

He thought bad of her. That had to be it. He thought she'd been unfaithful to Trenton, even though she honestly hadn't.

But she hated that he didn't know that. That he would probably be assuming the worst about the best kiss she'd ever had.

"I can hear you overthinking," Maisie told her.

"I'm not overthinking. I'm catastrophizing. It's different."

Maisie started to laugh. "You need to tell him the truth."

"What? Why? We just kissed. Nothing more."

"Oh honey, I know you too well. You don't just kiss guys. You don't do anything without your heart rushing in first. I can hear it in your voice. You're falling for this guy. And you're beating yourself up even though you shouldn't be."

"If you knew I wouldn't kiss another man lightly, why did you put it on the list?" Emery asked her.

"Honestly? I didn't think you'd do it," Maisie admitted. "I didn't think you'd do most of the things. I just hoped... I don't know. I wish I was there, helping you work through this. The list felt important somehow."

"You are helping me."

"No, you're helping yourself. The list, that's just the catalyst. Look at how you're changing. After all those years of being suffocated in a chrysalis, you're like a butterfly, being set free. Now tell me. How do you feel about him?"

"Hendrix?" Emery let out a soft sigh. "I feel... I don't know. Yearning, I guess."

"Yearning?"

"Like my heart is about to break out of my chest every time I look at him. But I can't feel that way."

"Yes you can. Fuck Trenton. I mean it, fuck him." Maisie sounded furious. "He's getting everything, and you're getting nothing out of this."

Emery stayed quiet. She still hadn't told Maisie about the lien. It felt too painful. Like it was her fault.

"I'm adding a number eight," Maisie said. "And you have to do it tonight."

"You can't add something to the list after you wrote it," Emery protested. "That's not how it works."

"Yes I can. It's my list and I can do what I want. Number eight, tell Hendrix that you're not engaged."

Emery's mouth turned dry.

"I'm serious, Em. You said yourself that the guy's out there thinking he kissed a taken woman. The least you can do is let him know he hasn't."

And there it was. Her friend had found her weak spot. The part that was worrying her the most. Because she was still the good girl she always was, even when she played at being bad. And she hated the thought that her actions had affected someone else.

No, that they'd affected *him*. He didn't deserve to be lied to. Not after he'd helped her so much.

He deserved so much better.

She looked out of her window at his farm. He still wasn't there. But he would be later.

She owed him an explanation. She owed him the truth.

But the thought of telling him made her want to hurl.

Hendrix had spent most of the day in his uncle's fields, finishing the bailing he'd lost time on yesterday with the repairs. And yes, technically he was only supposed to work until lunchtime on Saturdays, spending the rest of the time on his own farm.

But he didn't want to go home. And yes, he was avoiding Emery Reed. Because he was a damn pussy.

And maybe he preferred beating himself up to looking her in the eye, knowing he couldn't have her.

Last night, that kiss... he shook his head, because he didn't have the words to capture how he was feeling at the memory of it. All he knew was that as he lay on top of her sweet body, his mouth taking hers, he was a breath away from pulling her panties down and making her his in the sweetest, most delicious way.

Christ, the memory of her lips was making him hard. He could almost feel the silk of her skin against his palms, feel the way her legs parted for him as he slid his hands down them.

Her eyes had been wide, her breath had been short, and she hadn't tried to stop him. No, she'd encouraged him, kissing him harder, scratching her nails against his scalp.

She'd been as needy as he'd been hard.

"Don't you have a home to go to?" a voice shouted.

He blinked away the thought of Emery's curves, looking up to see his dad walking toward him.

"Hi." He forced a smile on his face, shutting off the engine to the bailer, climbing down from the high seat to hug his father. "I didn't know you were here."

"Just came to talk to Logan. Your mom wants to hold the launch for the charity here. I wanted to make sure it was okay with him."

"When is it?" Hendrix asked. He knew how excited she was about it. How nervous, too. His mom rarely made public appearances. She hated being in the news. But this launch would involve both, and he felt for her.

"In three weeks. We were planning to do it at our place, but you know what's she's like. Over thinking it. I said I'd ask Logan. He's good for us to do it at the restaurant." His dad smiled softly. His parents' love story was so clear to see in everything they did. From the moment he could see, he knew how much they cared for each other.

They were a good team. But where his dad loved the limelight – as a rock star he yearned for it, and even now that he was retired, he wasn't exactly a shrinking violet – his mom hated it.

The only reason she was dealing with a PR company and the media over the charity was because she was determined to get the right people applying for grants. He admired her for doing it, too. She was a good woman through and through.

"You're gonna come to the launch, right?" his dad asked.

"Of course." Hendrix nodded. "I wouldn't miss it."

"Good." His dad patted his arm. "It'll mean a lot to your mom, having you all there. She needs our support."

"She's always got it."

That was enough to put a smile on his dad's face. "Well,

I'd better go home and tell her the good news." He tipped his head to the side. "Come over and see her soon, okay?"

"Of course."

His dad nodded, turning to walk away. But then he looked at Hendrix once more, concern in his eyes. "And son?"

"Yeah?" Hendrix asked.

"You look tired. Go home and stop working so hard."

As soon as he pulled up outside the cottage, Hendrix could feel himself being watched. He kicked the stand into the dirt, cut the engine, and climbed off, grabbing some hay to fill up Frank's trough.

Once the goat was eating, he finally brought his gaze to Emery's house. And of course she was standing there, her body stock still as she stared at him from the porch.

It only took two beats of his heart for her to start walking down the steps toward him.

He didn't move as she got closer. Just waited for her to cross the lane and walk into his yard. Knowing this was inevitable.

Even if it felt so painful it hurt.

"Can we talk?" she asked, her voice soft. Her hands were curled into fists. She had her hair down, the gentle breeze lifting it at the ends.

"Here?" He looked over her shoulder. "Won't your mom see?"

Her lips parted and she let out a breath. "She's cleaning out some closets. But you're probably right. Can we talk somewhere private?"

The obvious response would be to invite her into his house. But he couldn't. It felt too personal. Especially when he knew she was about to give him the brush off.

Truth was, he wasn't sure he could be alone with her in an

enclosed space anymore. And wasn't that an advertisement for keeping away from him?

"I need to take some soil samples from the upper field," he told her. "Get them sent off. I'll grab the supplies then we can walk and talk."

He didn't wait for her to reply, just walked into the cottage and over to the table in the corner, rifling through the piles of paperwork he'd been ignoring for weeks, trying to find the soil testing kit the company had sent him.

He should have sent the sample off last week. But he'd put it off over and again. Mostly because he hated filling out the damn forms.

"God, you have a lot of paper."

Her voice made him jump. He turned around to see her standing in the doorway, staring at him.

"Just need to find the time to sort through it." He grimaced. "Paperwork isn't exactly my forte."

"I can see that." She nodded.

He found the kit and pulled it out, wincing when he saw the directions. They were in small print and the letters looked all jumbled.

"Can you read this?" he asked her.

Emery took the paper, her brows dipping as she took in the words. "You need a bucket and shovel. Then take four different samples from four different parts of the field, at a depth of four to six inches," she told him, her voice soft. "Mix them together in the bucket and let it dry out before putting the sample in the bag they've provided." She looked up at him. "Do you have that?"

"Yeah. Somewhere." He walked past her, back out to the yard and she followed him, watching as he grabbed a small spade and a pail from the shed next to the house. "Come on," he told her. "It's the field behind the house I want to test."

Usually, he'd jump on his bike to get there. But that would involve her riding with him. He couldn't stand that either.

"Can't you use home kits?" Emery asked, as they started walking up the lane. "I swear Dad used to use digital ones."

"Yeah, I have those too. But it's been a long time since this soil's been used. A long time since anybody fed it. I want to get it right."

"That's understandable."

He was walking fast. He knew that. She almost had to run to keep up. It was the perfect inversion to last night, when he was the one doing the chasing.

But she didn't ask him to slow down. Didn't ask him to do anything. Just matched his speed as he made his way to the gate that led to the field at the back of the house, pushing it open with a creak, before stepping aside to let her in first.

"Where are you going to take the first sample?" she asked him, looking out at the expanse of tilled soil.

"Here." He nodded at the first corner and handed her the bucket. He hunkered down, using the tip of the trowel to dent the dry soil, digging down to what felt like around half a foot, then scooped up a trowel full of the earth, turning to put it in the bucket she was holding out.

Their eyes caught and he could see the emotion in her gaze. Like she was trying to bring herself to say something.

"If this is about last night," he murmured. "I should apologize. For taking advantage of you."

Emery's brows furrowed. "You're sorry? For kissing me?"

"I put you in a bad position. And I shouldn't have. It won't happen again."

Her mouth parted as though she was going to say something. Then she let out a sigh and shook her head.

"You didn't put me in any position. Not one I didn't want to be in."

"Emery..."

She put her hand up. "Please, just let me say what I need to say. It's really hard and I've been worrying about it all day and I need to get it out."

It was his turn to let out a long breath. God, he hated this. It felt almost painful, knowing she regretted last night.

That she wished he hadn't kissed her.

"Okay." He nodded. "Go ahead."

She put the bucket down on the dirt, looking up at the sky as though the clouds held inspiration. Then she looked back at him, her eyes shining. And then her lips parted, words spilling out of them like she couldn't keep them in anymore.

"I've been lying to you. I've been lying to everybody. I'm not engaged to Trenton anymore."

CHAPTER
Eighteen

HE COULDN'T HAVE LOOKED MORE shocked if he'd tried. His brows were pulled tight, like he was trying to take in the words.

His lack of response was killing her.

"Did you hear what I said?" she asked him.

He nodded. "Yes, Emery, I heard what you said." Hendrix laid the shovel on the ground and stood up, like he'd forgotten all about the soil testing. Then he shoved his hands in his pockets like he needed something to do with them, before bringing his gaze to hers.

"What's going on?" he murmured to her.

She took a deep breath. She wasn't ready for this. But then she probably never would be. "Trenton and I broke up before I came back to Hartson's Creek."

Hendrix's expression didn't change. "So why are you pretending you're still engaged?"

Her legs felt weak. "Can we sit down?" she asked him, afraid she might fall if she didn't.

He nodded, watching as she pretty much collapsed onto the dry earth. He followed suit, being sure to leave a gap between them. For a second all she could think about was last night, the way her body felt pressed between his and the ground. The sureness of his touch as he trailed his hands over her thighs.

When she looked up, his gaze was locked on her face. Like he was thinking the same thing.

"My life is a mess," she whispered, trying not to cry, because this was excruciating. He watched her silently, his jaw tight. As she tried to explain the tangled web she'd managed to get caught in.

Her chest was so tight as she talked to him, telling him about the last few months of her relationship with Trenton, their split, his suggestion that they kept the end of their engagement quiet until his parents returned. Then his jaw went hard when she told him about the lien on the farm. Trenton's refusal to sign off on it until he'd been able to tell his parents about their split face to face.

And when she was finally talked out, she pulled her knees against her chest, wrapping her arms around her legs like she was one of her students. "So that's it," she told him. "You did nothing wrong by kissing me. I'm not taken. Just a liar."

Hendrix ran the tip of his thumb along his jaw. "So he's blackmailing you to keep quiet?"

"Until his parents come home from their cruise, yes."

"Why? He doesn't strike me as the kind of man who cares that much about what they'd think."

"He's a momma's boy at heart," she murmured. "He doesn't want to ruin their vacation." She looked at him, trying to make him understand. "I didn't think it was a big deal when I agreed to it. I might've even thought it was a good idea. My mom is going to be devastated, too. I figured if I got everything ready for her here, got her ready to sell the farm, before I told her, things would be easier."

"Can't you pay off the loan?"

"Not until the house is sold. And I can't sell the house until the lien is taken off. It's a catch twenty-two." She frowned, because she hated this. "The easiest and quickest way to solve it is to do what Trenton wants. By mid August, it'll all be over."

"So that's it. You're gonna let him win?" Hendrix asked her, his brows knitted. And she understood that. She felt it too.

"It's not about letting him win. It's about me not losing. And if he wants to, he can make my mom's life really difficult. It's just a few weeks, Hendrix. That's it. Then I can move on." She pressed her lips together. "I'm sorry I lied to you."

"I'm not angry about the lies. But I'm angry that you're letting him do it."

"I get that." She nodded. "You're not like me."

"What does that mean?"

"You're not scared of life. You're not afraid of making the wrong choices. Of having people think badly about you." She shook her head, looking at the cotton clouds in the sky above them.

"You're wrong. I *am* afraid of making the wrong choices. Mostly because I know the consequences all too well. I'm the king of bad choices. Just ask anybody."

"I think I just took your crown," she said ruefully. "So that's it. I just needed to tell you." She exhaled heavily. "Please don't tell anybody about this."

"Of course I'm not gonna tell anybody." He frowned. "I wish you would, though."

She gave him a soft look. They both knew she wouldn't. Then she scrambled to her feet, dusting the earth from her legs. "I'll let you finish up here. It's getting late. Thank you for listening to me."

She started to walk away.

"Emery?"

She turned to look at him. He was standing, too. His arms folded in front of him.

"Yes?"

"In a few weeks. When the truth is out and the lien is gone. What happens then?"

She ran her tongue over her dry lips. "Then I put my mom's farm up for sale."

"And after?"

"After?" she echoed, as though she didn't understand the question.

"After you've told everyone that you ended things with him? Then you'll be a free woman, right?"

Her heart thumped against her ribcage. "That's right."

He stepped closer to her. Enough that she could see the covering of dust on his skin. "Good. Then I'd like to take you on a date. *After.*"

"I'll be back in Charleston after. I have to work." Her lips parted. His gaze dipped to them, like he was thinking about kissing her again. He reached out and tipped her face up, his thumb beneath her jaw. She swallowed hard at the intensity in his eyes as he stared down at her.

And for a moment all she could hear was the blood rushing through her veins. She looked at his mouth, the same mouth that had kissed her like she'd never been kissed before. The one she stayed awake for most of the night thinking about.

Wishing he'd kiss her again.

"We'll work it out. But you need to go now," he told her, his voice thick. His message was clear. He wanted her, but not enough to get involved in this mess. And she couldn't blame him. It was hers and hers alone to deal with.

But after? The thought of it sent a shiver down her spine.

"I'm going," she whispered. And then she stepped back from his touch.

He couldn't sleep. Couldn't do much of anything. Truth was, he'd been a mess since he'd gotten back home, carrying the bucket of dirt with him. He'd taken a shower, made his dinner on autopilot, then he'd headed into his bedroom.

It was almost eleven. He should be asleep. After last night's tossing and turning, his body craved oblivion more than anything else.

And yet he couldn't stop thinking about the way she'd looked as she'd whispered what a mess she was.

Like she was so damn alone. God, he knew how that felt.

It was like listening to a song you know all the words to even though you've never heard it before.

And damn, how she called to him. He ached for her. He was hot and hard and his heart felt like it was too big for his chest.

Sighing, he climbed out of bed. He'd get a drink. Take another shower. Try to push her out of his mind. At least for a few weeks.

He could wait that long, right? The end of her deal with her ex wasn't exactly a lifetime away.

But it felt like it was. He felt like he couldn't go on like this for another minute, let alone for longer.

"Fuck." He dropped his head into his hands. He was losing his mind. That was it. Driven to distraction by this aching need. He strode to the window that overlooked the lane and pulled back the curtain, his gaze drawn like a magnet to her house, to the room he knew was hers. It was dark. The whole place was. She was probably fast asleep.

But that's when he saw it. The movement. At first he thought it might be an animal. A dark shadow was moving along her yard, toward the lane. It was only as his eyes adjusted to the darkness of the night that he realized it was a person.

Her. Walking toward his house. Like she was as messed up as he was.

Releasing the curtain, he strode to his front door, wrenching it open, before he stepped out into the sultry night. She was clearer now. Still walking fast, as she crossed the road, then walked into his yard.

Without saying a word, he started striding toward her. Like his mind had been washed of all reason, replaced by pure desire. And when their bodies met, he scooped her into his arms, lifting her up, his mouth pressing against hers as he lifted her against his chest.

This kiss wasn't soft. It wasn't gentle. It was hard, full of need. Full of the desire they'd both repressed for way too long. She let out a sigh, her hands curling around his neck, her fingers tangling, as he turned around and carried her into his house.

"You came back," he murmured, kicking the door shut behind them.

"I couldn't stay away."

The way she said it, her voice so full of honesty, sent a shot of desire through him.

"I couldn't either. I was coming to get you. Throw stones at your window until they woke you up."

She smiled against his mouth. "You could have called."

"Yeah, well I hadn't thought that part through." He put her down on the ground. Brushed the hair from her face. "Do you know how beautiful you are?" he asked her.

"Do you know how beautiful *you* are?" she said back to him. "I can't stop thinking about you."

Her words felt like the softest balm on his rough soul. He dipped his head, kissing her neck, feeling the drum of her pulse against his mouth.

"Come to bed."

Her breath caught. "What about waiting until *after*?"

"I'll take you to bed then, too." He looked up at her. She

was staring at him, her gaze dark. Full of the same desire that pulsed through him.

"Okay then," she murmured. "Take me to bed."

And that was all he needed to hear.

———

He carried her into his bedroom, his muscles tight as he put her on the bed. Emery looked around. He kept a neat bedroom. She wasn't sure what she'd been expecting, but not this.

"Oh, your room is pretty," she said to him, trying not to sound so surprised. It was simple, that's for sure. Old furniture he'd found in resale stores and refinished. The walls were whitewashed and the curtains were some flowery fabric.

"It's prettier now," he told her.

She smiled at him, feeling the softness of his coverlet beneath her palms. "For a man who says he's not good with words, you certainly know how to use them."

He shrugged. "It's easy when it's the truth."

Their gazes locked with a soft kind of yearning that made her feel hollow and full at the same time.

"Then come and show me how true it is," she whispered. He looked at her like he was trying to figure her out. She nodded, and could see understanding wash over him.

He knew her well enough to understand this was her way of giving consent. He stepped toward her, his gaze taking in the short pajamas with a flowered pattern on them, her scrubbed clean face and mussed up hair.

The shorts were bunched up around her waist, from where he'd put her down on his bed. He curled his hands around her ankles, his fingers tracing her skin like he was trying to imprint her into his brain.

And then, taking her by surprise, he yanked her legs apart.

The sudden movement sent a shot of desire through her. Reflecting the need in his eyes as he stared down at her. Her lips parted with a soft breath as he leaned in to kiss her thigh.

His mouth was rough against her skin as he moved his lips against her. She reached down, threading her fingers through his hair, murmuring his name.

"Is this okay?" he asked, tracing her thighs with his fingers. Then he slid them up until they were tracing the hem of her shorts.

She nodded. It was more than okay. It was what she needed. The connection she'd been searching for. She had to feel him touch her. To know he wanted her as much as she wanted him. He pushed his hands beneath the soft cotton of her shorts, his fingers grazing the skin where her thighs met her hips.

"I lied when I said I didn't know what to do with your panties," he said, his voice rough. "I kept them because I like you. I like this."

"I'm glad you kept them," she whispered. His touch was driving her crazy. Everything about her was on fire. "I like the thought of you looking at them. Thinking of me."

"That's good," he said gruffly. "Because you're not getting them back."

And then he touched her *there* and she let out a soft cry.

She was wet. She could tell by the way his fingers glided so easily against her. He was still gentle. Still soft, like he was learning her body inch by inch.

Then he found the tiny bud, the most sensitive part of her. His finger traced it, running the tiniest of circles over her.

"Oh my God."

"Okay?" he murmured.

"Kiss me."

He smiled, looking a little dazed as he lifted his head. Without stopping the teasing, circular movements, he leaned over her, claiming her mouth with his.

"So pretty. So wet for me." He slid his finger inside of her, making her body convulse around him.

"Hendrix..."

He smiled at her passioned cry. "I want to taste you," he told her.

"Please."

He grinned and tugged at her shorts, sliding them down her hips. "Take off your top," he murmured. "I want to see all of you."

She did as he asked, not bothering to unbutton it, just pulling it over her head. And then she was bare for him. Her body was pale compared to his. His gaze narrowed as he took her in, from the curve of her neck to the swell of her breasts. Her nipples were pink and hard as he leaned in to kiss one of them, teasing and flicking it with his tongue, before pulling it between his teeth.

It only took a few moments until she could feel her body start to heat up. He moved his hands between her legs, finding her most sensitive spot again, kissing her breasts as he teased her clit.

She was on edge. Her breath was short, her skin glowing. He kissed her lips softly again, then moved down, until his hands were on her thighs, pulling them apart so he could stare at her.

"I want to fuck you with my tongue."

Oh, she wasn't expecting that. Wasn't expecting how hot it was to hear him say it, either. She found herself blushing in a way that made him smile.

"You want that?" he asked her.

She nodded, her lips parting to let out a long breath.

"Say it," he told her. "Tell me what you want."

"I want your mouth on me," she told him, knowing he needed to hear this. That he needed her to say it. "I want you to fuck me with your tongue."

A smile pulled at his lips as he parted her legs. "You're

glistening for me." He looked hungry as he stared at her. And she liked that a little too much.

He pressed his face between her thighs. She could hear the sharp intake of his breath, like he was smelling her. Oh god, that's exactly what he was doing. Then he moved closer still, his tongue flickering against her clit, as he slid a finger along her, before pushing it inside.

"You're so tight," he whispered as he managed to push a second inside of her. She gasped at the intensity of it, her thighs tightening around his face as he buried himself in deeper.

"Oh God," she whispered. She wasn't sure how much of this she could take.

"He won't help you," he murmured, sucking her between his lips, alternating between hard and soft, curling his fingers inside of her until she started to flutter around him.

She pushed her fingers into his hair, her nails scraping his scalp as he found the sweet spot inside of her, the delicious shock causing her hips to lift off the bed.

"God, I love this," he muttered. She opened her mouth to reply, but she couldn't. Her breath caught as he started fucking her with his fingers, his mouth plundering her until every cell in her body felt like she was about to explode.

He was playing her like she was his favorite instrument. Finding the notes and making them vibrate. Then, just as she was reaching the crescendo he pulled his fingers out, making her cry out in desperation, before replacing them with his tongue.

"Hendrix!" Nobody had ever made her feel like this. Like she needed to be consumed. Like she was his last meal and he was determined to savor it.

He let out a soft groan, then flickered the tip of his tongue inside of her, pressing his thumb against her clit. He circled it until he could feel every part of her tightening. There was a pause, like the silence before the storm, then her back arched and she let out a scream.

The pleasure was so intense it was almost painful, coming in waves as he licked the sweetness from her, holding her tight as she convulsed around him.

As she started to breathe again, her hold on him loosened, like she didn't have the energy to control her muscles anymore. He clambered on top of her, claiming her mouth, kissing her through the end of her orgasm.

"Okay?" he murmured as she finally started to focus on him.

"More than okay," she murmured.

He moved up, stroking her face, kissing her softly. "Good. Because I plan on doing that again very soon."

———

They spent the next hour kissing and touching each other. He'd made her come twice more – once with his mouth and once with his fingers, and now she was lying on top of him, kissing him like she'd never get enough.

He loved the way she'd come alive in his arms. Like she'd been half asleep for the last few years, waiting for him to come along and wake her up.

He also let her lead the way. She liked it when he ate her, that much was obvious. She liked his fingers, too. But he'd been careful not to push her. He didn't want her to do anything she wasn't ready for.

Maybe that's why her circling her hand around his dick took him by surprise.

He let out a groan at the softness of her palm. "Emery, you don't have to…"

"I know I don't." She smiled at him. "I want to." She kissed him softly. Then she slid down his body until her mouth was pressed against his thigh. "Oh."

He realized what she was responding to. She'd finally found his tattoo. He swallowed hard, watching her as she read the words etched into the skin below his hip.

I walk alone.

He'd gotten the tattoo years ago. Not long after graduation. And yeah, he'd been in his feeling-sorry-for-himself phase.

She looked up, her lips soft and parted.

"You're not alone," she murmured.

The way she said it, like it was an absolute fact, made his chest tighten. But before he could think anymore about that, she slid her lips over him, her mouth warm and velvety, making him gasp because damn, this woman was going to kill him.

Moving back, she almost released him from her lips, her tongue trailing in a circle around him, making his body clench with desire.

"Emery."

She smiled, taking him harder, creating a rhythm, sliding up and down until he could barely think, let alone speak. Christ, she was perfect. Everything about her drew him in. His body tingled, his breath shortened, and she kept moving, her mouth so maddeningly warm and velvety, her lips making him feel so high he wasn't sure he'd ever come down.

He reached for her, murmuring her name, feeling the pleasure coiling inside of him like a serpent, ready to be unleashed. His fingers tangled into her soft hair as she reached down to cup his heavy balls.

"Fuck." His eyes widened. "Emery, I'm gonna come."

He tried to move her head away. To stop from coming inside of her mouth. But she wouldn't move. Instead, she flicked out her tongue, tasting him as his orgasm released from him in long, smooth pulses, his eyes squeezing shut with pleasure as she softly swallowed him down.

Christ. This woman was going to be the death of him. He

pulled her up to look at him, kissing her, loving the way her body fit so perfectly against his.

Within minutes, his eyes were closed, and he was falling into the kind of deep sleep he hadn't experienced for a long, long time.

And he didn't wake until the light was spilling through his bedroom window.

CHAPTER
Nineteen

YOU SHOULD HAVE WOKEN *me up before you left. – Hendrix*

Emery smiled softly at the message on her phone. She'd left his place while he was still sleeping, so deeply she couldn't bear to wake him to tell him she was heading home. It had been right before five and she wanted to get home before there was any chance of waking her mom.

Plus, she had a lot to think about. So she'd pulled on her clothes and softly tiptoed out of his bedroom, stopping to grab the paperwork that was piled on his table. Mostly because it was grating on her, seeing it all scattered and untouched.

She'd go through it for him. Find out if there was anything pressing in there.

He hadn't said as much, but she wondered if he had some form of reading disorder. She'd been a teacher for long enough to be able to spot it.

She also knew that some people hated admitting to it. Yes, he could type out a text message. But the reams of words on these long letters were possibly more than he could bear to look at.

You looked like you needed your sleep. – Emery

She tapped it out and hit send, trying not to grin. It was almost impossible not to. She hadn't stopped smiling all morning.

I'll see you tonight. – Hendrix

It felt like a promise. One that made her heart race.

"What are you doing?" her mom asked, leaning over the table. "Those aren't ours," she said, seeing Hendrix's name at the top of one of the letters.

"I know." There was no point in trying to hide it from her. "I'm just going through these for our neighbor."

"Why?" Her mom frowned.

"Because I'm being friendly. And I figure that having a working farm across the road can only be helpful for the sale."

"Oh, yes. I guess you're right." Her mom pressed her lips together. Like she was trying to find the right words to say.

Then she let out a sigh, and Emery knew something bad was coming.

"Do you think Trenton would like it if he knew you were going through another man's mail?"

Emery blinked. No, he wouldn't. He'd like it even less if he knew what she'd been doing with the same man last night.

But she didn't care what he thought.

Swallowing, she looked up at her mom. "Hendrix is a friend."

"But Trenton is your fiancé."

Her stomach tightened. She didn't want to have this conversation with her mom. For a second, she wondered if she should just come clean.

And break her mom's heart by letting her know about the blackmail and the lien? She blinked that thought away.

Yes, her mom wasn't as fragile as she had been when Emery first arrived home. But she still cried herself to sleep every night.

"You don't have to worry. I told you, I'm just being neighborly."

"Okay. But Emery… don't do anything you'll regret, all right?"

"Like what?"

Her mom's smile was weak. "You're going to be Mrs. Montclair next year. It's normal to think about what you might be missing out on. But you're a good girl, Emery. You've always been a good girl. Don't do anything that will make you less than that."

Her chest felt tight. "Mom…"

"It's okay." Her mom waved her hand. "I know you wouldn't do anything. I'm just being silly. Now, can you do me a favor and go get some eggs? I think I'm going to do some baking. Book club is tonight. I want to take a cake."

Sensing a reprieve, Emery pushed herself away from the table covered with paperwork and headed to the hallway.

Grabbing her sneakers, she pulled the front door open, sliding her feet into them before she ran down the steps to the chicken coop.

"Hey," Jed called out to her from the lane. "You look like you're in a hurry."

She pressed her lips together. "Just collecting some eggs. How are you?"

"Good." His gaze went to her face. "You look healthy."

"Is that a good thing?"

He shrugged. "I'm a farm man. Healthy is always good. And you've caught the sun."

"Hard not to here."

"True." Jed looked down at his sunbaked hands. "How's your mom?"

"About to bake a cake." It came out tight. Enough for Jed to notice the tone of her voice. He lifted a brow.

"It must be hard for you," he said, "coming home after being away for so long. After a while, it's not good for young people to be living with their parents. You want to live your own way, and it's tough when they still treat you like you're a child."

She swallowed, because he'd hit it right on the nail. She wasn't a kid. Hadn't been for a long time. But her mom couldn't see it sometimes.

"I guess she means well."

"I know she does." Jed nodded. "She's a good woman. She's just a little adrift, is all. She needs to find herself again." A smile ghosted his lips. "And that way she won't spend all her time thinking about you."

"You're a wise man, Jed." Emery grinned. "You know that?"

"I'm just a farm man." He shrugged. "But people aren't that different to cattle."

A low hum of an engine came from the main road. She turned to see a cloud of dirt lifting behind a motorcycle. And of course her breath stuttered, because even though she'd seen him a couple of hours ago, it felt like so much longer.

Like he could read her mind, Jed turned to see the motorcycle taking the curve from the main road onto the track that led to their farms.

"He's gonna hurt himself riding like that one day," he murmured.

"I think he knows how to take care of himself," Emery replied. For a second she could feel Jed staring at her, like he was trying to read something in her expression.

The bike took a turn into Hendrix's driveway, coming to a stop with a skid. He climbed off and looked over at her, a smile pulling at his lips.

And that was all it took for her heart to slam against her chest.

"Well, I'd best be getting back to work." Jed patted her arm. "Give your mom some time. She'll get used to the fact you're a grown up and can make your own decisions."

"I hope so." She gave him a soft smile.

"And honey?"

"Yes?"

"Your dad would be proud of you, you know? For trying to help your mom."

Her throat felt tight. "Thanks Jed."

"No problem." He winked. "Now go fetch those eggs. That cake isn't going to bake itself."

"Honey, I'm heading out to book club," her mom said later that day, walking into the kitchen to grab the cake she'd left on the table. "Are you sure you don't want to come?"

Glancing out of the kitchen window, Emery saw movement coming from Hendrix's house. The front door opened and he called something out to Frank, who turned his head to look at the stupidly handsome man walking toward him.

Her breath caught. He was fresh out of the shower, his chest bare, his jeans loosely fastened at his waist, revealing the band of his boxers. His hair was slicked back and he had a bottle of beer in his hands, beads of condensation clinging to the brown bottle.

He lifted his head, like he was looking straight at her.

Then he put the beer to his mouth, tipping his head back to take a sip. She watched, fascinated, as his throat undulated as he swallowed the ice cold liquid down.

"That man," her mom huffed, her voice making Emery jump, because she hadn't realized her mom had gotten up from the table and was right behind her. "He's always parading around half naked. Like he's some kind of... what did Rita-Mae call it? Thirst trap."

Emery tried not to laugh.

"He's probably just overheated," she murmured to her mom. "He's been working on the farm all day. Remember how Dad used to get bright red and sweaty?"

"He always wore an undershirt," her mom pointed out.

"Yeah, well, I remember you sneaking looks at him like he was the hottest thing this side of the Mississippi River," Emery told her.

A smile pulled at her mom's lips, like there was a secret memory there. For a moment she looked younger than her years. Like the woman Emery remembered from when she was a kid. So pretty in her dresses. Giggling every time her dad made a joke. The two of them would sneak kisses every time they thought Emery wasn't looking.

"Yeah, well he might be easy on the eye," her mom said, nodding over at Hendrix. "But he's still trouble."

"Aren't they all?" Emery said.

Her mom actually laughed. And it sounded so sweet that it made Emery's heart ache. Was this the first time she'd heard her mom giggle since she'd come home to help get the house ready?

"True," her mom agreed. She was still looking at Hendrix, who had his back to them now, filling Frank's trough. His muscles rippled in the light of the setting sun. And for a second Emery considered confessing everything to her mom.

How much easier her life would be if she told her what

was really happening. That Trenton was blackmailing her, that Hendrix was actually the good guy here.

"Your dad was so handsome when I met him," her mom said, a wistful note to her voice. "All the girls used to fight over him. But I was the one he asked to dance at senior prom."

"Yeah." Emery nodded, not wanting to break the spell of this sweet truce between them. "Of course you were. You've always been the pretty one."

Her mom hugged her from behind. "You're such a good girl, Emery."

Yeah, well she didn't feel like a good girl right now. And she liked that. She'd been shackled by the need to obey the rules for too long.

It was time to fly free.

CHAPTER
Twenty

IT WAS a few minutes after eight when Hendrix wandered out to his front porch with his second bottle of beer. The sun was slowly sliding to the horizon, casting an orange glow over the fields.

He sat on the swing hanging with rusty chains from the rafters, and looked over at the farmhouse opposite, his eyes full of speculation. Her mom's car was gone. And he was a little too pleased about that.

He hadn't messaged her since this morning. Things had been too hectic at the farm, and he also didn't want to come on too strong. For both their sakes. He wasn't used to this aching need, this constant feeling of wanting to touch her.

If he thought on it too long it was going to make him panic. So he threw himself into work instead.

The front door to her cottage opened and she stepped out, wearing a pair of cut-off jeans and a lace top that made her look both sweet and sinful all at the same time. He could see the tattoo on her ankle, all healed now, and a smile ghosted his lips at the memory of their trip to the tattoo parlor.

She had a pile of papers in her arms, holding them against her chest like a student running between classes.

"Hey," she called out. "Room on that swing for two?"

He tipped his head to the side. "Always."

She smiled and walked over, her hips swaying to a rhythm that matched his heartbeat. She opened the gate to his front yard and blew Frank a kiss before heading up the steps to the porch.

Her hair was tied back in a low ponytail, but the heat made some strands stick to her neck. She sat down beside him and he was so damn aware of her presence he had to curl his hand into a fist not to touch her.

"Where's your mom gone?" he asked her.

"Book club."

His mouth twitched. That was a good thing. His own mom went to book club – hell, half the town did – and he knew it always went long. Not because they were talking about the book, but because somebody always brought punch that hit harder than liquor, and book talk soon changed to local gossip.

He turned to look at her. Up close he could see a little trail of freckles along the bridge of her nose. She wasn't wearing makeup, but her skin still glowed. "How was your day?" he asked her.

"Long." She ran her tongue over her dry lips. "I spent a few hours going through these," she told him.

That's when he realized what the papers were. He hadn't even noticed they were gone from his kitchen table. That's what no sleep and a long day of work did to you.

"You took them?"

She looked uneasy, like she thought she'd done something wrong. "I just thought I'd go through them. Since you're so busy and all." She lifted the top few sheets up. "These are applications for grants. I've completed them for you. They just need your signature and I can mail them off."

He shifted in his seat. "You're not my secretary, Emery."

"I know." She gave him the most tentative of smiles. "I did

it more for me than you. Seeing that paperwork every time I go into your house is going to give me hives."

He knew she was lying. She'd done it for him.

"There are a couple of bills that you need to pay here," she said, pointing at a few papers with red sticky notes on them. "And the rest can probably be thrown in the trash."

His jaw felt tight. He didn't like that she'd done this. He didn't like her knowing that he couldn't cope with this stuff. It made him feel small. Like the kid he once was, wishing he could learn as easily as his brothers. Hating that he was letting people down.

Acting up, because if he was gonna be called an idiot, he might as well earn the damn title.

"Emery…"

"It's just paperwork," she murmured. "You've done so much for me. My list. Last night…"

"You did a lot for me last night too," he reminded her. The memory of her lips on his body made him shift on the swing. She took a long breath, her pink lips parted, like she could read his mind.

"You wanna come here?" he asked. Because he didn't want to talk about paperwork. Or about anything, really. He wanted to touch her. Wanted to feel her.

He'd always preferred action to talk.

Maybe she felt the same, because the words were barely out of his mouth before she was clambering on top of his lap. Her bare legs on either side of his denim clad thighs, her chest pressed against his. For a moment all he could feel was wonder. And the pulse of need that was more insistent, throbbing as she looked at him, her wide eyes locked on his.

He ran his hands down her sides, feeling the warmth of her skin through the thin fabric of her tank. Assessing his options, he tried to find the resolve to take this slow even though all he wanted to do was throw her over his shoulders and carry her to his bed.

Everything about her was beautiful. When was the last time anybody had done anything as sweet as going through paperwork for him? He had no idea. All he knew was he needed to show her his appreciation.

"Aren't you going to kiss me?" she murmured. Impatience was written all over her face. He liked that way too much. She was needy and he was the man who was ready to fulfil that need.

Before he could answer she pulled her tank over her head, exposing her upper body to the evening air. A smile pulled at his lips at her sudden bravery.

"So pretty," he murmured, kissing her throat. His hands spanned her bare waist, moving her closer. He kissed a trail to the swell of her chest where her bra pushed her sweet breasts up. She let out a gasp and his smile widened.

He palmed her breasts, feeling the hardness of her nipples against the rough palm of his hands. Then he dipped his thumb inside the lace cups, seeking them out, teasing them, pinching them until Emery whimpered.

Pushing her bra down to expose them, he dipped his mouth, capturing a nipple between his lips. He licked, the taste of her like nectar against his tongue. His ministrations made her breath hitch as he sucked her in, then he scraped his teeth against the hard nub until she started to rock her hips.

"Oh." She tipped her head back as he moved to her other breast, her hands moving to his hair, her fingers threading through the strands. She kept his mouth pressed against her, like she could never get enough.

Yeah, well, neither could he. He lifted his head, kissing her softly. "Shall we go inside?" he murmured. Mostly because yes, she was turned on right now, but she was also a good girl at heart. He didn't want her to feel exposed out here, even if they were all alone.

Her mouth opened, and she pulled her swollen bottom lip

between her teeth. "We could stay here..." she trailed off, her cheeks pinking up.

And fuck if that didn't make him even more excited. His good girl wanted to be bad.

"What if Frank comes out?" he asked, teasing her now, because Frank had disappeared behind the shed, like he was bored with them. But the rush of endorphins was making him feel heady. Like he wanted to make her laugh and make love to her at the same time.

"Fuck Frank."

The way she said it made him laugh out loud.

"I'm serious, Hendrix. Stop teasing. I'm desperate here. You're all I've been able to think about all day."

His eyes caught hers and he felt a little thud in his chest. Like something had broken and been fixed at the same time.

Reaching behind her, he unfastened her bra, pulling it off her slim arms, and throwing it to the deck.

"This is the second time I've seen you half naked outside like this," he told her. "The last time kept me warm for weeks."

Her cheeks pinked up at the memory of him seeing her post skinny dipping. "The way you looked at me kept me warm for weeks, too."

He didn't think he could get any harder. But the thought of her touching herself, thinking of him, was more potent than any aphrodisiac. He let out a groan, kissing her again, his tongue teasing hers as he reached for the waistband of her shorts.

"You first," she whispered, tugging at his t-shirt. He lifted his arms, making it easier for her to tug the fabric over his head, throwing it on the porch next to her bra.

And then she pressed her bare chest against his and it felt like heaven. Soft skin against hard. His breath felt ragged as she leaned in to kiss his jaw, his cheek, the corner of his lips.

There was such a sweet danger to being half naked with

this woman on the porch of his cottage. Sure, he wasn't expecting any visitors and neither was she, but it still felt like they were exposed.

He was so damn aware that if they were seen like this it would be worse for her than for him. It was an annoying fact that the world judged women and lauded men. But he knew that if it came to that he'd throw himself in the way. He'd do anything to protect this woman.

Even if she didn't need his protection.

She leaned back, her hands tracing the thick muscles of his shoulders, before trailing down to his chest. Her fingers brushed against his nipples and he gasped.

"You like that?" she whispered.

"I like everything you do." And wasn't that the truth? He would never get bored of this woman. He had to grit his teeth as she leaned in to kiss them, her tongue flickering at his like she was feeling him out.

"Fuck…" Every touch of her sent a shot of pleasure down to his dick. He slid his thumb under her chin, tipping her head up until their eyes caught. "If you keep doing that I'm gonna come."

"From me kissing your nipples?" Her eyes narrowed like she found that a turn on.

"From you being here with me." He brushed her lips with his again. "From being mine."

But he'd got it all wrong, he realized. It was so much more than that. *He* was *hers*. And that was the truth of it. All she had to do was say his name and he was gone.

"Then take what's yours," she told him, reaching down to unbutton her shorts. The band gaped open, revealing the taut skin of her stomach and the scalloped edge of her lace panties. She slid off of him, kicking off her sneakers before she pulled her shorts down her toned legs, kicking them away too.

And there she was, this piece of art, standing in front of

him, wearing the same kind of tiny panties he still had in his cottage.

"Do you know how beautiful you are?" he asked her.

A smile played at her lips. "Tell me."

But he preferred to show her instead. He pulled her back to his lap, kissing her, caressing her soft skin. His fingers played at her nipples, making her gasp. Then he slid his hands down, his fingers touching the lace of her panties.

"I need you," she whispered. Her hand reached for him, her fingers unbuttoning his jeans before sliding inside his boxers. Her eyes widened when she felt how rock hard he was for her.

He had been all day. Every time he thought about her.

Then she pulled him out, the warm air surrounding him as she kissed him back, her body so close to his he could feel her wetness.

"Emery…"

"I want you inside of me," she told him, her mouth soft.

"Birth control?"

"I'm covered." Her eyes met his. "And I had a test last month. I'm clean."

"Me too."

She smiled softly, her hand still circling him. She pulled those pretty lace panties to the side, like she couldn't wait long enough to pull them down. Then her hand lined him up, his thickness brushing against her most intimate place.

As soon as she slid down on him, it felt like a billion fireworks exploding in his brain.

She let out a gasp at the sudden intrusion.

"Okay?" He held her in his arms, brushing his lips against hers.

"Yes." She locked her own arms around his neck, letting him slide his hands to her hips and move her down. He took it slowly, filling her up, feeling her pulse around him as she got used to his size.

"You're inside of me," she whispered, a smile pulling at her lips.

"I know." The feeling was overwhelming.

"I didn't.. I haven't..." She shook her head. "I didn't know it could feel like this."

"Like what?" He had to grit his teeth as he attempted to stay still. Every cell of his body wanted to fuck like he'd never fucked before. It was exquisite torture, staying still, waiting for her to speak.

She inhaled, like she was short of breath. "So intimate. Like perfection."

This woman was going to kill him, sweet word by sweet word. He groaned softly, burying his face in the dip between her neck and her shoulder, breathing in the scent of her skin.

He curled his fingers around her hips, lifting her up until he was almost out of her, then slid her back down, making them both groan. She was so tight and so perfect. His mouth sought hers, kissing her softly as he started to find a rhythm.

"So good," she gasped.

"I know."

"Don't stop."

"Not sure I can."

She laughed softly against him, the shaking of her body causing him to groan in pleasure. And then he put one hand between them, finding the aching center of her nerves, rolling his finger against her until her eyes were wide with pleasure.

"Oh my god," she whispered as their rhythm increased. "I can't believe I'm so close already."

"Do it. Come for me." He could feel it. The tightening around his cock. She started to tremble on his lap, her head dropping against his shoulder, her breath warm on his skin.

And then she stilled, a strangled gasp escaping her mouth, her body tightening so hard around him that he couldn't move her even if he wanted to.

"Oh...." She bit down on his shoulder, the sudden pain so

close to pleasure that he felt himself thicken even more inside of her. And then she was coming, clinging onto him, calling out his name as he held her tightly.

He followed her seconds later, a low, aching groan rumbling through his chest as he spilled inside of her. And that's where they stayed, her straddling him, his arms around her, holding her tight, their lips moving together like they couldn't bear to stop.

It wasn't until Frank let out a bray that rational thought rushed back into his brain.

Emery started to giggle and fuck if that didn't send some aftershocks through him. His eyes caught hers and he grinned.

"I've never had sex outside before," she murmured.

For some reason that made him feel ten feet tall.

"Well we can have sex inside, in about half an hour," he told her.

Just as soon as he remembered how to breathe again.

CHAPTER
Twenty-One

"OH. MY. GOD." Maisie's voice lifted a whole octave. "I can't believe you did it. Everything on the original and the best list, except stay up all night talking."

Emery looked at the list. There were checkmarks against every one except number four. "I know. I'm expecting a gold star as soon as you're back on US soil."

"You should just ask him to not sleep," Maisie told her. "Get them all ticked off."

"I can't. The man has to work with heavy machinery. I'm not going to beg him to stay up all night talking to me. I like his body intact, thank you very much."

Emery was in the town square, heading over to the diner to grab a coffee before driving home. She'd spent the morning in the library. With only a month left before she was due back at work, she needed to start working on her lesson plans. They had a week of in-service at school without the students coming in, where she could get the classroom ready. That way the fall semester would start with a bang.

She'd been sneaking over to Hendrix's cottage every night. Waiting until her mom was asleep, then tiptoeing over like a teenager heading out for a booty call.

And during the days, she and her mom had finished getting the cottage ready to go on the market. They'd ended up paying the farmhands some extra money to take the trash away. And anything that could be burned was put on a big bonfire by Jed.

It was funny how attuned she was to the changing of the seasons. Part of that came from being a farmer's daughter. But some of it came from being a teacher. The summer had come to its peak. The long lazy days were slowly morphing into the feeling that something big was coming. Back to school. Back to work. Before she knew it, fall would be in the air.

And yeah, there was a pang in her gut about that. About going back to Charleston. She'd be staying with Maisie until she found somewhere to live.

"Then we'll just have to stay up all night when I get back," Maisie said. "I guess I can help you complete the assignment."

"Perfect." Emery felt her throat tighten. Going back meant the end of the summer. The end of sneaking across the road to Hendrix's cottage.

But it also meant the end of Trenton's hold on her. The start of her mom's new life. All these things felt so bittersweet.

"So have you and Hendrix talked about what happens next?" Maisie asked her.

"It's only been a few days," Emery pointed out.

"No, sweetie. It's been at least a month. You and him... you've been dancing around each other all summer. The sex might be recent but the rest isn't."

"The rest?"

"Your feelings for him." Maisie sounded so damn sure. The worst thing was, she was right. Emery did have feelings for Hendrix.

"There's the small matter of everyone thinking I'm still

engaged," Emery pointed out. "I can't have that conversation with him until that's over."

"When are Trenton's parents back?"

"In a few weeks. He's coming to town then." And he'd be signing the lien away. That was the agreement. She felt so twisted at the thought of seeing him. Yes, it meant the end of everything. Once the loan was resolved there'd be nothing left between them.

But he'd still hurt her. And wounds ran deep.

"And then you'll be coming back home. At least Charleston isn't that far a drive from Hartson's Creek."

"I guess not," Emery murmured. But the tightness in her chest was still there.

Come over once your mom has left for Chairs. I want to cook for you. – Hendrix

Emery stared at the message. Of all the things he could have proposed for tonight, she wasn't expecting that. She didn't even know the man could cook. And yet she was ridiculously excited at getting to spend the evening with him. Yes, she would need to head home before her mom got back, but until then they had a few hours of freedom.

Sure, it was hot sneaking out of the house and into his bed for a few hours late at night when her mom was asleep, but she ached for more.

For *after*.

As soon as she pushed his door open, she could smell the warm aromas of onions and garlic. She walked inside, her lips curling when she saw him standing behind the stove, in a fresh t-shirt and jeans, his hair damp from a shower.

He turned to look at her, taking her in. "Hope you're hungry," he told her. "I'm making pasta."

"It smells amazing." She slid her arms around his waist, leaning her head against his back. He smelled of pine trees on a summer's day. For a second she closed her eyes and breathed him in.

"Are you making amatriciana sauce?" she asked him, watching as he added a can of Italian pomodoro tomatoes to the pan.

He stirred them in, and she could feel his back muscles tighten against her chest. "Yeah. You had it before?"

"I took a cooking course in Charleston a while back. My mom bought it for me for Christmas one year." She wrinkled her nose. All part of her mom's dreams to make her a better housewife, she guessed. "We learned about the four roman sauces. Amatriciana was my favorite."

"I visited Italy for a few months," he told her. "I paid my way by working at a vineyard up in the hills. The Wi-Fi was terrible, so I had to entertain myself. Ended up getting taught how to cook by the grandmother of the family."

She tried to picture him being bossed around by a beautiful older Italian woman. There was so much more about him to learn. She couldn't wait. "I figured you'd be more of a steak man."

"I don't like eating beef."

Well, that surprised her. "You don't?"

He turned to look at her, and she let go of his back. Hendrix leaned down to press his mouth against hers.

His kiss was hungry. And short, because the tomatoes were starting to bubble.

"I rarely eat meat," he told her. "I don't even put it in this sauce, though you're supposed to. I use mushrooms instead, though I'm pretty sure Nonna Gabriella would beat me over the head with her least favorite pan if she knew."

"Do you not like the texture?" she asked him.

He shrugged. "I just don't like eating the animals I spend all day taking care of."

It was weird how that made her chest feel tight. He had such a masculine, *don't care* exterior. And yet there were all these little clues that led to one conclusion. Hendrix Hartson was a good man. Even if he pretended otherwise.

He grabbed a teaspoon from the drawer and scooped it into the pan before lifting it to his mouth so he could taste the sauce. "Needs a little more salt," he murmured, grabbing the salt grinder and sprinkling some in.

"Where's the recipe?" she asked, wondering if he had it on his phone. But it was nowhere to be seen.

"Here." He touched his head. "I'm not good at reading recipes. You've already seen what I'm like with paperwork." He looked suddenly shy, like he'd said something he wished he hadn't. "Anyway, it's simple. No recipe book needed. Want to try a bit?"

"Absolutely." She watched as he grabbed a fresh spoon and dipped it in, then lifted it up, blowing on it before he offered it to her. The simple intimacy of the action made her breathless. Then she opened her mouth and tasted it.

"Oh God," she murmured, once she swallowed it down. "That's delicious."

"Right?"

She shook her head. "I could go to culinary school for a year and never make it that good. I'm never going to be able to cook for you now."

"In that case, you can set the table," he told her. "Silverware is on the counter."

"On it." She grabbed the forks and spoons – because of course he ate the Italian way – and walked over to the tiny kitchen table in the corner of the room. The papers she'd sorted through for him were neatly piled on the surface.

"I sent the grant applications off," he told her. "I still have to go through the bills."

A jolt of warmth went through her. She liked knowing she was helping him. Her dad had taught her how important federal grants could be to the running of a farm. Especially a small one like Hendrix's.

"Are you dyslexic?" she asked him. Because it felt like the right time to ask.

It was like watching the doors slam shut. His face literally closed down in front of her eyes. There was no expression there, no nothing. "Drop it," he said.

She blinked at the harshness of his tone. It contrasted so badly with the way he'd treated her up to now. "I was just asking…"

"And I was just saying I don't want to talk about it. Do you want a drink? Wine?"

Emery let out a breath. "Just water, please." After the bar dancing debacle, she'd be happy not to drink alcohol for the rest of her life.

He nodded and poured them both a glass from the refrigerator, then carried over the glasses followed by the bowls of pasta.

They both pulled out a chair, and she felt herself squirm at how fast the atmosphere between them had changed. She wanted to take back her words. To stop him from scowling. Taking a deep breath, she looked at him.

"I'm sorry. I should have thought before I opened my mouth."

For a second he closed his eyes. Like he was trying to find the right words. When he opened them again, she saw that vulnerability she'd seen earlier.

"No, I'm sorry. I just…" He shook his head. "I shouldn't have spoken to you like that."

"I've had worse," she joked, but that only made him wince.

"And you've deserved better. You deserve better from me." He shook his head. "Yes, I'm mildly dyslexic. I was diagnosed as an adult. For most of my life I just thought I was stupid."

She hated the way he said that. Like it was a fact, not a feeling.

"You're anything but stupid," she protested. "Look at the way you can take care of a farm. The way you can cook. The way you take care of me."

His gaze narrowed as he looked at her. "Yeah, well it all comes down to nothing when you can't do well academically. My mom was beside herself when I was finally diagnosed. She thought she'd let me down by not finding out earlier. But I'd hidden it pretty well. Just made it seem like I didn't care about school or learning. I was all about sports and being outside and she was okay with that."

"Because she loves you."

"Yeah." His voice was thick. "And I had my brothers. They helped with my homework enough for me to scrape by." He shrugged his shoulders, like he didn't care even though she knew he did. "So there you have it. I'll never be the kind of guy who can provide luxury. I'll never be a bank manager and I don't want to rely on my folks to keep a roof over my head. This is me. What you see is what you get."

"Do you think I care that you have dyslexia?" she asked him, frowning. "Because I don't. I just told you I can't cook. I also can't seem to figure out my own life. And here's you, running a farm all by yourself. Succeeding against the odds." She reached for his hand, squeezing it. "You take care of me. You make me smile. You protect me, even when I'm not sure I need protecting."

His jaw tightened but he said nothing. Maybe he just needed to listen right now.

"All the book learning in the world doesn't make you a good person," she told him. "Ask me how I know." Her voice cracked, because she didn't want to think about her past.

She just wanted to move forward. With him.

"Emery..." His voice was thick.

"What?"

"Can you come over here before I drag you across the table?"

She laughed softly, then did as he asked, walking over to him, letting him pull her onto his lap. He held her close, burying his face in her hair, like he was trying to breathe her in. She slid her arms around him, hugging him like she thought he needed to be hugged.

Fiercely. Unashamedly. She needed him to know that she didn't care. That nobody who really knew him would. It was a diagnosis, not an affliction. His heart was pure, and that's what mattered to her.

He'd shown her more kindness in the last few weeks than she ever thought she deserve.

"Are you hungry?" he asked her, his voice rough as he lifted his head, his gaze catching hers.

"Not really," she admitted. Her stomach felt too tight for food.

"Good." He stood, pulling her into his arms. "Because I need you."

She stroked the hair from his brow, her heart doing that little flip it always did whenever he touched her. "You've got me," she whispered. And he had no idea how true that was.

He had her, and she never wanted him to let go.

"Stay with me tonight," he murmured an hour later. They were both naked and sated, her body curled against his as they came down from their highs. He was holding her tight, the way she'd learned he liked to, his fingers playing along the ridges of her spine. The way he softly kissed her brow made her chest tighten.

He'd made sure she felt good again – more than once – but

it had been the way he'd stared into her eyes as he spilled inside of her that made her feel like there was this unbreakable connection buzzing between them.

They'd both shared their secrets. Laid themselves open to each other. And somehow the honesty between them had made sex even better.

"My mom will be home from Chairs soon." She took a deep breath, because part of her was afraid. Of upsetting her mom, of destroying her hopes and expectations.

But the bigger part of her needed this. "Let me send her a message telling her I'm heading to bed."

"Won't she check on you?" he asked.

"Probably not." She turned her head to the side. "But I could always run over and make it look like I'm under the covers."

In the end, he came over with her, the two of them sneaking into her mom's house like naughty teenagers, rolling up some clothes and pushing them under the covers until they looked vaguely like a human form all curled up sleeping.

"Grab some fresh clothes for the morning," Hendrix instructed her.

"Good idea." She nodded. "I can get my toothbrush, too."

He tipped his head to the side, looking amused. "Didn't you ever sneak out for the night as a teen?" he asked.

She frowned. "No. Can you tell?"

"Yep. Bad boy one-oh-one. Don't take your toothbrush with you. It's a dead giveaway."

Emery blinked. "How many times did you sneak out?"

"Too many. Best not to ask." He winked. "Shit, there's a bit of a t-shirt sticking out. We need to tuck it in." He pulled at her pillow, and she realized what he could see.

Not her clothing, all piled up to look like her. But the t-shirt she'd been sleeping with every night.

He lifted it up then looked at her, his lip quirking.

"Shut up," she said, grabbing it back. "I like to smell it, all right?"

His smirk turned into a full-on grin. "You can smell the real thing tonight." He folded it up and put it back under her pillow. "If you're short of clothes, Emery, all you have to do is ask."

She laughed, because she liked how lighthearted he was right now. Their talk earlier felt like it had cleared the air. He was so handsome when he was chilled out. It made her heart feel tight.

"I thought tonight was all about not wearing any clothes," she teased him.

"My thoughts exactly. Now, are you coming back to mine, or do I have to carry you there?"

She glanced at her watch. Another half an hour and her mom would likely be home. "Carrying would probably be faster," she told him. But before she could tell him she was kidding, he was lifting her over his shoulder, strolling out of her room with her in his arms like she was no weight at all. And she knew that to be untrue.

Still, he managed to get down the stairs without dropping her, and closed the front door behind them without letting go. She was still upside down, her face against his back, when they made it back through his own gate.

Frank let out a low noise. Like they were disturbing him.

"Sorry, fella," she murmured. "Now I know how you feel when he carries you."

The goat didn't even open an eye as Hendrix made it through the front door, not letting her go until he'd closed it firmly behind them.

And once she was upright – and a little dizzy – her stomach let out a low grumble.

"You're finally hungry," he murmured. "Let me warm up the pasta. Get you fed and back to bed."

"Every woman's dream," she told him. "Now get to it."

CHAPTER
Twenty-Two

"DAMN." Hendrix widened his eyes, his vision focusing on the clock beside his bed. It was almost eight o'clock. "Emery, you awake?"

"Five minutes," she muttered, rolling over onto her side. She looked so damn comfortable in his bed, her hair a hot mess, her cheeks pink, her skin soft. He hated having to wake her.

But she'd hate the consequences of sleeping in even more.

"It's almost eight o'clock," he told her, leaning over to kiss her cheek.

That did it. A second later her eyes opened wide. "Wait, what?"

"We slept through the alarm." It was Saturday morning. He was supposed to work until midday like he did every Saturday. And he swore he'd set the alarm for six.

He couldn't remember the last time he hadn't been woken up by the blast of his clock radio. But then again, he couldn't remember the last time he had sex three times in one night, either.

His appetite for this woman was insatiable.

"Oh my God!" She sat up straight, her soft body coming clear of the sheets. "Why didn't you wake me?"

"I just did," he pointed out, trying not to smile at the bird's nest her hair had turned into. A mixture of too much sex and sleeping, he guessed. And he wouldn't have it any other way.

The next ten minutes were a frenzy of showers and putting clothes on. It was funny, watching her get ready so quickly; jumping in his shower, pulling her clothes onto her still-damp body, tying her hair into a messy bun that exposed the arch of her neck. She ran out of the bathroom and came up short, because he was standing there, a mug of coffee in hand.

He held it out to her. "I figured you might need this," he said to her. Emery grabbed the cup gratefully, swallowing half the hot liquid in one gulp. Good thing he'd added extra cream to cool it down.

She looked out of his window, her eyes wide, as she saw her mom opening up the chicken coop, no doubt searching for eggs.

"Ugh, I'm going to have to wait until she's back in the house," Emery murmured. "I can sneak around the back and hang out in the fields for a bit to get an alibi." Her eyes caught his. "If she asks you, you haven't seen me, okay?"

"Your mom won't ask. I don't think she likes me."

Emery let out a soft breath. "Well *I* like you," she told him.

And wasn't that like an injection of adrenaline straight to his heart? "I like you, too." He grinned at her. Damn, he could get used to this, sleeping with her in his arms, watching her get dressed.

"You're coming back over tonight, right?" he asked, as she shoved her feet into her shoes.

She looked up, her warm eyes meeting his. "That's the plan, yeah. I need to pick up my clothes. I figure it'll blow my cover if I carry them home now."

He put his mug down and kissed her softly, her mouth tasting of mint and coffee. He could get used to having her in his bed. To waking up next to her every morning.

Stupid how much more enjoyable it was making coffee for two than for just him.

Emery looked at him, shifting her feet. "Last night. I was planning for us to talk…"

His stomach tightened.

"And then I got carried away." Two discs of pink appeared on her cheeks. "That seems to happen a lot."

"What did you want to talk about?" he asked, checking his watch again because every minute really did count right now. He cared about her. He didn't want her to panic about her mom. And he knew she would.

He already knew a lot about this woman.

"About after." Her eyes caught his. A smile pulled at his lips, remembering the way he'd said it to her.

After.

After she'd gotten the lien removed from her mom's farm. After she stopped pretending to still be in a relationship with a jerk.

Fuck, he couldn't wait.

"Then we'll talk tonight."

She bit her lip. "We're going to need to sit on opposite sides of the room and not touch each other or something. Every time you kiss me I seem to forget how to form a sentence."

He looked over at her house. Her mom was walking back up the steps to the porch, carrying some eggs. "Your mom's going back inside. You should make a run for it."

"Maybe you can distract her while I head around the back. Just walk around naked on the porch or something," Emery suggested. It made him grin. Mostly because he'd have no qualms about doing it.

Especially for her.

If his brothers could hear his thoughts, they'd be teasing him the way he'd teased them over their wives. He hadn't known you could feel like this. So damn protective yet vulnerable at the same time.

Like you had to take care of the only thing your heart beats for.

"I should go. Wish me luck." She walked over to him, rolling onto the toes of her sneakers as she tipped her head up, her lips slightly parted. He put his arm around her waist, pulling her closer, loving how warm and soft her skin was.

Then his mouth brushed hers and everything inside of him felt like he was on fire. She curled her arms around his neck, her body arching into his as he deepened their kiss, his body hardening with need at the way this woman felt.

"Good luck," he murmured against her lips. "I'll open the door, make sure the coast is clear." Because her mom wasn't the only one who could catch her sneaking out. There was Jed and the farmhands.

It would be just their luck for one of them to catch them after they'd been so careful. Until now, at least.

"My hero."

He winked at her, then yanked the door handle, still distracted by the soft way she was staring at him. Maybe that's why he let the door swing wide open before looking out.

And when he saw the dark-haired woman in a pair of slim-fitting jeans and a checkered shirt standing there, his stomach dropped.

"Mom."

"I didn't even knock," she said, smiling at him from the stoop. "Do you have a sixth sense or something?" The sun was behind her, illuminating her hair. In her late fifties, Maddie Hartson was still a beautiful woman, her face untouched by any of the fillers or surgeries so many of his friends' parents had gotten. Sure, there was a little gray streaking in her hair nowadays, but she still looked like the mom who'd adored him when he was a kid.

Fuck. The word lingered on his tongue. He barely managed to bite it away. His mom looked over his shoulder, the smile on her face wavering when she saw who was behind him.

He could have played it off if he'd thought about putting some damn clothes on. But he was standing here in his underwear and nothing else, his hair mussed from a night with Emery, his fingers curled around a coffee mug.

His mom blinked. "Oh, I've interrupted." Her cheeks flushed as she tried to pull her gaze away from him and Emery, pressing her lips together like she was trying to figure out how to get out of this.

He heard Emery's breath catch.

"Emery was just leaving," he muttered, because he had no idea what else to say. And if this was bad, Emery's mom seeing the three of them would be a thousand times worse. He turned to look at the woman he'd just spent the night with. Her face was pale.

"Oh, hi Emery," his mom said, her voice sounding so falsely light that at any other time he would have teased her.

"Hi, Mrs. Hartson." Emery sounded just as awkward.

Okay, so now it was almost funny.

He stepped aside so Emery could pass by. She had her hands curled into fists, like she couldn't quite believe this. He had to stop himself from grabbing her, kissing her again.

She gave his mom a tight smile, and his mom nodded back as Emery passed her, standing stock still as Emery walked down his steps, turning to look at him over his mom's shoulder.

"Oh. My. God!" Emery mouthed.

His lips twitched. If he laughed, she'd probably kill him. So instead he just widened his eyes at her. She shook her head and walked toward the side of her house.

Letting out a low breath, he brought his gaze back to his mom, who still hadn't moved.

"Coffee?" he asked her. "I just put some on."

She blinked. "Oh. Um…"

"Come in," he said. "I promise I don't have anybody else in here."

She looked supremely awkward as she walked inside. The place was still a mess, from last night and this morning. He picked up the towel Emery had placed on the couch and threw it into the laundry room, before walking into the kitchen and pouring his mom a coffee.

"Do you want cream?" he asked her.

Finally, his mom let her gaze land on his face. "Hendrix…"

He shook his head. "I don't want to hear it." Because he knew his mom didn't like what she just saw. Right now he didn't like it either. Not the fact that Emery stayed the night – hell, he *loved* that. It was the fact he could feel his mom's judgment, even if she was trying so hard not to let it out.

And she could judge him all she wanted. But not Emery.

"I know you don't," his mom said softly. "And believe me, I don't want to be here saying it either. I can't tell you how much I wish I'd called before I stopped by. Or at least been a few minutes later." She sighed. "But I didn't. And here we are…"

He leaned against the counter, his jaw tense. "It's not what you think."

"So I didn't just see an engaged woman leave your house while you're half naked?"

He squeezed his eyes shut tightly for a minute, trying to think of the best way to proceed. He'd promised Emery to keep her secret, and there was no way he'd betray that promise.

Opening his eyes, he could see his mom had moved from the kitchen. She was standing by the window, looking out at the farm on the other side of the road. Emery must have made it to the fields, because there was no sign of her. As soon as his mom left he'd check that she was okay.

"Yes, you saw her leave. But…" he shook his head. "It's not her fault. I'd prefer if you didn't go spreading it around."

His mom's eyes widened. "Of course I wouldn't spread it around. I can't believe you said that."

"I didn't…" Christ, he was only making this worse. He pinched the bridge of his nose between his fingers.

"What was it, just a one-night thing?" she asked him. "Or is it an affair?"

His chest tightened. It was too early and he was too exhausted for this. "I don't think that's any of your business."

She recoiled like he'd slapped her. And he hated that, because his mom didn't have a bad bone in her body. She was a good person, a kind one. She loved him and his brothers fiercely.

"I didn't mean it like that." He let out a long breath. "I just… I can't explain it right now. That's all."

"She's getting married, Hendrix. To Trenton Montclair."

He winced as she said *his* name.

"What if somebody else had seen you two?" she asked him. "What if he found out? You remember what happened the last time the two of you went head to head?" Her voice cracked, like she was lost in her own memories. "I lost you. For years. You just left…" She pressed her lips together, like she was trying not to cry.

"I was a kid, mom. I'm grown up now. I can handle things. I can't tell you more than this, but I promise it's not what you think."

"Is she still engaged to him?" his mom asked pointedly.

He sighed, because he hated doing this. "Yes."

"Then it's exactly what I think. And it's what everybody else will think."

"Not if they don't know." He glanced at the clock on the

wall. It was almost half-past eight. He should've been at his uncle's farm hours ago. Sure, Logan was relaxed as long as he got his work done before coming home to tend his own farm, but there was only so much time in the goddamn day.

"I have to shower. Then I need to get to work," he told her.

"I know." She nodded, still looking wary. "I only popped over to check that you're okay. I was at Logan and Courtney's for breakfast. We were going through the plans for the charity launch." She held up a pad she'd obviously been taking notes on. "He said you hadn't come to work." She gave him a small smile. "And of course I wanted to see you. It feels like it's been too long."

"You could have called me. I would have picked up."

Her eyes caught his. "Ditto."

That made him feel even worse. He knew it had been a while since he'd stopped by to see his parents, but had it really been that long? He had no excuse for it, other than he was an ass.

"I'm sorry," he said softly.

"I'm worried about you," she told him, her brows furrowed.

"You don't need to be."

"I'm a mom. That's my job."

He tipped his head to the side. "Don't you ever get time off for good behavior?"

That made her smile.

"Seriously, Mom, you don't need to worry about me. Everything's fine. Sure, I think we all wish you hadn't seen what you did, but try to forget about it."

"I can't do that."

"I wish you would."

"Yeah." She nodded, looking wistful. "I do too."

"Let me get dressed, okay?" he said, because standing here half naked talking to his mom didn't seem right. He didn't care that he was only wearing boxers – his mom had seen a lot worse, after all. Growing up with three sons and a husband that the entire country adored, there was usually at least one man half naked in the house at any time.

But she was still his mom. She deserved respect.

"I can go," she told him.

"Just one minute." He walked into his bedroom, letting out a groan at the situation he'd managed to get himself in. He pulled on yesterday's clothes before he walked back out to his mom. She was still holding the coffee cup. It was hardly touched.

He gently took it out of her hand, and put it on the table, before he pulled her into his arms.

It was like she needed this hug more than either of them knew. She exhaled heavily, her head against his shoulder.

"I love you," he told her. "But you need to stop worrying so much about me. I'm all grown up now." He was the youngest and she'd always mothered him more than his brothers, but he didn't need that from her anymore. Hell, the twins were married with kids, fathers themselves.

And yeah, for the first time in forever, he was thinking about that. Thinking that maybe someday that's what he wanted, too.

"I can't help it," his mom said. "I let you down. When you were younger…"

He cupped her face in his hands, his expression almost stern. "Mom, you never let us down. You were the best mom. You still are." He meant it, too. Yes, he'd made mistakes, but they were never hers.

"I just want you to be happy," she told him. Her eyes were watery now, like the emotions were finally seeping out.

"I am," he told her firmly. "I'm so happy."

"But you can't base your happiness on somebody else's misery."

He knew she was talking about Emery again. About her

being engaged to somebody else. "Can we agree not to talk about this?"

"If you promise me you won't get hurt, then yes."

His eyes caught hers. He could see the anxiety in them. The same emotion he used to see when they were kids off doing reckless things, like climbing too high up a tree or fighting each other in the yard.

"Well that's easy," he told her. "I promise you I won't get hurt." He was a big boy. He'd left that kind of pain behind. There were only good things ahead.

She patted his face, her lips pressed tightly together. "You're such a good man," she told him. "And I wish that you could see that."

Yeah, well. Bad boys didn't always become good men. But he was trying his best here.

CHAPTER
Twenty-Three

TAKING A DEEP BREATH, Emery picked up the phone and pressed on the phone symbol next to Trenton's name, counting the seconds until it inevitably went to voicemail.

Her mom had barely paid her any attention when she'd walked back inside an hour ago. She was nursing a hangover, of all things. The woman who never drank had managed to get through three glasses of punch last night before she realized it was spiked.

"Didn't you ask?" Emery had said, trying not to smile, because her mom looked horrified.

"No. I assumed the sign next to it was true."

"What did the sign say?"

"*Drink me and be happy. Very, very happy.*" Her mom frowned.

"And that didn't give you a clue that it was spiked?"

Her mom groaned, putting her palm against her brow. "No. Why would anybody add alcohol to a perfectly good punch?"

Emery had suggested her mom rest, so she was laying upstairs, a cold compress on her head.

Which was a good thing. Because she didn't need to overhear this call.

"You've reached Trenton Montclair. Leave a message."

The sound of his voice was enough to make her grit her teeth. But she wasn't going to let the fact that he was obviously still avoiding her stop her from doing what she needed to do.

He'd called the shots from the start. Looking back, from the moment they'd started dating there'd been a power imbalance between them. He'd been slightly older and a lot more sophisticated, with the money and social class that came from being born into a long established family. And she'd been the young, naïve farm girl.

He'd managed to pick away at her confidence bit by bit. Suggesting he take over their finances because she could make mistakes. Overruling her suggestions on where they should go to eat or on vacation. Making suggestions that she'd be more attractive if she ate less or if she talked less when he took her out to dinner with a client.

She'd made herself so small for him that she felt like she'd disappeared.

But she wasn't going to do that anymore. And it wasn't even like she was disturbing him at work. It was a Saturday. Plenty of time for him to get used to what she had to say.

"This is Emery," she told him, her voice clear as she spoke down the phone. "I want you to know that the deal is off. I'm tired of lying to people to make your life easier. I'll be telling my mom next week that our engagement is over. I suggest you do the same with your parents." She paused, her heart racing. "And I expect you to sign off the lien. Because I'm putting the farm up for sale on Monday."

She ended the call, knowing that Trenton would be furious when he listened to it. But that wasn't her problem. Not anymore. She wasn't his verbal punching bag. It wasn't her job to make his life easier.

Her only concern was herself and the people she loved. And that didn't include Trenton, not anymore.

It might include the man who'd held her all night, though.

His mom had left about twenty minutes after Emery arrived home. Not that she was looking.

Okay, she was totally looking. Maddie Hartson hadn't looked upset with her son. She'd hugged him on the stoop and walked away, a smile on her lips. Five minutes later she'd seen Hendrix get on his motorcycle and leave – presumably to catch up on the work he'd missed by sleeping in.

He'd sent her a message, though. Probably when he was taking his first break.

Did you make it home without your mom noticing? By the way, you're hot when you're sneaking around. – Hendrix

She liked the way his messages sounded exactly like him. He'd told her he typically used voice to text to reply. It was easier than trying to work through his dyslexia with his fingers.

So she'd started replying to his texts with a voice message. Her lips curled as she whispered into her microphone. "You're pretty beautiful yourself."

It took a minute for him to reply.

"Nobody's ever called me beautiful before." His voice was thick.

That made her heart tighten. It was funny, because they could probably call each other rather than message. Since they were both so clearly on their phones right now. But there was something special about this. The way she could save his voice notes and listen to them when she was alone.

"Then you'd better get used to it, buddy."

They messaged a couple more times before he told her he

needed to get back to work. But not before he sent her one last voice recording.

"What time can you get to mine later?"

"Not until late. I need to wait until my mom's gone to bed." She smiled at that. "I'll come over as soon as I'm free."

This time his reply was typed. Like there was somebody around listening.

Good. – Hendrix

And yes it was. Very, very good.

―――

It was almost seven by the time he'd gotten all his work done. It had been a scorching hot day, too, the sun so strong that despite the fact he'd worn a cap and sunscreen, his skin had still turned a deeper gold.

Hendrix showered, ate some dinner, and went out to the yard to check on Frank. The goat was laying underneath a tree on the dusty grass, his legs folded beneath him. When he spotted Hendrix walking over to fill his trough, he slowly rose to his hooves, then walked over, nuzzling Hendrix in the stomach.

"Hey buddy." He tickled the goat beneath his jaw. "You have the right idea. When it's this hot, the only thing to do is lay in the shade on the grass."

The goat let out a little bray, then ambled over to his food trough, sniffing at it before he dipped his head to scoop some pellets into his mouth. None of the farm animals had been active today. Unlike humans, they knew to rest when the sun started to beat down in the middle of summer.

He spent the next hour sitting on his deck, on the porch

swing. His legs gently rocked it back and forth as he drank a bottle of beer and stared out into the distance, thinking about last night and this morning. The way it had felt so damn good to wake up with Emery in his arms.

And the way his mom's face looked when she'd discovered them made him feel like he was that bad kid, again. Making her cry.

You're pretty beautiful, too.

The memory of Emery's voice on his phone made his chest ache. It wasn't a lie. Nobody had called him beautiful before. He wasn't an idiot. Physically, he knew he was doing okay. Mostly thanks to his genes and the hard, unrelenting, physical work of being a farmer that sculpted his body more than any gym could.

And yeah, he'd never had any problems attracting women. If anything, they liked the way he didn't give a damn about life. The way he was casual. Hard to keep.

Women liked the chase as much as men. More sometimes.

Not Emery, though. She was like the firefly etched on her ankle. Breathtaking to look at. Impossible to capture.

Twenty minutes later, like his mind had tried to conjure her up, he noticed her walking onto the porch to get something. Her head was inclined and her lips were moving, like she was talking to her mom inside the house.

And then she saw him on his own porch, watching her. And stopped, her hand in mid air.

He swallowed hard, unable to tear his eyes away from this woman. Her hair had taken on a curl from the heat, tumbling around her shoulders in waves.

She'd changed into a dress. Was that for him? For later? Styled her hair, too. Stupid how much he liked that thought, but he did. His heart slammed against his chest, all thoughts of their moms pushed away.

He didn't care what anybody else thought. He wanted her like he'd never wanted anything else. But more than that, he wanted to be good for her. Not the man everybody else thought he was.

Hendrix Hartson. Town bad boy. Keep your daughters locked up.

Emery's mom said something to her, and she nodded, but he could see her gaze was still on him. He grinned at her, because fuck, he was the luckiest man around.

His breath caught as she smiled back. A small, half-curl, secretive kind of smile.

The kind of smile that held a promise of more.

Then her mom said something else, and Emery pulled her gaze from his, lifting her hand as though to wave goodbye, as she turned her back to him.

And that's when he knew. He'd do anything for her. Including tell her the truth of who he was. Because if she was going to make sacrifices for him, she deserved for him to do the same.

He felt like he was falling. And he had no idea if he could stop.

Or if he wanted to.

———

"I think I'm going to head up to bed," Emery's mom told her an hour later. They were only half way through the movie they'd been watching, but her mom's eyes were half-closed. "Can we watch the rest of this tomorrow?"

"Good idea," Emery said. "Hopefully, you'll feel better in the morning."

"Fingers crossed. All I know is that I'm never going to drink Mary-Ellen's special punch ever again. That thing is bad for my health." Her mom let out a sigh. "Will you be okay to check on the chickens and lock everything up tonight?"

"Of course." Emery looked at her watch. "I might go out for a nice long walk now that it's cooling down."

Her mom nodded. "Don't stay out too late."

As soon as she heard the creak of her mom's bedroom floorboards, followed by the groan of the springs in her mattress, Emery slid her feet into her sandals and checked herself in the mirror by the door.

She'd put on a dress and curled her hair while her mom had napped earlier. Her mom had said something about her always looking nice in a dress, but hadn't asked her why she had one on.

The truth was, she wanted to look pretty. Wanted to dress up. She'd never felt more feminine than she did now that she'd finally taken control of her life. She felt powerful and attractive.

And stupidly hot at the thought of being in Hendrix's arms again. The man made her ache from the inside out.

The chickens had put themselves to bed in the coop earlier, as tired of the heat as she was. They barely looked up when Emery peeked her head around the door to check on them. Opening the little boarded window above the door, so the night air could provide some ventilation, she topped up their water with some ice cubes from the outdoor freezer, then locked the door closed behind her, turning her head to make sure her mom's curtains were closed.

They were.

Frank didn't even lift his head when she walked past him. So instead she reached down to ruffle his fur. "Hey cutie."

He lifted an eyelid, then closed it again, like he was way more interested in sleeping than flirting with her tonight.

Anticipation raced through her as she lifted her hand and rapped her knuckles on his door. She'd barely pulled her hand away before the door was wrenched open and Hendrix scooped her into his arms, making her giggle as he carried her inside like he was some kind of Neanderthal.

"Is this how you greet all your visitors?" she asked him, loving the way his hard muscled arms held her tightly against his chest. Her sandals fell from her feet, clattering on his wooden floor.

He grinned at her. He was freshly shaved, in a pair of jeans and a clean t-shirt. Her stomach did a little twist at just how handsome this man was.

"I don't get a lot of visitors," he told her. "So no."

"Your mom was here this morning," she pointed out.

"And you know I didn't pick her up like this." He pressed his mouth against hers, like he couldn't stop himself from kissing her. His happiness at seeing her was so plain on his face. "Do you know how much I hate you having to sneak over here?" he asked her, gently letting go of her so her feet were back on the ground.

"You want me to go home?" she teased, reaching up to muss his hair.

He shook his head. "I just want to be able to come over and pick you up. It doesn't feel right that you have to make sure nobody sees you walking over."

"You can do that next week," she told him.

"Won't your mom get suspicious?"

She took a deep breath. "I called Trenton today. Told him I'm sick of this. I'm telling Mom it's over on Monday. And after that, I don't care who finds out."

He blinked, looking pleased. "How did he take that?"

She shrugged. "I don't know. He didn't answer so I left him a voicemail." Her eyes met his. "But I don't care, either."

That was the truth. She couldn't make everybody in the world happy. No matter how good she tried to be. All she could worry about were the people she allowed into her life.

People like her mom, who'd get over the upset. And Hendrix, who right now was reaching for her, pulling her into his arms and kissing her until her legs felt weak.

"And you're okay with people knowing about us?" he asked her when they finally parted to get some air.

"I'm absolutely okay with it." She jutted her chin out and a smile played at his lips.

"When did you get so damn brave?"

"I guess staying here has given me a lot of time to think. About what I want in life. About how I'm the only one who's been holding me back." Her eyes met his. "I know this thing between us is still at the beginning. And I know me going back to work next month will complicate things."

"It won't complicate things. Charleston isn't that far away."

"Far enough when you're a farmer," she murmured. She took a breath. "But if you want me…"

"Of course I want you." His eyes were dark. "There's no question about that."

"Then we can try to make it work. Long distance or…"

"Or?" Hendrix prompted.

She pressed her lips together. "I don't know. There are schools everywhere. I'm not tied to Charleston."

He cupped her face with his hands, leaning in to press his warm mouth against her brow. "You'd move back here for me?" he asked, his voice thick.

"I'd consider it. And for my mom."

This time when they kissed, she could feel the ache rush through her. The need for him, so hot and thick inside of her, felt like it was almost impossible to ignore.

"Wait," he murmured, as she pulled at his t-shirt. "I want to say something, too."

"Is it bad?" she asked him.

"No." He paused. "Well yes. But not the way you think it is. I just wanted to tell you. About me."

Oh. That made her heart slam against her chest. "What do you want to tell me about you?" she murmured, noticing how his eyes didn't leave hers.

"Everything."

CHAPTER
Twenty-Four

HIS HEART WAS RACING way too fast, despite the fact that he wasn't moving. Just leaning on the wall, staring at the woman he was quickly becoming addicted to.

"You're worrying me," she murmured. "You look so serious. Is it about your mom? About her catching us? You never told me what she said this morning."

"She thinks we're having an affair."

Emery winced and he shook his head.

"Don't worry," he added. "I made it clear that it's all my fault."

"I'm not worried about that," Emery said softly. "I'm worried because you look like you're about to throw up."

"I don't like talking about myself." Wasn't that the understatement? And yet he needed to. She'd been so damn brave, telling her ex she was coming clean. Telling him that she'd think about moving back to Hartson's Creek.

She'd put herself out there. He couldn't pull back now. He wanted her to know him. The good and the bad. He'd been hiding behind his mistakes for too long. Pretending he didn't care what people thought about him.

But he cared what *she* thought. That was the truth. And she deserved it.

"I moved back here because I'd been breaking my mom's heart for way too many years." He let out a breath, trying to figure out how to explain the constant dread he felt that he was letting her down.

He was a grown man. But he loved his mom. And she'd always deserved better.

"You know about the drugs being found in my locker at school?" he asked her. Because he might as well start from the beginning.

"I remember hearing about it."

"Trenton put them there. Him and his friends. They were pissed because I'd gotten onto the football team and taken the place they thought he deserved."

"Trenton planted the weed on you?" Her mouth dropped open.

"He was one of them."

"I didn't know," she told him. "I didn't, honestly."

"Of course you didn't. Why would you? Even my friends thought it was me who'd brought it to school. It fit. I was always the bad kid. The one who couldn't read. The one who acted out because I was so shit at school. It wasn't a great leap to believe I was also the kid who hid weed in my locker."

"You didn't tell the principal it wasn't you?"

"No." He shook his head. "And this is all old history, anyway. The only reason I'm telling you about it was because the day it happened was the day before my dad was inducted into the Rock and Roll Hall of Fame. He and my mom were so damn happy. They were going to attend, just the two of them, have some time together alone to celebrate. And then my mom got the call from the principal and she told my dad to go without her." He swallowed hard. "She didn't blink, didn't think, just rushed to be with me. And he went there alone and she missed it."

"I'm so sorry…"

"That night, when he was inducted, I caught her crying. She was in the kitchen, in the dark. I could hear her softly sobbing, like she was trying not to let me know how much I'd fucked things up. And I promised myself, right then, that I wouldn't hurt her like that again."

His throat felt scratchy, because he knew how fickle that had been.

"That's why I left home so young. They thought I wanted to explore. To spend time in different countries. Go from one farm to the next, working, learning." His eyes caught hers. "But I guess more than anything I was running away from being the family mess up."

She took his hand in hers, staring at him with soulful eyes. "Your mom must've hated that."

"She did. But I figured that way I couldn't hurt her anymore. She blamed herself for me getting in trouble at school. Then blamed herself again for not knowing about my dyslexia earlier. The way I saw it, I needed to be an adult. Live my life without causing her problems." His jaw tightened. "And then last year happened."

"Last year?" Emery asked.

He took a deep breath, like it was taking all of his effort to form the words on his lips. "I had a fling with a woman. It was a mistake."

Emery gave him a weak smile. "I know all about those."

"You do things with a good heart, baby. I had no heart at all. I was only interested in no strings. I didn't want a relationship. I thought I'd made it clear. But she got a little… attached. And I didn't care. Hell, I didn't even notice."

"What happened?"

"I tried to break it off. And then she told me she was pregnant."

Emery's mouth dropped open.

He winced at the memory of it. How oblivious he'd been.

How self centred. He hadn't realized he was hurting her. But he should have.

"She wasn't pregnant, though. Her best friend came to tell me that it was all a lie. But when I told her it really was over, she decided to contact my parents. She called them crying, telling them they were going to be grandparents. That I was treating her horribly and she needed them to talk to me.

"She had my mom completely convinced she was going to be a grandmother. It was only when Mom was heading to the airport to fly out to meet her that I found out what was going on. She'd built this whole alternative reality where we were going to have a kid and she'd get my mom and dad to persuade me to marry her."

"Oh my God," Emery whispered.

"Yeah." He let out a breath. "It was a mess. After that, I decided to move back here. It felt like the right time, and this place was up for sale. Uncle Logan helped me with the mortgage and a business plan and here I am."

"That wasn't your fault," Emery told him. "You didn't know she was going to do that."

"I treated her like shit. I should have noticed she was getting attached. I spent most of my life not taking notice. Just thinking that I could be casual with people's emotions. That it wasn't my fault I kept causing pain to the people I shouldn't."

Emery stepped toward him, putting her arms around his waist, resting her face on his chest. "It wasn't your fault," she repeated. "You have to know that. Somewhere deep inside."

He dipped his head against her hair, breathing her in. "I just wanted you to know."

She looked up at him, her eyes shining. "I know you're a good man," she whispered. "That's all I need to know."

He kissed the top of her head. "I want to be good for you."

"You're so good for me," Emery whispered. "You're perfect for me, in fact. You're all I can think about. I don't care what anybody else thinks about us. I know the truth. You do too. We're good together. And I don't just mean in bed." She moved her hands to his shoulders, feeling the tension in his muscles. "I mean you understand me. More than anybody ever has. And I think I'm getting to understand you, too."

"I want you to understand me," he murmured, looking her right in the eyes. "I want you to know me." He needed it.

"I *do* know you." She kissed him softly, moving her hands to his chest. "I know you love animals. Especially goats who flirt too much. I know you love your family, and I know, despite your ideas to the contrary, that they love you fiercely, too." She traced her fingers over his stomach, making his breath catch in his throat.

"I know what you look like when you're sleeping. Like you don't have a care in the world, even though that's not true." She reached for the hem of his t-shirt. Pushing her hands underneath it, she made contact with his skin, her palms against his stomach.

"I know how you look at me, like I'm a perfectly good girl you're corrupting," she whispered. "But I'm not good, Hendrix. None of us are completely good. Sometimes I'm bad. Like really bad."

"Oh yeah?" God, he was aching for her already. Just one touch from her and he was a goner. "How so?"

"Sometimes I touch myself thinking about the guy who lives across the street," she whispered, tracing the ridges in his stomach. "Sometimes I imagine him touching me. And sometimes I imagine what he'd do if I dropped to my knees and unfastened his jeans and slid my lips over the hardest part of him."

His jaw was tight as she looked up at him. "Maybe you should try it and find out."

Her lips curled into a smile. "See? We even think the same." She dropped to her knees, her fingers tracing the hard ridge of him pressed against the denim, her fingers curling around his zipper and pulling it down.

"You look pretty good right now," he said thickly, as she pulled him out of his boxers, her warm hand circling him before she kissed the hot, hard tip.

Her eyes met his and he saw the desire there. The kindness, too. This woman understood him, and for the first time in forever it felt like he wasn't alone.

Then she slid her mouth over him, and all rational thought went out of his mind.

Hendrix saw the for sale sign at the end of the lane on Monday morning, as he rode over to his uncle's farm. It was flapping in the heat of the summer breeze, and he stopped to look at it, so damn proud of Emery for going through with it.

"It's finally happening, huh?" Jed, the Reed's farm manager, called out to him.

"Yeah. Good for them." Hendrix nodded. "You okay with it?" he asked Jed. He knew his uncle had already offered Jed a job, but the man was set on retiring. Still, it was one thing talking about it happening, another seeing the for sale sign in front of the farm you'd worked on for decades.

"It's time," Jed said, running his hand over his jaw. "It'll be good for Alice. She needs to get out of here. Emery too."

Hendrix nodded. "She's taken on a lot this summer."

"She has." Jed tipped his head to the side. "She's changed a lot, too." He looked Hendrix straight in the eye. "Seems happier than I've seen her in a long time."

There was something in the way he said it that made Hendrix realize Jed knew about him and Emery. He shifted his feet.

"She deserves happiness," Hendrix said.

"That she does." Jed pressed his lips together. "Especially after her dad…" He cleared his throat. "Anyway, in his absence, I guess I'm the closest thing she has to a father. And since that's the case, it's also my job to make sure nobody endangers that happiness. Like a guy who was taking advantage of her, for example." He looked Hendrix dead in the eye. "If she was involved with somebody like that, I'd need to tell him to back off."

Hendrix nodded. "You and me both. I feel protective of her, too. Not that she needs it. If anybody can protect themselves, it's Emery."

"Very true." Jed eyed him warily. "I guess I just have to hope this guy has good intentions."

"You don't have to hope, sir. I know he has good intentions. The best kind of ones." It should have been funny. The way they were dancing around the facts. Neither one of them admitting to what they knew. Neither one of them wanting to.

It was so stupidly masculine. Emery would probably laugh her head off if she knew they were doing this.

"Well, that's nice to hear." Jed nodded. "Very nice."

"I think so."

"And if this guy, whoever he is, keeps being good to her, unlike that asshole she's engaged to, then I'll be able to retire and not get involved."

Hendrix's lips twitched. "I think you can retire without worrying." He looked at the for sale sign. "Just as soon as this place is sold." He inclined his head at the road. "Well, I'd better get to work before my uncle sends out a search party."

"Of course." Jed nodded. "Oh, and Hendrix?"

"Yes, sir?"

"You deserve to be happy, too."

"So, have you told her yet?" Maisie asked Emery. It was early evening in Hartson's Creek, which meant it was almost midnight in Norway, which was Maisie's second to last country of her tour. She'd video-called Emery to show her the midnight sun. Even though it was almost the next day, the sun was still a burning ball of orange hanging above the horizon. It didn't set at all during the height of the summer there.

"I'm going to tell her tonight. No ifs, ands, or buts. Mom spent most of the day fielding calls from people who've seen the for sale sign and didn't realize we were planning on moving. And then the realtor sent over a bunch of home listings for her to look at, which she insisted on going through right away."

The truth was, her mom was dealing with the for sale sign going up outside the farm better than Emery had hoped. And yeah, she was nervous as hell about telling her that her engagement was over. But tonight was the deadline. She was going to tell her mom everything.

She was so ready to get on with the rest of her life. And that life started today.

"How about the asshole? Have you heard from him?" Maisie asked her.

"No. But the ball is in his court. I've told him what I'm doing, how he reacts to that is up to him."

"And how's the hot farmer?" Maisie murmured, leaning in.

"Perfect." She glanced up from her position in her mom's front yard. "In fact, he's just arriving home from work."

"I want to talk to him," Maisie said excitedly. "Take me over. Introduce me."

"Hell no. That would be weird."

Maisie gave her a pointed look. "You wouldn't be with him if it wasn't for me. I'm the one who gave you the list and made sure you went skinny dipping."

"He lives about thirty yards away," Emery said dryly. "I'm sure we would have talked eventually."

"Oh come on. It's daylight for almost twenty-four hours here. I can't sleep. The least you could do is provide me with some entertainment." She pressed her lips together. "I could add it to the list. What are we up to, number nine?"

"You're not adding anything more to the list," Emery said firmly. Then she looked back to check if there was any sign of her mom, but there wasn't. "Okay, I'll introduce you."

"Yay!" Maisie beamed. "Ask him to take his top off. I need the full effect."

Rolling her eyes at her friend, Emery walked through the gate and across the lane. Hendrix was climbing off of his motorcycle, and he smiled softly at her, making her heart thud.

"Hey." He tipped his head to the side.

"Hi." She felt stupidly breathless. Would it always feel like this? Like she couldn't remember how to breathe around him? "My friend Maisie is on the phone. She wants to say hi."

"Point me at him," Maisie's tinny voice shouted.

"Sorry," Emery mouthed at Hendrix. He winked at her, then walked up to his house. She followed behind him, letting him usher her through the front door.

It was good thinking. If Maisie was going to embarrass them all, it was better to do it in private.

Once they were fully inside she lifted the phone up until the screen was facing Hendrix.

He looked stupidly amused. "Hi Maisie," he said.

"Hi Hendrix." Maisie sounded breathless. "It's nice to meet you."

"It's nice to meet you, too. I've heard a lot about you."

"What did Emery tell you?" Maisie asked him. "It's all lies. Unless it's nice, in which case it's all true. So… I hear you look good without a shirt."

"Aaand that's my cue to end the call," Emery said, turning the phone back around. Hendrix was trying not to laugh.

"Bye Maisie. Go to bed, get some sleep."

"I'll see you in the flesh soon," her friend shouted out,

presumably to Hendrix as well, before Emery ended the call and rolled her eyes.

"I'm so sorry."

"Don't be. I like that you introduced me to your friend."

"She's even worse in real life."

"I think I can cope with that." He stepped forward until there were only a couple of inches between them. "How's your day been?"

"Pretty good." Emery let out a breath. "Did you see the for sale sign?"

"Yeah, I saw it. Jed was out there when I went by, actually. We had a very interesting conversation."

"What kind of conversation?" she asked him.

"The kind of conversation where he pretty much admitted that he knows about us."

"He knows?" Her eyes widened. "He never said anything." Thank God. Her cheeks pinked up. "What did he say?"

"Just that you seem happy. And he thought there might be a guy involved. And whoever he was better treat you right."

"So what makes you think he suspects?"

"Because the way he was looking at me made it clear he knew it was me."

"Oh." She put her hand over her face. "I'm so embarrassed. First him, now Maisie. Have they managed to scare you away yet?"

He gently peeled her hand away. "No. It's funny. And sweet. And I like that people care about you." He caught her eye. "I care too."

There it was, that little thud of her heart against her ribcage. She looked at her watch. "I need to get back. My mom…"

"She doing okay?" he asked.

And if that didn't make her want to swoon, she wasn't

sure what would. He cared about her. He cared about the people she cared about.

She was starting to get used to it.

"I'm going to tell her about the engagement ending when I get back."

His eyes caught hers. "You want me to be there?"

"It's probably best if I do it alone. And anyway, you need to stop being so sweet."

"I can't. I'm naturally that way." He grinned. "But if you need me just let me know."

"I will," she breathed. "I really should go."

He walked her to the door and she stepped out onto his deck. God, she wished they could stay here all night.

"Soon," he murmured, like he could read her mind. "This will all be out in the open. We won't have to hide anymore."

He looked so happy at that thought that she couldn't help but grin, too. She threw her arms around him, rolling onto her tiptoes to kiss him. "God, I can't wait."

His mouth was warm. Welcoming. The way he moved it against hers sent a shiver down her spine. He slid his hand down her back, pulling her closer, until their bodies touched. She could feel the thick ridge of his excitement pressed against her belly.

"Come over later," he told her.

"I'll try."

"And if you don't come over, call me."

"I'll definitely do that." She kissed him again and stepped back, a grin pulling at her lips.

It reflected the smile he was giving back to her.

God, this man made her feel good. "I'll see you later, Only Farms."

"Yeah," he said gruffly. "You better."

She turned on her heels, still smiling. Because the sun was shining, Hendrix Hartson was beautiful, and the rest of her life was in front of her.

Maybe that's why she didn't see Trenton standing in her mom's yard, waiting for her, until it was too late.

CHAPTER
Twenty-Five

"WELL, YOU TWO SURE SEEM COZY."

Emery's stomach rolled at the sound of Trenton's voice. He sounded pissed. Of course he did. Thoughts were rushing through her head. How much had he seen? She'd kissed Hendrix, she'd definitely kissed him.

He'd absolutely seen too much.

"What are you doing here?" she asked Trenton, trying to ignore the panic in her veins. He must have driven here right from work, because he was still in a suit, the pants perfectly cut for his slim body. He'd taken his tie off, though, and the top button of his white shirt was unfastened. But that was his only concession to comfort.

"I got your message. I figured we needed to have a conversation face to face." He looked over her shoulder. "Your voicemail didn't sound like you. And I guess now I know why." Trenton looked her dead in the eye. "How long have you been fucking Hendrix Hartson?"

Her cheeks pinked. "That's none of your business."

"So you *have* been fucking him, then?"

She winced at the volume of his voice. Her mom was inside. And yes, hopefully she wasn't listening, but still.

"Is this why you split up with me?" he asked her. "I should have known what a bitch you were, whoring yourself all over the place behind my back."

His accusation boiled her blood. "Stop projecting. I never cheated on you," she snapped. She had no reason to feel like she'd done something wrong. And yet he was looking at her like she was the one who'd caused all their problems.

"I should have known you'd end up back in the gutter. You can take the girl away from the farm, but she'll always act like an animal."

There was movement over Trenton's shoulder. It took her a moment to realize it was Hendrix, striding over, like he was afraid she needed help.

No, please no.

She widened her eyes at him, trying to tell him that his presence would only make it worse.

But like a bull in a damn china shop, he stormed toward them, oblivious.

"Is everything okay?" Hendrix asked.

"What the fuck does it have to do with you?" Trenton spat out at him. "Go back to your house, farm boy. The grown-ups are talking."

Ignoring him, Hendrix looked at her. "Emery," he said, his voice soft. "Are you okay?"

No, she wasn't. So far from it that it wasn't funny. But they were in her mom's yard. It was only a matter of time before her mom noticed that Trenton's car was here. "I'm fine," she told him, trying to keep her voice steady. "Let me talk to Trenton. I'll talk to you later."

"She means she'll suck your dick later," Trenton told him.

Hendrix's eyes narrowed. "What did you say?"

"You heard me. You enjoy getting my sloppy seconds?" Trenton asked, turning to face him. "I would say you could do better, but we both know that's not true. Maybe you two deserve each other."

"If I hear you say one more disrespectful thing about this woman again, I'll make you regret it." Hendrix's voice was low.

The corner of Trenton's lip lifted, like he was actually enjoying this. Mortification pulled at Emery. This was her worst fear, all wrapped up in a testosterone bow. She knew Trenton. His pride was more important than anything else. Certainly more important than she'd ever been to him.

"She's. A. Whore," Trenton said slowly, his eyes dancing.

It was like watching a train crash in slow motion, knowing that the worst thing in the world was about to happen. Knowing she couldn't stop it, but still trying anyway.

"Hendrix..."

His hand was already curled into a fist.

"Let him hit me. I look forward to calling the cops," Trenton goaded.

But she couldn't do that. "Please." She looked at Hendrix with soulful eyes. This had to stop.

She reached for his arm, her touch gentle as she curled her fingers around his wrist. "Hendrix, please. Stop. I'm okay, it's okay."

She could feel the fury vibrating from him. His muscles were tight, his jaw tense. She wasn't sure if he could even hear her.

"Hendrix?" she said again. This time he brought his eyes to hers, blinking at her like he'd just realized where they were, what was happening. "Let me talk to Trenton," she said, her voice low. "Go back to your place. I promise I'll call you later."

"Emery?"

Oh God no. She wanted to scream. Her mom's voice was the last thing she needed to hear in this mess.

"Is that Trenton?"

For a second, all she could do was close her eyes and wish she could disappear into the ground. "Yes." Somehow, she got the word out. It still felt like it was strangled, though.

"Aren't you going to invite him in? I'll pour some sweet tea."

"I'd love some of your sweet tea, Alice," Trenton called back to her. "But I thought Emery and I might take a drive. I haven't seen her for weeks. I just want to be alone with her."

Hendrix's eyes narrowed.

"Oh, of course," Her mom said. "I'll leave you to it."

Emery looked over her shoulder to see her mom hovering at the front door. Her gaze landed on her daughter, then on the two men in front of her. "Is everything okay?" her mom asked.

"Everything's fine, Mom. Just go back inside."

For the first time in forever, her mom actually did what Emery asked. Maybe she was tired from the emotion of today, or maybe she sensed that Emery needed her to disappear right now.

There was only so much a woman could deal with at once.

Trenton pulled his keys from his pocket, unlocking his car. "Get inside," he told Emery, his voice icy cold.

"You don't have to do this," Hendrix told her. "You don't have to do anything you don't want to."

Her eyes caught his. She could see the anger still inside them, coupled with something softer. It looked like worry. Emery forced a smile onto her face. "It's fine. I'll be okay. I'll call you later, all right?"

Trenton was already striding to the driver's side, ignoring Hendrix completely as he yanked open the door.

"Emery?" Hendrix murmured.

"Yes?"

"If he lays one finger on you, if he hurts you…"

"He won't," she promised. Yes, Trenton was a controlling ass who'd broken his promises. But he'd never hurt her. Not physically at least. And she wasn't the woman she used to be – she wasn't going to let this man walk all over her anymore.

"Call me if he does. I'll be there so fast he won't know what hit him."

She nodded, pressing her lips together because she was afraid she was going to cry.

And then she got into Trenton's car, and he silently started the engine.

———

Trenton didn't say a word as he pulled his sleek car out of her mom's driveway, taking the lane to the main road.

"Where are we going?" Emery asked him.

"Somewhere we can talk and you can tell me what the hell is happening here."

It turned out that somewhere meant the town square. Not exactly private, but maybe that was a good thing.

He climbed out of the car, not bothering to pull her door open for her, and strode over to the bandstand.

This was good, she told herself. At least he wasn't making a scene in front of her mom. Plus they were in public. He couldn't get away with burying her body here.

Her mouth twitched at that thought.

"So how long has this been going on?" Trenton asked.

She didn't owe him an explanation, but she wasn't afraid for him to know either. It felt good, just getting it out there. "A few weeks. We were already split up."

"And you expect me to believe that?" She could hear the hurt in his voice. And that was so much worse than the anger.

"It doesn't matter. It's the truth." She looked him in the eye. "You were the one who downloaded a dating app while we were still together," she reminded him. "Not me."

"Because I was lonely. But I didn't do anything."

Yeah, well she still had her suspicions about that. But it

didn't matter anymore. None of this did. It was old history. She just wanted to move forward.

"I'm sorry you had to find out that I've moved on like that. I'd have liked to tell you about it face to face." And no, she didn't owe him that. But that would have been for her. She was still a good girl at heart.

"But you're not sorry for fucking him."

She grimaced at him. "Can you stop saying it like that, otherwise I'm leaving."

"What do you want me to call it? Making love?" Trenton's nose wrinkled up. "Because assholes like him don't make love, Emery. They just take what's not theirs." He shook his head. "What do you even see in him, anyway?"

"That's none of your business."

"Is it his parent's money?"

She shook her head. "He doesn't want their money." And she'd never been interested in that. Did Trenton really not know her at all?

"Of course he does. His parents are loaded."

"And they're not leaving him any of it," she replied, infuriated by his insinuation. "His mom is setting up a charity with their money. Hendrix won't see a penny of it."

"He's gonna end up hurting you. You know that, right? You know what kind of man he is."

No, she wasn't going to take this. Not from *him*. She lifted her chin, refusing to let him make her feel bad. "Yes I do. A good one."

Trenton scowled. "What is this? Are you trying to make me jealous? Make me look bad? How do you think my parents will feel, knowing that you're knocking boots with the guy who smoked weed in school?"

"He didn't. He told me everything." She squared her shoulders. Because she was sick of this. "About what you did to him at school. The way you made him take the blame."

Trenton didn't wince. He knew exactly what she was talking about. "That was a long time ago, Emery."

She looked him straight in the eye, her jaw tight. "What are you doing here anyway? Why did you come?" It wasn't because he suspected she was seeing somebody else, that's for sure. She'd never seen him so blindsided.

"To talk. I wanted to ask you to wait until the weekend to tell people about us. My parents are arriving home early, and I want to tell them face to face." He shook his head. "Not that it matters now. I don't want anything from you."

"Trenton…"

He put his hand up. "No. I'm over this, Emery. I'm over you calling the shots and making decisions without me. So I'm making one without you." He leaned closer. "I saw the for sale sign. Good luck selling that place without me removing the lien."

"But you promised…" Her stomach tightened.

"I promised nothing. I'm not signing anything for you. You can tell your mom that she can't sell her house because her daughter can't keep her legs together."

"You should have let me hit him," Hendrix murmured through the phone. He'd been pacing the cottage ever since she'd left. Even Frank had felt his tension and wandered up to the front door to check that everything was okay.

He hated her being in the car with that asshole. Hated not being able to protect her from him.

Every minute that he didn't know where she was felt excruciating.

"What would that have solved?" Emery was in her bedroom. He'd seen her arrive home and walk straight into the house. She'd sent him a message telling him she was taking a shower and putting her pajamas on and would call him in ten minutes.

And now here she was, sounding anxious and emotional. He wanted nothing more than to wrap his arms around her, but her mom was still up and the last thing Emery needed was for him to storm over and make things worse.

"It would have made me feel better," he told her. And yes, that was selfish. He knew that. Hitting Trenton Montclair wouldn't have only been for the pain he'd put Emery through. But also for the disgusting way he'd described her.

It would have been for himself, too. And the satisfaction would have been worth it.

"So he's gone now?" he asked her.

"Yeah. He's on his way back to Charleston, I guess. He has work tomorrow and there's no way he'll miss that."

It was clear she wasn't going to tell her mom about them tonight. And yeah, he understood why. Everything was a mess.

Didn't mean he liked it, though.

"So what happens now?" he asked her.

"I guess I tell my mom that the farm has to come off the market." Her voice cracked and it about killed him.

"Emery…"

"It's okay. I'll work it out. I'm just so tired."

"Let me speak to my parents. Or my uncle. They can loan me the money. I'll pay the thing off."

"He won't let you." She let out a long, unsteady breath. "He's going to string this out as long as he can. Make me pay. He can make things impossible, refuse to take payment. And anyway, you can't ask your family for help. I know you'd hate that."

Yeah, he would. He'd always prided himself on paying his own way. Being the son of a rockstar had its benefits, sure, but everybody assuming you're rich thanks to your dad wasn't one of them.

Like his brothers, he didn't want their money. He wanted to build his own life without relying on his parents.

But he'd do it for her. There was no doubt in his mind about that.

"Maybe I can talk to him. Make him see sense…"

"No," she said quickly. "He hates you. He's made that more than clear." She was silent for a moment, like she was trying not to cry. "This is my mess," she told him. "I just need to get some sleep and think things through. I'll figure out what to do next."

She didn't sound so sure. And he wasn't either. He knew first hand what a conniving asshole Trenton could be.

It killed him that he couldn't protect her. That he couldn't make this right for her. She was a good person, she didn't deserve this.

And worse than that, he couldn't help but feel that this was mostly his fault. Everything he touched went to hell. He might not mean to, but he broke people. He'd broken his mom, his family, and now he was breaking her.

The thought was like a knife twisting in his stomach. It made him want to hurl.

"We'll work it out," he told her, his voice low. "We can do it together. You're not alone, not anymore."

She inhaled raggedly. "You don't know how good it is to hear that."

CHAPTER
Twenty-Six

EMERY'S MOM was waiting for her when she came down the stairs. She looked as tired as her daughter, like she hadn't gotten much sleep either.

"Hi." Emery shot her a smile. She needed coffee. And lots of it. She walked past her mom and reached for the pot.

"What was going on between Trenton and Hendrix last night?" her mom asked.

Get straight to it, why don't you? "Nothing," Emery said. "Just some old enmity coming out."

"Well, maybe Hendrix should stay away," her mom said, shaking her head. "I can't believe Trenton came all the way here to see you and our neighbor butted in." She looked at Emery. "Why didn't Trenton come in when he dropped you off?"

Emery tried not to sigh. "I told you, he has work. He needed to get home."

Her mom frowned, like she was completely confused. "I just don't understand why he didn't tell you he was coming. I could have made dinner. I'm sad he didn't come in to say hello."

Yeah, well Emery wasn't. After more recriminations he'd

driven her home, he barely let her get out of the car before he was spinning his wheels and heading away from the farm and back to Charleston.

The last thing she needed was for her mom to know that he'd pretty much threatened to scupper any sale of the farm.

Taking a long sip of the coffee – black, because she needed the energy boost – Emery looked out of the window to see that Hendrix's motorcycle was gone. She felt a little pang. She'd been so happy last night before it all went to hell. So ready to fight the world. And now she felt like she was at sea again.

He'd been sweet, offering to see if he could help pay off the lien. But this was her problem, not his. She wasn't going to depend on somebody else to pull her out of the hole she'd made for herself.

If only she'd said no to Trenton's pleas at the very start.

"The realtor called," her mom told her. "He's already had some interest in the farm. He's setting up the viewings." She gave Emery a half-smile. "And I've looked through all the listings he sent over. I'm going to make some appointments to view three houses in town." She looked at Emery. "You'll come and look at them with me, won't you?"

"Of course."

"Are you sure everything's okay?" her mom asked. "You look pale. Was it seeing Trenton? You must miss him?"

Like she missed a hole in her head. "Everything's fine." She forced a smile on her lips. Because it would be. She was going to make some phone calls. This time to a real estate lawyer. Figure out how to get that damn lien removed. "I'm just a little tired."

Her mom tipped her head to the side, looking concerned. "Are you sure there's nothing troubling you? You seem... I don't know? Distant, I guess. It's okay if you can't come with to see the houses with me. I know I have to do some of these things alone now."

"No, of course I'll come with you." That wasn't even in question.

Her mom nodded. "If there was something wrong, you'd tell me, right? Because you don't have to bottle everything up. I know the past few months have been tough. I haven't been the mother you've needed."

"Mom, you've been fine." Emery put her arms around her mom, holding her tight. "It's me that's all over the place." She forced a smile onto her lips, determined not to let her mom know that inside she was panicking. "It's just that end of summer feeling, you know?"

"I know." Her mom patted her back. "Not long until you go home to Charleston. I'm dreading it, too."

The field was warm and dusty, the sweet smell of the late harvest clinging to the air as his uncle's workers loaded their baskets full of sweetcorn, their silky outer cases golden and ripe. This was the final harvest they'd do in the field. Next month they'd be busy with the corn his uncle grew for animal feed. But Hendrix couldn't think about next month.

He could barely think about tomorrow.

Last night he'd tossed and turned, unable to sleep, unable to do anything apart from think about Trenton's threat to Emery.

No, not a threat. A promise.

It wasn't just that Trenton was an asshole. He'd always known that. It's that he thought he could treat Emery that way. That he could go back on his promise to sign away the lien. And yes, she was the one who'd broken their agreement first, or at least she'd threatened to.

But she didn't deserve this. And he couldn't help but think this was his fault.

The flatbed of the truck was half full with corn cobs. In an hour it would be full, thanks to the eight men picking the long rows of golden ears. Once full, he'd drive it to the barn to be sorted. Some of it would go to his uncle's restaurant – the menu was always locally sourced and in season – and others would go in vegetable boxes they sold to local stores. But the majority was earmarked for the local canning plant to fulfill the contracts his uncle had signed last year.

Next year he'd have his own small harvest, if things worked out as he'd planned. It would be a one-man job for the first few years. He wouldn't have the money to pay anybody else, and he didn't want to grow too fast.

But he couldn't wait to see the first fruits of his labor being sold.

"Did you hear me?" his uncle asked him. He was waiting by the flatbed, holding out a can of ice cold soda. He must have arrived to hand them out while Hendrix was picking corn.

"Sorry. I was a million miles away. What's up?" Hendrix asked him. He took a long, cool sip of soda, but it did nothing to soothe the ache in his soul.

"I asked if everything was okay. You've been distant all morning." He'd barely listened to his uncle when he was briefing him about the harvesting. "You coming down with something?"

"No." He shook his head. Not unless you counted a bad case of annoyance as a sickness. And wishing he could stop the woman he cared about from getting hurt.

"You sure?"

He let out a breath. This was the problem with being a man of few words and a lot of actions. He wasn't great at putting into words what he needed to say. He just needed to do things. To make things right.

To stop Emery from getting hurt.

He let out a breath, looking at his uncle again.

"Actually, I think you might be right. I might be coming

down with something." He ran his hand through his hair. "Would you mind if I disappeared for a few hours? I'll make it up tomorrow. Be here before everybody else."

"Of course." His uncle nodded. "Are you sure there's nothing I can do? I don't like seeing you like this."

He shook his head. "Thanks, but it's not a big deal. I'll be better tomorrow." He gave his uncle a smile.

"No worries. Feel better."

His uncle turned to call out to one of the farmhands, leaving Hendrix to grab his phone from his pocket as he walked back through the dusty field, heading for the edge where he'd left his bike.

He pulled up Google, tapping his big fingers on the screen keyboard as he typed into the search box.

Trenton Montclair. LinkedIn.

And there he was. The smarmy bastard, grinning at the camera like the cat who ate the cream. Strategy Director. Montclair Estates.

It took less than thirty seconds for his second search to bear fruition.

Montclair Estates Charleston Office
500 Kanawha Boulevard E, Suite 1203
Charleston, WV 25301

He slipped his phone back into his pocket, climbing onto his motorcycle. It was time to take a trip to Charleston.

He and Trenton Montclair had unfinished business.

———

Montclair Estates, Charleston division, was housed in a brownstone office building overlooking the Kanawha River. Hendrix parked his truck – it had been too hot to ride his bike in the scorching heat – in the lot beneath the twelve story tower, then walked to the lobby, fully aware of how he must look walking into the pristine building.

He hadn't bothered to change, and a few people turned to stare at the man in his old, battered jeans and black-t-shirt, covered in dust from a morning in the fields.

"Montclair Estates," he told the receptionist.

"Of course. Are they expecting you?"

"Yeah." It wasn't a complete lie. He had to know Hendrix wouldn't take it lying down. "Tell them it's Hendrix Hartson here to see Trenton."

The receptionist picked up her phone and spoke softly into the mouthpiece. She nodded and looked at Hendrix. "Do you have an appointment, Mr. Hartson?"

"No. But Trenton will know what it's about."

She did, pausing as she listened to the reply.

"Mr. Montclair's assistant says to go on up." The receptionist pointed at the bank of four elevators set into the marble wall. "You'll need the twelfth floor."

"Thank you."

When the elevator arrived on the twelfth floor, he stepped out into the sprawling suite, taking a left to the door that led to Montclair Estates.

"Mr. Hartson?" a blonde asked him.

"That's right."

"Mr. Montclair is just through there. He's expecting you."

Hendrix bet he was.

"Can I get you a drink?" Trenton's assistant asked him.

"No, I'm fine." A complete lie. He was parched after a morning's hard work, followed by a two-hour drive, but he needed to get this done. He walked over to the oak door with Trenton's name written in gold on a black plaque at the center, and pushed it open.

Trenton was sitting behind his desk, in front of the floor-to-ceiling windows that overlooked the sparkling river. He had his arms crossed, and didn't bother to stand up as Hendrix walked in.

"What do you want, Hartson?"

Hendrix looked him dead in the eye. There weren't going to be any pleasantries. Not that he wanted any. Until last night he hadn't laid eyes on Trenton for over a decade. Hadn't wanted to. There was still a resemblance to the kid he used to be in high school. His hair was still floppy, though a little shorter. For a second he could remember Trenton as a cocky teen, when he'd pull into the school parking lot in his jet black BMW, rap music thumping from the speakers like he thought he was a badass.

Some people grew up after high school and left childish things behind. Others still clung to the top dog they used to be. He suspected Trenton was the latter.

What the hell did you see in him, Emery?

"I've come to tell you to leave Emery alone." Hendrix murmured. Outside the window he could see an osprey circling high above the river, stalking the prey it would no doubt be swooping down to catch at any moment.

"You don't need to worry about that. I wouldn't touch her with a ten-foot pole now that you've had your greasy hands on her."

Hendrix frowned. God, it really was like being back in high school with this guy. "And you need to release the lien."

Trenton tipped his head to the side, his thin lips pressed together. "I won't be doing that."

"Why not?"

"Because I don't do favors for people who fuck me over."

"Emery hasn't fucked you over. She's done nothing but be nice to you. You asked her to pretend you were still engaged. And she did." Hendrix shook his head. "She's done everything for you that she didn't need to do because she's a good person. She doesn't deserve this."

"And I don't deserve to be cheated on."

"You haven't been cheated on. I know she explained that to you."

"But I don't believe her." Trenton lifted a brow. "I have no idea why you're here. I have nothing to say to you."

"Release the lien," Hendrix said, his voice low.

"Or what?"

The way he said it, like a dare, sent a warning shot through Hendrix's brain. Trenton had a smirk on his face, like he was enjoying this way too much.

"Here's the thing, Hartson. You've always thought you were better than me. Always thought your daddy being a rockstar made you king of the school."

Hendrix sighed. "You're a dipshit. We left school a long, long time ago."

"Yet here you are, trying to get your revenge on me." Trenton ran his thumb across his jaw. "Does she scream out your name like she used to scream mine?"

"Shut the hell up."

"Why? Does it hurt, knowing I had her first?"

"You might have had her, but you didn't keep her. You broke her."

"Oh no. I didn't do that." Trenton finally stood, walking around his desk so he was in front of Hendrix. The contrast between them couldn't have been anymore different. Hendrix in his dirty farm clothes, Trenton in his sharp suit. "I'll tell you what. I'll release the lien, but only if you do something for me."

"What?" Hendrix asked abruptly.

"Break it off with her."

He shook his head. "You really are delusional."

"I'm just protecting myself. My reputation." Trenton lifted a brow. "Of course, there's the other problem," he mused. "The issue of you and Emery having an affair behind my back. I'll have to make it clear she's the reason we split up. I don't expect she'll like that very much, when everybody in Hartson's Creek finds out that you two are cheaters."

"But we're not. You two were split up."

Trenton shrugged. "But nobody knows that. I know Emery. She's been very careful to keep it quiet." He brought his eyes up to Hendrix's, a flash of victory in them. "Emery said something about your mom's charity last night. I've been looking it up today. What a noble endeavour. She sounds so excited about it. Wouldn't it be awful if her family had some kind of scandal right when she was launching it?"

Hendrix's mouth went dry. "You wouldn't do that. She's never done anything to hurt you."

"Of course I wouldn't. Unless I was forced to." He lifted his chin. "The ball's in your court, Hartson. Either you break it off with Emery, or by the end of tomorrow everybody will think you had an affair with my fiancée."

"You think she'll be okay with that? With you making me do this?" Fury rushed through him.

"I don't think we need to tell her." Trenton gave him a pointed stare. "You break things off and I'll sign that lien off on Saturday. Emery and her mom will be free to sell the farm. And if you don't, then I'll make sure the whole of Hartson's Creek knows exactly what you've been doing with my fiancée. It's your choice. Take it or leave it." He grabbed a business card from the silver case on his desk, passing it to Hendrix. "Let me know your decision. I'll do the rest."

When Hendrix had taken the card, he leaned over his desk and pressed a button. "Catherine, Mr. Hartson will be leaving now."

CHAPTER
Twenty-Seven

"IF YOU STARE at that computer for too long your eyes are going to fall out," her mom said, folding her arms across her chest as Emery finally closed the lid of her laptop. She'd spent most of the day emailing and calling lawyers, trying to find somebody who dealt with agricultural property and debts.

Not a single one of them had replied to her messages. Even the phone calls were useless – just promises of a call-back when the lawyer was available. Time moved slowly here, especially in the summer. Nobody was ever in a rush.

Except her.

"You're right," Emery murmured. "I'm going to head out for a walk. Clear my mind."

"No wonder you're all worked up," her mom said, her voice soft. "Seeing Trenton must have reminded you of how much you miss him. But it won't be long now. You'll be going back home soon."

Yeah, she would. And one way or another she'd tell her mom the truth. She'd been so ready to do it last night, before he'd arrived.

It was almost six, and there was no sign of Hendrix when

she walked over to his farm, seeing Frank resting his head on the fence. He let out a bray as she stroked his wiry head.

"Why can't life be easier?" she asked him.

Frank pushed against her hand, clearly wanting more stroking. She covered his head with both hands, petting him, a smile pulling at her lips, when the sound of an engine coming from the main road pulled her attention.

It was Hendrix's truck. Her heart started to speed, because she hadn't seen or heard from him all day. She knew they were busy harvesting, but it felt like a balm to her soul to see him pull into his driveway and climb out of his car.

"Hey." She gave him a wide smile, because yes, her life was a clusterfuck right now, but he was the one good thing in it.

Okay, there were a lot of good things. But this man was definitely the best.

He shoved his hands into his jeans pockets, the action squaring his shoulders, and walked over to where she was cuddling Frank.

"Hi." There was an awkwardness to him. She assumed because her mom could be looking.

"How was your day?" she asked him.

"Long. Yours?"

"Pretty terrible. I spent most of it trying to track down a lawyer to get me out of this lien."

He blinked but said nothing.

"Nobody is calling me back, of course. I hate the way life moves so slowly here sometimes. I just need this to be over."

He nodded, looking strangely thoughtful.

"Hopefully, I'll get to speak to somebody tomorrow," she continued, barely noticing that he wasn't replying. Was barely looking at her, actually. His gaze was set over her shoulder, but his eyes were hazy.

Like he was caught in his own mind.

"Sorry for going on about it, you must be tired. How's the harvest?"

"We were picking sweetcorn." He looked down at the earth, at the work boots he was wearing, covered in brown dust. "Emery…"

"Is everything okay?"

They both spoke at the same time. And she gave a little laugh, but he didn't.

"I just…" He shook his head. "I think we should cool things a bit."

Emery blinked, his words taking a moment to sink in. "Of course. Though I think we're doing pretty good at keeping this thing under wraps."

He shook his head, still not meeting her gaze. "I mean… it's all a little fast, right?" He took a breath, then blew the air out. "You're just out of a relationship. You and I are going to be living hours apart in a few weeks. Maybe we should take a break. Give you a chance to concentrate on getting the farm sold."

Her mouth dropped open. "Are you breaking up with me?" she asked, her voice low. It was impossible to hide the hurt on her face.

He ran his hand through his hair. "I'm not good with words. I told you that."

"Yeah, and you hide behind that," she told him. "If you want to split, say so."

God, this was the last thing she was expecting. And maybe that's why it felt like her chest was being crushed.

"I don't understand," she managed to whisper. "You said you were all in. That you'd be here for me."

He winced at the pain in her voice. "I'll always be here for you," he told her. "Just… as a friend."

"I don't need any more friends, Hendrix," she told him. "I have enough." She shook her head, the realization washing through her. He was ending their relationship because she was too much. Her situation was too much. He wasn't willing to fight for her, and that hurt.

But she still had her pride. It might be the only thing she had left. And she was damned if he was going to take that from her, too. "I guess that's it then," she said, giving Frank one last stroke. The goat nuzzled her like he knew something bad was happening. "I'll see you around."

She turned, managing to stop the tears from falling. She wouldn't give him the satisfaction of seeing that. *One foot in front of the other*, she told herself. *Just keep walking*.

"Emery?" he called out when she was halfway across the lane. The sound of his voice felt like a blanket and a knife.

But she didn't turn back. Didn't stop walking. Sometimes, moving forward was the only thing you could do.

———

He stood there watching her until she reached the gate to her mom's farm. She didn't walk up the steps to the porch, though. Just walked around the back, to where the fields sprawled out with their golden corn. Once she disappeared from view, he let out a long, painful sigh.

It was the right thing to do. He knew that. It was the only way for the lien on her mom's farm to be removed.

You could have told her the truth.

No, he couldn't. He couldn't give her another burden to carry. Another lie to tell. He knew she hated this whole situation. The very least he could give her was the ability to sell her mom's farm and move on.

And he definitely couldn't let Trenton ruin his mom's charity launch. The memory of her face that night when he'd seen her sobbing in the kitchen was enough for him to know that.

They were the two women he loved the most. He knew

that now, even if he'd never told Emery the truth of his feelings. He loved her.

And sometimes love meant making sacrifices. It meant walking away because they deserved better than you could give them.

Even if it felt like every cell inside of him was being crushed right now.

A nudge against his stomach brought him out of his thoughts. Frank was staring up at him with soulful eyes.

"I know, buddy," he murmured. "It's a fucking mess."

Frank tipped his head to the side, like he was agreeing, then pushed against Hendrix's stomach again. Harder this time, like he was annoyed.

No, goats couldn't talk. Nor could they understand the words you said out loud. But from the way Frank was glaring at him right now, maybe he knew that Hendrix had just lost the one person that had made him feel whole in the last few years.

And yeah, he deserved to feel like shit.

Taking his phone out of his pocket, he walked up the steps to his house, finding the number for the man he hated the most.

And when he found it, Hendrix sent a message containing two words.

It's done.

How she managed to keep her tears inside until she made it out to the pasture, Emery would never know. And yet she'd done it, her body stoic, her face still, until she collapsed against the fence and let the tears flow.

Of all the things she'd expected him to say, ending things wasn't one of them. She was blindsided, unable to breathe. And for a moment all she could do was sob. Why was this so painful? It felt a million times worse than when she'd broken up with Trenton.

Because he made you believe in him. And for the first time in forever you didn't feel so alone.

She pulled out her phone. It was almost seven. Which meant it was after midnight in Europe where Maisie was.

She couldn't call her. But she sent her a message, anyway. Hopefully, her friend would see it in the morning.

Hendrix ended things between us. Can you call me when you wake up? – Emery

She hit send, knowing that she'd still be awake in the middle of the night when Maisie woke.

Before she could put her phone away it rang. For a second her heart did a little twist, knowing that her friend was still awake to hear her tales of woe. But then she saw the name on her phone.

Trenton Montclair.

Her stomach twisted. What the hell did he want?

"What?" She didn't bother to try to sound nice.

"Emery." His voice was soft. "I called to apologize."

She blinked. Of all the things he could have said, she wasn't expecting that. He never apologized. He didn't do it after she found the dating app on his phone, nor after she ended their relationship.

"Apologize for what?" Her voice was thick. Half her mind was still on the farm opposite her mom's. And the man who lived inside it.

"For being so rash last night. I was hurt." He exhaled heavily. "And I said some things I shouldn't have."

"Like you were going to ruin my life?"

"I would never do that. I know things between us… were

messy. But we still spent years together. You'll always be part of my heart. And I shouldn't have treated you like that."

"No you shouldn't have."

"I'll be back in town on Saturday," he said. "My parents will be back from their cruise. I'll be telling them about out breakup. And then I will release the lien."

"You will?" She frowned.

"You have my word. There's just one thing I'd like you to do."

Oh, here we go. She rolled her eyes, knowing she never should have answered the damn phone.

"Will you come with me?" he asked her. "I'd like you to be there. Give everybody some closure."

"Will they even want to see me?" She loved his dad. But his mom, well not so much. He was a mommy's boy, after all, and they both knew it.

"I just think, after all this time, it will be good for us to stand as a team. One last time. Before we both walk away."

"I don't know…"

"Think about it," he suggested. "I can sign the lien documents at the same time. Kill two birds with one stone."

"Okay. I'll think about it."

"Thank you." He paused for a second. "Let me know before Saturday."

"I will."

CHAPTER
Twenty-Eight

"WHAT A DICK," Maisie said the next morning, after Emery told her everything that had happened in the past few days. "Actually, scratch that. What dicks, because it sounds like the two of them are as bad as the other."

Emery had spent most of last night lying on her bed, wide awake and staring at the ceiling, trying to figure out what had gone wrong. Only a few days ago she'd been on top of the world. Taking control of her life. Moving forward.

And now she felt like she was stuck. More than that, she felt rejected.

Like she wasn't good enough to fight for. And that hurt really bad.

Tears pooled in her eyes and she tried to blink them away, because she was already sick of crying. She'd spent last night boomeranging between anger and despair, trying to cry quietly so her mom wouldn't hear.

This morning she just felt wrung out. She had no energy, no push. She wanted to lie on this bed forever.

"So when are you going to tell Trenton you're not going to his parents?" Maisie asked her.

"I'm not. I've decided to go."

"What?" Maisie sounded appalled. "Why would you do anything that asshole asks you to do?"

"I'm not doing it for him. I'm doing it for me. I figure that if I'm there, he'll actually tell them. And this way I can make sure he doesn't lay all the blame at my feet." Because the one thing she knew was that Trenton was a coward at heart. He didn't like upsetting the status quo and he hated emotions.

And now she'd discovered that Hendrix was just as much of a coward. And that was like a knife to her heart.

"I'm going to go, watch him tell his parents, then make sure he signs off the lien. That way I know everything is done. I can move forward, get this house sold and then come back to work."

"I wish I was there to help," Maisie told her.

"You'll be home soon." That was the one bright light in the darkness.

"I can't wait to see you." Maisie took a long breath. "I'm sorry, too, though."

"What do you have to be sorry about?"

"I wish I'd never given you that list. Then you wouldn't be going through this." Maisie sighed.

"I'm glad you gave me the list. It made me feel... I don't know... alive. Like I'm finally able to take control of my future." Emery swallowed down the anxiety she felt about what that future would look like. Yes, right now she was in a bad way. But she still had hope.

That was something, wasn't it?

"Anyway, I never did complete the list," Emery reminded her.

"When I get home we are definitely staying up all night talking," Maisie promised her. "Just not on a school night. Listen, I have to go. Call me once everything is done with Trenton. Let me know if you need me to come and chop his balls off."

"I will." Not the ball-chopping part, though. Truth was,

she'd been over wishing him pain for a while. She was over *him*.

The man living in the farmhouse opposite her mom's, though? She wasn't sure she'd be over him for a long, long time.

And that hurt more than she could say.

———

Two days. That's how long it had been since he'd told Emery it was over. A couple of times he'd seen her in her front yard, collecting eggs or making phone calls. But as soon as she'd seen him looking, she'd turned away, refusing to meet his gaze, let alone return the wave he'd give her.

He'd done the right thing. He knew that much. His chest felt tight at the way she'd looked so broken when he'd ended it. But she would have been more broken if her ex had done what he threatened and never signed off the lien.

Or if he'd spread the kind of gossip that Hendrix knew he could. The type that would paint Emery as a cheater and make everybody in town treat her differently.

He knew what it felt like for everybody to assume the worst of you. He'd learned how to deal with it. But Emery? She never could.

And she shouldn't have to.

Maybe that's why he wasn't prepared to see her out on the lane when he rode home from work. She must have been taking a walk, because she was in the middle of the rocky, white road, wearing a pair of shorts and a tank, her hair tied back in a bun.

He came to a stop, his chest feeling tight at the sight of her. There was no smile on her face, no life in her eyes.

You did that.

He hated the way she wouldn't meet his gaze.

"How are you?" he asked her softly, putting his foot down

on the road to balance himself. He didn't bother getting off the bike. She looked like she was ready to run away from him, anyway.

Can you blame her?

No, he couldn't. He'd spent a lifetime running away from himself, after all.

"Fine." She nodded, keeping her chin high. "You?"

Feeling like shit without you. "All good. We finished the sweetcorn harvest." And it had been backbreaking work. Like he'd promised his uncle, he'd gotten there earlier than anybody else, and worked after the rest of the farmhands had gone home every evening.

If he was honest, it was mostly to avoid coming home and having to sit in his empty house, missing her.

"How's the sale going?" he asked her. After he sent the message to Trenton, he'd gotten a reply the next day.

I'll keep my end of the deal. – Montclair

"It's fine. We've had a few people interested. It'll be easier once the lien is removed this weekend."

"It's being taken care of?" Dammit, he had to go there. He couldn't stop himself. Yes, he'd pulled away but he still wanted to know everything about this woman.

"Do you care?" she asked him. She was so clearly trying not to let him see she was hurt. And it was killing him. He wished she'd just shout at him, rip into him about how much of an ass he was. All those things he could take. Hell, he could secretly seethe because he was doing this for her own good. For his mom's good.

And yes, he was playing the martyr, but what choice did he have? He couldn't be responsible for them losing to that asshole.

But the way this woman was keeping her pride? That was like torture.

"Of course I care," he told her.

"Because you want me to leave?" she asked. "That'll make

things easier for you, won't it? When you won't have to look out of your window and see me." She let out a long breath, not meeting his eye. "Well, you don't have to worry. I'm taking care of everything. As soon as I meet with Trenton's parents and get that lien removed, I'm packing my things and getting out of here."

Wait. What? "You're meeting with Trenton's parents?"

"That's what I just said."

"Why?"

Her mouth dropped open. "Excuse me, I don't know if you got the memo, but once you end things with a woman you don't get to ask them questions anymore."

"I still care about you," he told her, his voice low.

"Oh, no." She shook her head wildly. "You don't get to play that card. You don't get to pretend you care when you broke my damn heart into tiny pieces just days ago." Her voice cracked, and it killed him. "Now excuse me, I have things to do. And they don't involve looking backward."

She turned to walk away, but he couldn't let her. He couldn't let this be it. There was no way he could make things better, he knew that. Not without making things worse for her. But it still killed him to see her like this.

He reached for her arm, shocked as ever at the softness of her skin. Her wrist was warm from the sun's rays, but so damn delicate he could more than circle it with his fingers.

"Emery…"

"What?" She lifted her eyes to him. He could see the tears reflecting there.

Tears he'd caused.

"I just… I want you to be happy. That's all. You're a good person. You deserve that."

She wrenched her wrist away from him. "But clearly not good enough," she told him before she walked away, leaving him standing in the dusty lane, wishing he knew how to make things right.

"Is there something wrong with your phone?" Pres asked him, as Hendrix climbed off his motorcycle. It was Friday evening and he was beyond exhausted. He'd been starting work right after dawn and had stayed in the fields long after all the other workers had left for the evening. In the end his uncle had chased him out, telling him in no uncertain terms it was time to leave the bailing alone.

But home was the one place he didn't want to be.

Especially not when his brother was outside his cottage waiting for him, having let himself inside to grab a beer. Pres had made himself completely at home. He was sitting on the porch, Frank curled up at his feet, like he was settling in for the long haul.

"I've been busy." Hendrix walked up the steps. Frank stood to greet him, nuzzling his chest.

"Just a quick message to let us know you're alive would have helped," Pres told him.

Stroking Frank's maw, Hendrix looked at his brother. "It's harvest time," he pointed out. "Do I bother you when you're neck deep in construction work? And anyway, you know I'm alive. Uncle Logan would have told you if I wasn't."

Pres sighed. "Okay, so mom sent me over."

And there it was, the crux of the matter. "You can tell her I'm fine."

"But you're not. And she needs some papers signed for the charity."

"What kind of papers?"

Pres rolled his eyes. "I don't know, man. Maybe if you answered her damn calls you'd know." His brother stood and looked Hendrix right in the eye. "What's with this stupid rollercoaster, anyway? You've been fine for weeks. More than fine, happy. Now you're doing your usual bullshit and disappearing in full sight."

"I'm working," Hendrix snipped back, annoyance rushing through him. "I told you that."

"And I wouldn't care if you were just ignoring me. But mom? That's a low blow, even for you." Pres shook his head. "You're a real asshole sometimes."

Hendrix's mouth dropped open. "Seriously?" His brother had no idea what he was going through. With his perfect wife and beautiful kids, why would he?

But to accuse him of trying to hurt their mom when all he was trying to do was protect her? Well, fuck that.

"Just call her." Pres looked him straight in the eye.

"Since when do you get off telling me what to do?" Hendrix asked him.

"I'll stop when you start doing the right thing." Pres shook his head.

The problem was, he was doing exactly that. He'd just never expected to feel so bad about it. Hendrix let out a deep sigh. He didn't need this from his brother, not now.

"Shit, man, what's going on with you?" Pres asked him. "You look... I don't know... beaten."

"Nothing. There's nothing going on with me." Automatically, Hendrix glanced across the road. He hadn't seen Emery since she walked away crying from him two days earlier. He'd made sure of it. Leaving early, arriving home late, locking himself up in between. This wasn't living, this was surviving.

It was enduring the worst days of his life. Bar none.

Pres let out a breath. "I'm not the best at talking... and absolutely not the best at giving advice."

"Then don't."

Pres put his hand up. "But I'm gonna do it, anyway. Because you're my little brother and I love you. But also because Mom worries about you way too much, and I'll do whatever it takes to make her life easier."

"Would you give up everything to make her life easier?" Hendrix asked him suddenly.

Pres blinked at his question. "I… ah…" He ran his hand through his hair. "I don't know."

"Let me put it this way. Would you give up everything to make Delilah's life easier?"

Pres frowned. "Of course I would. You know that."

"Then don't question me about what I'd do for Mom. I'd do anything, you know that, right?"

Pres stared at him for a long minute. "Is there something I'm missing?"

The door to Emery's mom's farmhouse opened, and Emery stepped out. Seeing her for the first time in a couple of days felt like a size ten work boot to his gut. She stopped suddenly, seeing Hendrix and his brother on his porch, then turned on her heel and walked back inside, closing the door behind her.

For a second Pres was silent. It was clear he'd seen her from the expression on his face.

He looked at Hendrix, then back at Emery's house.

"Is there something going on between you two?" he asked Hendrix.

Hendrix swallowed. "No."

But Pres wasn't buying it. "She walked outside then walked right back in when she saw you. I've never seen anything quite so obvious."

"There's nothing going on," Hendrix said stubbornly.

"But there was, huh?"

He opened his mouth. Then closed it again.

"Wasn't there?" Pres asked.

"It's complicated," Hendrix told him.

"How complicated?"

"The kind of complicated where I don't even know where to start," Hendrix told him, a wave of dizziness washing over him. "And I'm so damn tired. I haven't slept in days. I haven't done anything but work in the fields and if I don't get inside and lie down I think I might collapse."

Pres stared at him. "Okay. Go inside and get some sleep. But come to Mom's tomorrow. You can sign those papers. We can talk." His brother's voice was soft, for once. And yeah, maybe that's what he needed.

A friend. A brother. Somebody who understood that he'd given up the one woman he loved to make sure she and his mom had the future they deserved.

CHAPTER
Twenty-Nine

"OH MY GOODNESS," his mom said the next day when he arrived at his parent's ranch at the edge of town. "Pres was right. You do look tired." She took Hendrix's hand in her own. "You need to slow down, sweetheart. I'm worried about you."

"You don't need to worry. I told you that." He forced a smile onto his lips, following her inside the house he'd grown up in.

He and his brothers had experienced a privileged upbringing, no matter how much their parents tried to keep things real. Sure, they'd gone to public school, had to work for their allowances, and were never allowed to slack off from helping out around the house, but not many kids got to grow up in a sprawling ranch complete with its own recording studio at the back.

"Where's Dad?" he asked when they made it to the kitchen at the back of the house.

"Fiddling about in the studio. He'll be in soon. Coffee?" his mom asked.

"Yes, please."

For a second they were both silent as she grabbed two

mugs from the cupboard and started up the machine their dad had bought her for Christmas. It was a bean to cup model, and she loved it.

"Pres said you have something you need me to sign," Hendrix reminded her when she passed him his cup. Black, no cream or sugar. He took a long sip, enjoying the hit.

He'd left home early again this morning. Heading to the farm before coming here. Sure, he told himself it was because he was busy, but there was also the fact that the thought of watching Emery go to Trenton's parents today would kill him.

He wanted to protect her. Wanted to run over and tell her to be careful, to watch out for that devious asshole.

But why would she listen? Hendrix was the one who'd hurt her more than anybody. She'd made that clear.

The only person he should be protecting her from was himself.

His mom pulled out a brown envelope, passing it over to him. "You'll be a signatory on the charity bank account along with me, your dad, and your brothers."

Hendrix took the pen she offered and signed his name on the line, dating below it. She smiled softly at him and put the form back into the envelope.

"So…" She let out a breath.

"So." He lifted a brow.

"Emery Reed…"

She was really going there.

"Mom, we don't have to talk about this. Whatever you saw, it's dealt with. Over and done. I promise I won't do anything else to embarrass you."

Her brows pinched. "That wasn't what I was going to say."

"It wasn't?"

She shook her head. "No. I was going to apologize. I was wrong to say anything to you about her at all. What you do in the privacy of your own home is your business, not mine. I've been feeling terrible about it ever since I left your place." She let out a breath. "I didn't mean to judge you."

"Maybe you were right to judge me," he told her.

"So you and Emery? You're… a thing?"

"Not anymore."

"Because she's engaged?"

He winced at the mention of that.

And fuck it, after today all of Hartson's Creek would know the truth. "She's not engaged. She's broken up with him. Has been for a while, just not publicly." He winced. "It's a mess."

Her mom looked at him with soft eyes. "I've got time to listen if you have time to talk."

"It's okay. It's all over, anyway."

"You don't look too happy about that," she said softly.

He frowned. Wasn't that the understatement of the year? "I just keep messing things up, you know? Hurting the people I love." He let out a breath. "You. Dad. Emery…"

His mom's face softened. "You love her," she said. Not as a question but as a confirmation of the truth. She took his hand. "You look so sad. Please talk to me. Let me help."

So he did. And it hurt, admitting to his mom who he adored what a mess he'd made. Admitting about his bad choices, about the pain he'd caused. The damn agreement he made with Trenton Montclair not to blast his relationship with Emery all over town.

And in consequence, losing the one woman that meant everything to him.

No, not losing. He pushed her. He pushed her so hard he wasn't sure she'd ever stop running away from him.

And when he was talked out, his mom let out a long, soft sigh.

"You've got it all wrong," she told him. "You don't have to protect me. That's not your job. It's never been your job. I'm your parent. It has always been my job to protect you." She shook her head, her eyes shining. "That day you saw me crying. You shouldn't have seen that. But as a mom I've smiled about you three boys a hundred times more than I've cried over you."

"I don't want him to ruin the charity launch for you. Not after everything you've put into it," Hendrix told her.

"I understand, sweetheart, I do. But he won't. I'll speak to our publicist. They'll make sure it's dealt with. That's what publicists are for." She leaned forward, cupping his face with her hands. "Please tell me you didn't ruin this relationship to protect me?"

"For you and for her. He agreed to release the lien on her mom's farm if I backed away."

"And that's what she wanted too?" his mom asked.

"I don't know. I didn't ask her."

His mom winced. "Oh, honey…"

"I didn't want to put her in that position. It was for the best…" Or at least that's what he kept telling himself.

His blood turned cold. He hadn't even asked her. He hadn't given her the chance to say what she thought.

He'd just made the decision for both of them. Decided to be a martyr, to lose the thing he loved most, because it was better than watching the woman he loved lose her home.

Fuck. He'd made a mistake. No, more than a mistake, he'd made the biggest fucking wrong decision of his life.

"Mom…"

"You need to go." She nodded. "Of course you do." She smiled at him softly. "Now you go and get your girl, and do whatever it takes to win her back."

Well, here went nothing. Emery took a deep breath, and

climbed out of her car, trying not to show her dismay at Trenton waiting for her in his parent's driveway.

He'd wanted to pick her up, but she was done sitting in the passenger seat where that man was concerned. Today was about getting what she wanted and moving on.

Even if that meant moving on without Hendrix. That thought made her heart twinge.

"What's that?" Trenton asked, a frown in his voice.

"What's what?"

"That thing on your ankle." He pointed at her tattoo. It had healed so well she'd almost forgotten it was there. And she certainly wasn't planning on covering it up for him.

"None of your business," she told him. "Do you have that form for me?"

"It's here." He lifted up a manilla envelope. "But I need you to sign something first."

"You never mentioned anything about that." She frowned, sensing a trap. Why did this man never make things easy?

"Yes, well, I'm just covering myself." He pulled out a form. "It's a simple NDA. You agree not to tell anybody about our arrangement this summer, and I'll rescind my lien on your mom's farm."

She took the paper he was holding out. "You want me to keep quiet about when and why we actually split up?"

"Of course. Otherwise, what's stopping you from dragging my name through the dirt as soon as you sell the farm? I have to protect my reputation in this time of social media. Reputation is everything in my business. So sign the paper and you get everything you want."

"I wouldn't drag your name through the dirt. I don't want anything to do with you." She glared at him. "I just want this to be over."

"Then sign the NDA, Emery." He gave her a supercilious smile.

"I'll sign it after you've told your parents about us. Not before." Because no, she wasn't giving up her power to this man. Not anymore. She'd come too far to let him browbeat her again.

She'd worked too hard on herself this summer to let that happen. "Now, are we going inside or what?"

Looking furious, Trenton opened his mouth to answer her, but his voice was drowned out by the sound of an engine behind them.

No, not an engine. A bike. The kind of dirt bike that workers use to travel their farms and check on irrigations and errant goats and skinny dippers whose clothes were stolen.

And when she turned, her heart skipped a beat, because it was Hendrix, riding toward them like some kind of messed up knight in no armor, his jaw tight as he came to a stop at the end of Trenton's parents' driveway.

He kicked the stand out and climbed off his bike, striding toward her like he meant business.

It was only when he was a couple of yards away that she remembered she was mad at him.

No, furious.

"What are you doing here?" she asked him.

He stopped, his warm, soft eyes meeting hers. And yes, she felt that ache deep inside of her. The one that wouldn't disappear, no matter how hard she tried to tell herself he was an asshole and she hated him.

"I'm here to beg you to forgive me."

"Get out of here," Trenton shouted at him. "This is private property."

But Hendrix didn't move. Didn't stop looking at her.

She couldn't stop looking at him, either.

She was confused. He'd made it so clear she wasn't worth fighting for.

But now he was here. And he looked like he wanted to fight.

"Excuse me, did you hear me?" Trenton strode forward,

his eyes flashing as he glared at Hendrix. "You need to leave. Before I call the cops."

"Do what you have to do," Hendrix murmured, still staring at Emery. "Please, can we talk?"

Her head said no. He'd hurt her so much. But her heart wasn't listening. "Okay."

He nodded. "I need you to know that I'm in love with you. I've been an idiot. I pushed you away because I thought I was being noble, but now I realize I was just protecting myself."

"Noble?" she whispered. "How was pushing me away noble?"

Hendrix looked so vulnerable it touched her. She'd never seen him more attractive. Or been more confused.

"I went to see Trenton," he told her. "After he caught us. I went to ask him to release the lien and let you go."

She frowned. "What? Why didn't you tell me?" She turned to look at Trenton. "Is this true?"

Trenton threw up his hands. "I'm done with this. She's delusional. You both are."

"It's true," Hendrix told her. "And he told me he'd only do it if I broke things off with you." He lifted a brow. "He also added in a few threats about ruining your reputation and my mom's charity by telling everybody you'd been cheating on him."

"You threatened that?" She glared at Trenton.

"He's lying."

"I'm not, Em." Hendrix stepped forward. He was only a couple of feet away now. "Why would I lie? I was the idiot for agreeing to it. I never should have. I should have come to you. I should have talked to you. I had this stupid idea that if I did it my way, I'd be protecting you."

"You hurt me," she told him.

"I know. I know that and I hate it."

She let out a ragged breath, trying to process what he was

telling her. He'd gone all the way to Charleston to try to save her mom's farm sale. He'd agreed to end things so she could be free of the lien.

"I thought I was too much for you," she whispered.

"You were never too much," Hendrix told her. "You never could be. You're everything."

"Then why didn't you say something to me?" she asked him.

"Because I'm an idiot. I should have talked to you, not made a decision without running it past you. And if you can find it in yourself to forgive me, I promise you I'll never ever do that again. I'll never take away your agency, Emery. I'll never assume that I know best. Because I think we both know that I don't."

The way he said it made her heart tighten. He got it. He'd apologized. And no, it wasn't going to make the past few days of heartache disappear. But it was a good start.

"I've had enough of this," Trenton said, reaching for her arm. "We're going inside, we're telling my parents, and if you're lucky and you sign the NDA, I'll sign that fucking lien away."

"What's all the shouting about, son?" The front door opened to reveal Trenton's dad standing there, his face bronzed from his long cruise, his white hair stained gold by the blaring rays of the hot summer sun. His wife joined him, frowning as she saw the three of them in her driveway.

"Mom, Dad, go inside," he said.

Ignoring him, Emery smiled softly at Hendrix, then turned to walk up the steps to the Montclair's front door.

"Hi, welcome home. Did you have a lovely cruise?" she asked them.

"Oh, yes." Trenton's mom nodded. "But what's happening out here? Is everything okay?"

Emery's stomach twisted as she looked at them both. She'd known them since she was a teenager. Yes, they weren't always the closest, but she didn't mean them any harm.

They hadn't done her any, after all. Unlike their son.

"I'm glad you had a good time. I just wanted to come see you one last time. And to say thank you for all your kindness over the years," she told them.

"What?" His dad frowned. "What does that mean?"

"Trenton and I broke up. Months ago. We agreed to tell you once you were back from your cruise, because we didn't want to ruin your trip," Emery told them, figuring it was better to rip the bandaid off rather than gently pull it. The truth, the whole truth and nothing but the truth. "Our engagement is over, but we're both okay, and that's all that matters, right?"

"Right..." Trenton's dad said uncertainly, looking from her to his son.

"So I'll leave you three to talk." She took a step back, ignoring the dirty look that Trenton was shooting at her. "Oh, Trenton, don't forget to give me that release."

"What?" Trenton asked.

"Trenton has been very kind," she told his parents, lying through her teeth. "He loaned my mom some money when she was at her lowest. She wants to pay him back, but he has to release the lien so she can sell the house to have the money."

"Oh, that *was* very kind of you," his mom told Trenton. She looked proud.

Yes, it was a gamble. She wasn't certain he'd go through with it. But it was a risk worth taking. She knew enough about her ex to know he wouldn't want to lose face in front of his parents.

For a second, Trenton said nothing. But then she could see it sinking in. He'd lost. She'd won. Just by staying true to herself. He pulled the legal form from the manilla envelope and passed it to her.

And there it was. Signed and dated and notarized. She felt almost sick with relief as she stared at it.

"Thank you," she said softly. Trenton didn't reply. But maybe she didn't need him to. He was her past, and she was so ready to leave that behind.

It was time to face her future. Just as soon as she'd done one more thing.

CHAPTER
Thirty

HENDRIX WAS WAITING for her as she walked down the steps, leaving Trenton talking to his parents. She reminded him of that little girl in the meme, the one who is walking away while the world is burning behind her.

She was beautiful. And strong. And he didn't deserve her. But damn, he wanted to try.

"You okay?" he asked her.

She nodded. "I need to get this filed," she said, her voice low as she lifted the signed document Trenton had given her. "But first of all I need to talk to my mom. You know how news spreads around here."

"Of course." He wouldn't expect anything else of her. "Are you okay to drive? I'll follow you."

She nodded, giving him a weak smile. She looked as tired as he'd felt all week. "Yeah, I think so."

He resisted pulling her into her arms even though every cell in his body wanted it. Instead, he walked her to her car, and opened the driver's door for her, closing it once she was safely inside. He watched Trenton walk into his parents' house and close the front door behind them, as Emery started her engine up.

A moment later he was on his motorcycle. Like he promised, he let Emery lead, following behind her like some kind of secret service agent keeping her safe. Not that she needed it.

She'd been so strong back there. She was breathtaking.

He was still kicking himself for not being truthful with her from the start.

They were about a mile away from the farm when she turned on her blinker and pulled over to the side, coming to a stop at the edge of the country road. He pulled up behind her, frowning.

"Everything okay?" he called out, climbing off his bike as she opened her door.

She nodded. "I'm just... can you pick the car up later?"

"You planning on walking home?"

Emery shook her head, letting her gaze meet his. "Can I ride with you?"

She could do whatever the hell she wanted as far as he was concerned.

"I don't have a helmet," he realized.

"I know." She nodded. "But I need to be on the back of your bike right now."

"Okay."

He got back on his bike, trying not to react as she climbed on behind him, her body warm against his back. She fitted against him like they were made for each other, her arms wrapping around him, her head against his spine.

It warmed him more than he could say that she was letting him take the strain right now. There were times for words and there were times for actions. She was better with the former and he was always so much more at ease with the latter.

But right now her actions were telling him that he had some hope. For their future together.

It was only a couple of minutes before he turned onto the

lane leading to their farms. She kept her tight hold on him, like she needed this closeness as much as he did.

And when they reached the offshoot that housed their farms, he slowed down to a stop, turning to look at her.

"You want me to pull up outside your place or mine? Or let you off here?" he asked her.

Because if he pulled up outside hers, and her mom saw her climbing off his bike, she'd have a thousand questions. He needed to know that Emery was ready to answer them.

Their eyes caught for a moment. God, she was beautiful.

"Mine," she said.

There was a stubbornness in her jaw that warmed him. She might have just gone ten rounds in the ring with her ex, but she was ready to face her mom, too.

"Let's do it."

Her arms tightened around his waist as he took a right into her mom's drive, stopping next to her steps, cutting the engine and kicking out the stand. He climbed off, turning to look at the woman he loved sitting on his bike, her hair flowing down her shoulders, her eyes shining.

Then he helped her off, his hands warm and strong on her waist, and she took a long breath in as he kept them there.

"Emery?" her mom said, opening the front door, looking confused when she saw her daughter standing in Hendrix's arms. "What's going on? Where's Trenton?"

Emery frowned at the mention of his name. Like she was trying to make a point, she put her hand in Hendrix's, squeezing it tight. "You're coming in with me, right?" she asked him.

"I wouldn't have it any other way."

"Emery? What's going on?" Her mom sounded almost frantic.

"It's a long story," Emery told her. "Can we come inside? And maybe get some sweet tea?"

"Him too?" Her mom asked, frowning at Hendrix.

Emery winced at her mom's tone. "Can you at least call the man I love by his name?" Emery said.

And for a second, there was complete silence. Her words felt like a mac truck hitting his chest. But in a good way.

The best of ways.

She loved him. After all he'd done. He didn't deserve it, but he would take it.

He'd work so damn hard every day to be the man who deserved her.

"The man loves you, too," he said, his eyes meeting Emery's. Her lips parted as she exhaled softly.

There were tears in her eyes.

Emery's mom was still staring at them, completely confused.

"Mom, I know this is a shock. There's a lot I have to explain to you and I will," Emery promised. "But you need to know that Hendrix is a good man and I'd like you to treat him that way."

Her mom looked from her to Hendrix, like she wasn't sure what to do next. "But Trenton is your fiancé. How can you be in love with another man?"

"We split up a while ago. I'll explain it all to you, but I assume you prefer not to do it out here."

Her mom nodded, her sense of hospitality overriding her confusion. "Very well." She looked at Hendrix. "Please come in."

The corner of his mouth lifted. "With pleasure."

CHAPTER
Thirty-One

IT WAS ALMOST EIGHT. It had taken more than an hour this afternoon for Emery to explain everything to her mom, telling her the truth, the whole truth, and nothing but the truth.

She hadn't held back. Hadn't tried to sugar coat that she'd been as wrong to hide the end of her engagement from her mom as Hendrix had been to hide Trenton's demands from her. One thing she'd learned is that being underestimated by those you love is the most upsetting thing of all.

There had been tears, because this was all new for her mom. And she was desperately upset that Emery had gone through so much alone.

But there was also a new dynamic between them. One that could only come from being completely truthful and open. They were mother and daughter but they were also equals.

And it felt good.

Hendrix had left in the late afternoon to give his family a heads up that the news about Emery and him might spread through town very soon, and then to check the farm, feed and water Frank, and to give Emery and her mom some space.

But now her mom was heading up to bed, claiming she was exhausted, and Emery was walking over to Hendrix's house, where he was waiting for her with two bottles of ice cold beer in his hands.

She took one from him. "I needed this," she said, smiling at him.

"I thought you might." He pulled her down next to him on the swing, and she was trying really hard not to remember what they'd done that night when it was just the two of them.

"Your mom okay?" he murmured.

"Getting there. She took it better than I thought she would," Emery mused, resting her head on Hendrix's shoulder. "I underestimated her. And that was wrong." She looked at him, her brows dipped. "I made so many mistakes…"

"And you made so many good decisions, too. You're a good daughter to her. You're a good person." He kissed the top of her brow and it sent a shiver down her spine. "You only did what you did because you love her."

"How about you?" she murmured.

He tipped his head to the side. "Are you asking me if I did what I did because I love you?"

Her chest tightened. Hearing him say it again felt like the sun warming her skin.

"You spent an hour with me trying to explain to my mom all about my bad decisions. If that's not love, I don't know what is."

He chuckled. "You don't get it do you?" he asked her.

"Get what?"

He tucked his finger under her chin, lifting it up until her lips were a breath away from his. "That I'd do anything for you. Fight dragons, put on armor. Chase goats that steal your underwear."

"Are you calling my mom a dragon?" she teased, because he wasn't that far off.

"I'm just telling you that you don't have to worry. It's not a chore trying to win you over. I'm going to keep doing it every day of my life."

Her breath caught. "I thought you said you weren't good with words."

"Maybe I'm trying to change that, too." He brushed his warm lips against hers. "Tell me, what you said earlier. Is it true?"

"Which part?" she asked, trying to ignore the way her heart was pounding as he slid his arms down her sides to hold her waist. His hands were strong, she could feel the warmth of him through the thin fabric separating his skin and hers.

"The part about loving me."

"Yes." She nodded, because she'd promised herself she'd tell the truth in all things. "I know it feels so soon, and maybe it is too soon for you. And I can shut up about it if you want me to. But yes, I love you. I'm in love with you." She let out a long breath. "And now I wish I'd chosen a better…"

Before she could finish her sentence, Hendrix was lifting her against him, until she was straddling his legs, her body facing his. He pressed his mouth against hers, his lips moving with hers, like he was so desperate to kiss her that he had no idea how to stop.

She had no idea either. Truth was, she didn't want it to stop. Didn't want to ever stop kissing this man who was willing to fight dragons and chase goats for her. She rocked her body against his, and he let out a guttural groan, his excitement growing beneath her as they plundered each other's mouths.

When he pulled away, Hendrix was smiling at her like she was the best thing that ever happened to him. And she was grinning right back, because she knew *he* was.

He cupped her cheeks with his hands, his lips parted, his

eyes on hers. "Emery Reed, I love you so damn much. You're my first thought in the morning and my last thought at night. I have no idea what I did to deserve you, but I can promise you I'll never take your love for granted. Not now or ever."

As declarations went, it was pretty breathtaking. Enough for her to grab his face between her soft palms and start kissing him again, her body hot against his as she showed him just how happy he made her. He held her tight, kissing her back, murmuring her name as her fingers tangled into his hair, her nails scraping his scalp.

"You think your mom likes me enough for me to stay over tonight?" he asked her, once they ran out of breath and had to part.

"Unless you have a death wish, I'd probably say no." She wrinkled her nose, leaning up to kiss him again because damn, this man sent her pulse soaring.

"Then you're going to have to stay at my place," he said. "There's that matter of your list."

"My list?" She frowned, looking confused.

"You didn't complete it, remember? There's one more item left."

She wasn't sure why she was so happy that he remembered her list. She should have known that he would. He'd been there since the beginning – the skinny dipping disaster – and all through her attempts to find herself completing Maisie's challenges.

"Staying up talking all night," she murmured.

He grinned at her. "We can talk. But there are other things that can keep us awake too. I have plans for you."

"We've already ticked that item off," she said.

"Wait, what? Sleeping with me was on the list? You never said that."

She shook her head. "It's a long story. Maisie is a pain in the ass sometimes."

Hendrix kissed her softly. "I'm looking forward to meeting her."

"Not as much as she's looking forward to meeting you." Emery grinned, because Maisie had screamed with the latest update she'd given her. "Now this talking thing. Can it start later? Because I have other plans for you first."

The words were barely out of her lips before he was scooping her up from the swing and carrying her inside, because he was always so damn impatient. She started to laugh as he kicked the front door open. Frank lifted his head up from his favorite spot at the corner of the house, seeking out the cause of the noise that had awoken him.

Seeing it was them, he laid back down and closed his eyes again.

Hendrix headed straight for his bedroom, laying her on his bed and stepping back, like he was trying to take everything in.

"Don't move," he murmured, as she tried to sit up to ask him what the delay was for. "I just need to take this in."

"What?" She smiled, confused.

"Emery Reed on my bed. Publicly unengaged. Single."

"Not single," she whispered. "I'm yours now, remember?"

"I remember," he said roughly, leaning down to take her mouth with his. "And I'm never gonna forget it."

"Don't look so nervous," Hendrix told Emery the next weekend, as they drove in his truck to officially meet his family. To be fair, he'd struggled to hold them all at bay for the last seven days. Word had spread fast around the Hartson clan after he'd called his mom to let her know what had happened on Saturday, and he'd spent the last week being grilled by them all, desperate to know when they'd officially get to meet the woman who'd managed to tame him.

Or in some of their cases 're-meet' her. Because his mom was determined to make a good impression this time.

"What if they don't like me?" Emery asked him, looking anxious as she smoothed down her skirt. "They must have heard the rumors, after all."

Because yes, there had been some gossip going around town that she had been cheating on Trenton all summer.

But the Hartson network had hit back. As soon as she heard the whispers, Hendrix's mom had launched into action. She'd pulled in all her best grapevine users – including his sisters-in-law, Kate and Cassie, along with his aunts, uncles, and of course, his brothers who could never keep their mouths shut.

Suddenly all of Hartson's Creek knew that Trenton had tried to blackmail Emery, and she and Hendrix were in love.

It was one way to introduce a new relationship, that was for sure. And Emery clearly hated the extra attention they were getting.

"It'll be yesterday's news soon enough," he told her. "We just have to ride it out. And anyway, they don't believe the rumors. You know that. My mom's desperate to meet you."

"I hope I don't disappoint her."

He took her hand, squeezing it tight. "Look, all you gotta do is talk baseball with my brothers and my dad, talk music with Cassie, talk books with Kate, and you'll be part of the family."

"What do I talk about with your mom?"

"Me."

Emery started to giggle. "You have a high opinion of yourself."

"You had a high opinion of me too, this morning," he reminded her. "When I had my head between your legs."

"Hendrix!" Her cheeks broke out in a blush. And he loved it. Loved the way he could embarrass her with a few words in public, yet when they were in private she was as desperate for him as he was for her.

"Come on, let's go in. The sooner we get this over with, the sooner we can leave."

She shook her head, biting down a smile as he walked around to open her car door, helping her out, his hand firmly holding hers. He didn't let go as he locked the car and they headed over to Murphy's Diner, which already had a line formed outside.

"They already got tables," Hendrix told her, leading her past the crowd of people. And sure enough, taking up one whole corner was the Hartson family. As soon as they saw Hendrix, their chatter halted, and they all stared at him and Emery as they walked toward the tables.

"Hey." A man who looked just like Hendrix called out. One of the twins? "Pres," he said, holding his hand out.

"Thank you for telling me." She smiled at him. "I wasn't sure which one of you was which."

His twin laughed. "It's easy," Pres' doppelgänger told her. "I'm the good-looking one."

"You are so not." Pres shook his head.

"They're both assholes," Hendrix whispered in her ear. "I'm the good-looking one." He held out his arms and a pretty almost-teenager jumped into them. "This is my niece, Delilah," he told Emery.

"I'm so happy to meet you," Delilah said to Emery, beaming. "Now he's got a girlfriend, maybe he'll stop skipping family get togethers." She lowered her voice conspiratorially. "They can't give him lectures about needing a girlfriend anymore."

Emery laughed, completely charmed. "I've heard so much about you," she told Delilah. "And Club Solo."

"You can join if you want," Delilah said. "Even if you don't know the misery of having twin brothers."

"I'd be honored."

Emery smiled softly, as Hendrix led her to the seat next to his mom. "Maddie Hartson," his mom said, her eyes crinkling with pleasure as she held her hand out to Emery. Emery took it, and then Maddie shook her head. "Come here," she said, hugging her. "It's so lovely to officially meet you. I've heard a lot about you. Tell me, how's your mom doing? And how is the sale going? Has your mom seen any houses she likes yet?"

Emery started to tell her about the viewings they'd already had, while Hendrix's cousin Sabrina called out to him.

"Hey, you look annoyingly happy," she said. "I told you that she was your type."

Hendrix smiled. "Next time remind me to listen to you," he told her.

"Who is that man?" his mom whispered to Emery. "He never listens to anybody."

"He listened to you," Emery told her. "He told me about the talk you two had. I think it meant a lot to him." He'd told her all about it that night when they'd stayed up talking. How he'd thought he was doing the right thing for her and his mom. How talking to his mom made him realize what a fool he'd been.

Maddie's eyes were soft. "It was so lovely that he actually talked to me. That's because of you. You've softened him. Made him more open." She smiled at Emery. "I'm so grateful for that."

"I think he did that for himself," Emery replied, though she liked that way too much. One thing was for sure, he'd taught her to think much less. To stop worrying all the time. To learn to enjoy the moment.

They were a good team. She already knew that. Since last Saturday she'd been staying at his place. Hadn't even bothered hiding it from her mom. Not that her mom cared. She was too busy packing things up to think about Emery's sleeping arrangements.

And secretly, Emery thought she might be getting a soft spot for their soon-to-be ex neighbor. Her mom even made him some lemonade today, without being asked. Hendrix looked like he'd just won a prize when she pressed the glass into his hand.

"I'm Kate," one of the women opposite Emery said, smiling widely at her.

"And I'm Cassie. Married to the less good looking twin." She wrinkled her nose.

Emery laughed.

"We should get together," Kate told Emery. "Cassie and I have a WhatsApp group you should join,."

"What kind of group?" Emery asked her.

"A Stop-The-Hartson insanity support group. We compare what idiots the guys can be. Then we grill our husbands for all the dirt on their brothers so we can use it against them." Cassie smiled. "It's guerilla warfare, basically."

Emery grinned. "Count me in."

"Why am I not a member?" Hendrix's mom asked. "I'm married to a Hartson, too."

Cassie typed something into her phone. "You're in, too."

"Add me," Sabrina begged. "I know I'm a Hartson, but I have to live with Hartson men. I need all the support I can get."

Emery laughed softly.

"Everything okay?" Hendrix murmured in her ear.

"Everything is fine," she told him. And it really was. His family was lovely. So welcoming and funny.

"You know, next time we get together, you should bring your mom," Maddie said to Emery. "It would be lovely to get to know her a little better."

Emery nodded, her throat tight. And for a breath or two she was silent, just appreciating this moment. Everybody was talking over each other. Hendrix was getting teased by his brothers. And a few of the children were playing a game in the corner.

Hendrix looked up, his eyes catching hers.

"I love you," he mouthed at her, and it sent a shiver down her spine.

"I love you too," she mouthed back, and he gave her that little smile he always saved for her. The one that had shyness in it, and a hint of promise for later.

A promise she'd be sure to hold him to.

Epilogue

"SWEET BABYCORN, you must be Only Farms," Maisie said, flinging the door open to her apartment. Her eyes scanned Hendrix from head to toe, spending extra time on his flexed biceps. They bulged perfectly as he carried one of Emery's very overfull boxes into Maisie's apartment.

Hendrix lifted a brow, glancing over at Emery. She shrugged, trying not to smile. "I only mentioned calling you it once."

"It's the perfect nickname," Maisie told him. "Those arms deserve their own zipcode. Or possibly their own kingdom." She winked at Emery, who shook her head.

"Can I come in, or would you like to take a few photos?" Hendrix asked, his voice full of amusement.

"I'm absolutely going to need some photos," Maisie teased, but she stepped aside and let him walk in, squealing as she ran to Emery and gave her the biggest of hugs. "Oh my God, you didn't tell me he's from the GQ farm."

"You've seen him on FaceTime," Emery reminded her dryly, but she couldn't keep the smile off her face. She hadn't seen her best friend for months, after all, and she was just so damn happy she was back from her trip. Maisie was glowing, her skin tan, her eyes sparkling.

"Yeah, but the screen distorts things. Like the way it makes Tom Cruise look like he's tall." She slid her arm through Emery's, leading her to the living room where Hendrix had put down the box he'd been carrying. There were six more in his truck, waiting to be unloaded. And it felt bittersweet, because the summer was coming to an end and school was right over the horizon.

She loved her students. She loved teaching. But she hated that she and Hendrix were going to be apart during the week.

He'd made it clear he was happy to do the long-distance thing for as long as she needed him to. She'd drive home to see him on the weekends, and when she couldn't, he'd drive here to see her.

And in the meantime she'd look for a school that was closer, and talk to her principal about finding a replacement here for her. It made sense for her to move back home where he was, along with her mom and his family. But for now she was so grateful that Maisie was letting her stay in her guest bedroom, so that she had the flexibility to move home at anytime.

"I'll go grab the next box," Hendrix told Emery. Tonight, he'd stay with her and tomorrow he'd leave early, because there was way too much to do on the farm. "You stay here and catch up."

"Wait!" Maisie said, walking toward him, a mischevious expression on her face. "I need to hug you first."

Before Hendrix could say anything else, she threw her arms around him. Over his shoulder, her eyes met Emery's. "It's like hugging a steel column," Maisie mock-whispered, before she looked up at Hendrix, grinning. "Do you have any friends you can introduce me to?"

"There's always Frank," Hendrix said deadpan.

Emery bit down a smile. There was something so damn

sweet about her boyfriend and best friend getting along. For one, they were going to be seeing a lot of each other over the next few months – whenever Hendrix came to stay.

But also because they were two of the most important people in the world to her. And she needed them in her life.

Maisie released Hendrix, her face turning suddenly serious. "Thank you," she said.

"You're welcome. I'm available for steel hugs anytime."

She pushed his chest, then winced, like it hurt her hand. "I mean for bringing my friend back. For making her happy. For completing her list."

His eyes locked with Emery's. She smiled softly at him, feeling the familiar warmth wash through her. This man *did* complete her. In every way.

"Yeah, well she completed my list, too," he said gruffly.

"You didn't have a list," Emery pointed out.

"Not one I knew about," he said, still staring at her. "But it was there, waiting for you to come into my life."

"Okay, now you two are getting sickly sweet." Maisie shook her head, though she was still smiling. Like she was delighted for her friend. "Go get some more boxes, Only Farms. I'll have my camera ready."

"She's joking, right?" he asked Emery.

"I think so." She shrugged.

When he walked out of the apartment, heading down to his truck, Maisie turned to Emery, her mouth open with excitement.

"Oh my God, Em, he's perfect." She grabbed Emery's hands, squeezing them with delight. "And he's so in love with you. He can't stop looking at you. I'm jealous and ecstatic all at the same time. I'm so happy for you both, but I'm so sad I only get you for a little while longer."

"I promise you can come visit anytime you like once I've moved back home," Emery told her. "And we have the long summers too."

"Thank God." She tipped her head to the side. "If I come and see you, will you introduce me to Frank? I bet he's hot."

Emery couldn't help it, she burst into laughter.

"What's so funny?" Maisie asked her.

"Frank's a goat. Hendrix's goat. The flirtiest little sex-driven animal you'll ever meet."

"A goat?" Maisie frowned. "Why that little..."

"I'm ready for my close up," Hendrix said, walking into the living room with another box in his arms.

"I got a bone to pick with you," Maisie told him. "I know who Frank is. And I'm not happy about it.

Hendrix didn't miss a beat as he put the box on top of the first. "Hey, *you* asked if I had friends. I didn't say they were human."

Maisie narrowed her eyes. "You're lucky you're pretty."

As Hendrix disappeared down the stairs again, Maisie gave her one last squeeze. "Seriously, Em. I know you'll be leaving again, but it's different this time. You've got your forever waiting back home."

Emery nodded, her chest swelling with something that felt like peace. "Yeah," she said softly. "I really do."

Maisie sniffed and wiped her eyes with dramatic flair. "Ugh, stop making me cry. I'm trying to look cute for when Biceps McFarmerson walks back in."

They both started giggling as Hendrix's boots echoed up the stairwell again.

And just like that, everything felt exactly right.

The next year...

"What time is it?" Emery murmured, rolling over in their bed. She could hear the sounds of the animals outside, like they were just waking up. But she wanted to keep sleeping. It was the country air. It was better than any sleeping pill she'd ever tried.

"Almost six. Time to get up, sleepyhead." Hendrix kissed her cheek. She looked up to see him fully awake, golden rays of sun spilling through the curtains, illuminating his smooth skin. He was wearing a pair of boxers and nothing else – his usual nighttime clothes, if he wore any at all – and she took a moment to enjoy the view.

"Eyes off the body, Reed," he told her. "You don't want to be late for work."

"I have an hour and a half before I need to be there," she protested. "Now come here and wake me up properly."

He smiled at her. "When did you get so insatiable?" Not that he seemed to care. He was the insatiable one of the two of them. Grabbing her for kisses whenever he walked past her, pulling her into the shower with him when he got home after a hard day on the farm, carrying her to bed at night then loving her until she was screaming out his name.

"You unleashed the beast," she whispered, as he crawled over her, leaning down to kiss her. "It's your fault."

"Maybe I like the beast." He ran his hand down her silky nightgown, dipping his finger beneath the hem. He groaned when he felt her bare beneath it. "Christ, you're wet."

"I was having a good dream," she murmured, letting out a gasp as he slid his finger along her. "A dream you interrupted."

"Was it about me?" he asked.

She rolled her eyes as he slid a finger inside of her. "Of course."

"What was I doing to you?" He kissed the corner of her lip, her jaw, then trailed his mouth down her neck to the swell of her breasts. He started to circle her with his thumb, repeating the rhythm with his mouth as he kissed his way down her chest, using his nose to nudge the neckline of her nightgown down, exposing her breast.

He captured her nipple between his lips and she gasped.

"Nothing."

"Uhuh." She could feel him smile against her. "Was I doing this?" He curled his fingers inside of her. Finding the right spot that made her thighs start to tremble.

"No," she managed to stutter. "But it feels good."

"So what was I doing?" he whispered against her breast.

"Unloading the dishwasher," she said, deadpan. "It's so sexy."

He started to laugh, looking up until her eyes met his.

"Okay, you were inside of me," she said softly. "You had my legs on your shoulders. You were rough."

"And you liked that?" He lifted a brow.

"So much." Truth was, she liked him any way. Hard, soft, anywhere in between.

"Well, baby," he told her. "We don't have time for me to take you rough right now. But you be a good girl at work…" He pressed his thumb harder against her, enough to make her cry out. " And I'll show you just how rough I can be."

He scraped his teeth against her nipple, like it was a promise, then kissed his way up to her lips, claiming her mouth as he brought her to the edge with his fingers. And when she tipped over, he held her, kissing her, whispering her name, telling her how beautiful she was.

She clenched around him as he slowly brought her back down to earth, sliding his fingers out from inside of her, then slipping them into his mouth like the dirty man he was.

"Your turn…" She reached for him. But he stepped back.

"Nope. Tonight. Leave me hanging. You know that's how I like it." He grinned at her. "Now get in the shower and get yourself clean. You have a busy day."

The man was so giving. That was the first thing she'd noticed after she moved in with him two months ago. He simply liked giving pleasure. Yes, he liked receiving too, but the giving was always his favorite part.

She could live with that kind of generosity. Selflessness wasn't what she'd expected from Hendrix Hartson. But it was what she got.

When she walked out of the bathroom, he was waiting for her with a mug of steaming coffee and a pastry.

"Seriously?" She grinned. "Are you competing for the boyfriend of the year award or something?"

He shook his head. "No." But there was a smirk on his face. It made her heart clench. "I made lunch for you, too."

After a year of long distance dating – with her coming home most weekends to spend them with him and her mom – Emery had finally gotten a job at the local elementary school in Hartson's Creek. She'd left Charleston at the end of May, trying not to cry as Maisie had hugged her tight, making promises they'd see each other as much as they could.

And true to her word, Maisie had been down to visit them a few times. She hadn't quite loved the country life the same way Emery did – she screamed the first time Frank wandered into the cottage – but she'd tried.

And now it was August again, and after a week of getting her classroom and lessons ready, Emery would be welcoming her students into school this morning. With her mom happily living in town in a little bungalow, and the new owners working on the farm opposite, their lives were starting to come together.

Their only problem was that this cottage really wasn't big enough. It barely fit the two of them, and she and Hendrix had already agreed they wanted at least three children. So he'd sat her down and showed her the plan he had his brother draw up for extending his cottage. Building it out and up until it was family size.

They'd live in the annex in his parents' yard while the

construction was going on. They were due to start in a few weeks and they couldn't wait.

But for now they were both working their jobs during the day, then coming home in the evening and working on the farm. He had plans for that, too. Emery had been working on the financials with him. She loved how he wanted to create a working farm that also had an educational side to it, where kids could come and learn about animals and agriculture.

He was passionate about the land. And she spent her free time helping him, seeing his vision come to life. He had so many ideas for the future. Her favorite part of every night was when she laid her head on his chest and he'd tell her about his day.

Okay, her second favorite. But it definitely came close.

"Ooh thank you." She took the lunch bag he was holding out. "What did you make me?"

"A bologna sandwich and a little sweet treat."

"What kind of sweet treat?" She tipped her head to the side. He knew how much she loved cake.

"Take a look," he said. She took a gulp of her coffee and handed the mug to him so she could open the sack. And when she did, she saw exactly what kind of sweet treat he'd made.

A little red velvet box was nestled on top of her wrapped sandwich.

"Hendrix?" Her eyes widened as she lifted her head to gaze at him.

But he was already dropping to his knee.

"I decided to stop competing for boyfriend of the year," he murmured to her, taking her hand in his. "I figure husband of the year is a loftier goal." He kissed her knuckles, his eyes shining as he gazed up at her. "Emery Reed, will you marry me and let me show you just how good I can treat you?"

She swallowed down the lump in her throat. "Yes." She

nodded, a tear running down her cheek. "Absolutely and completely, yes."

He grinned, standing up, taking the ring from the box and sliding it onto her slender finger. Then he kissed it. "You make me so damn happy."

"You make me happy, too," she told him. "And just so you know, I'm going to be competing for wife of the year, too."

"You already won it." He kissed her softly, stroking the back of her head. "Just by saying yes."

She couldn't help but admire the ring. Sparkling as she moved her hand in front of her face. Then she caught sight of the time. "Dammit, I have to go to work." She pouted, because yes, she loved that he asked her, but what a time to do it. "I guess we can celebrate later?" she said, hopefully.

"That's the plan. I'll pick you up after school and we can head out for dinner." He lifted a brow. "And I figure on the way home you'll want to stop by and tell your mom."

"And your parents," she pointed out. Because this was Hartson's Creek, after all. If they didn't tell them right away, the rumor mill would. But she couldn't help but smile at his words. He and her mom were firm friends now. Last week, while she was at work, he'd helped her mom hang artwork around her house.

"Of course," he murmured, pulling her close.

Emery rested her head against his chest, listening to the steady beat of his heart, letting the warmth of his arms settle around her like home. This was it – this was forever. The life they'd dreamed of was right in front of them. Late nights on the farm, laughter filling their growing cottage, a future big enough to hold all of their dreams.

And as he pressed a kiss to her temple, she knew one thing for certain – she'd never been more sure of anything in her life as she was of the bad boy farmer with a heart made of pure gold.

. . .

THE END

Dear Reader

Thank you so much for reading THAT ONE NIGHT. If you enjoyed it and you get a chance, I'd be so grateful if you can leave a review. And don't forget to check out my free bonus epilogue which you can download here: **DOWNLOAD YOUR BONUS EPILOGUE BY PUTTING THIS URL INTO YOUR WEB READER:** https://bookhip.com/RQGJMCQ

I can't wait to share more stories with you.

Yours,

Carrie xx

Also by Carrie Elks

THE HEARTBREAK BROTHERS NEXT GENERATION SERIES

That One Regret

That One Touch

That One Heartbreak

That One Night

THE FITZGERALDS

Must Have Been Love

In Case You Didn't Know (Coming soon)

THE SALINGER BROTHERS SERIES

Strictly Business

Strictly Pleasure

Strictly For Now

Strictly Not Yours

Strictly The Worst

Strictly Pretend

THE WINTERVILLE SERIES

Welcome to Winterville

Hearts In Winter

Leave Me Breathless

Memories Of Mistletoe

Every Shade Of Winter

Mine For The Winter

ANGEL SANDS SERIES

Let Me Burn

She's Like the Wind

Sweet Little Lies

Just A Kiss

Baby I'm Yours

Pieces Of Us

Chasing The Sun

Heart And Soul

Lost In Him

THE HEARTBREAK BROTHERS SERIES

Take Me Home

Still The One

A Better Man

Somebody Like You

When We Touch

THE SHAKESPEARE SISTERS SERIES

Summer's Lease

A Winter's Tale

Absent in the Spring

By Virtue Fall

THE LOVE IN LONDON SERIES

Coming Down

Broken Chords

Canada Square

STANDALONE

Fix You

About the Author

Carrie Elks writes contemporary romance with a sizzling edge. Her first book, *Fix You*, has been translated into eight languages and made a surprise appearance on *Big Brother* in Brazil. Luckily for her, it wasn't voted out.

Carrie lives with her husband, two lovely children and a larger-than-life black pug called Plato. When she isn't writing or reading, she can be found baking, drinking an occasional (!) glass of wine, or chatting on social media.

You can find Carrie in all these places
www.carrieelks.com